SEEKING APRIL

Seasons of April Trilogy: Book One

KJERSTI AICKEN

Seeking April

Cover design by Jannaya Jensen
Cover photo by Bryan Aicken and © HC Fotostudio/ Adobe Stock
Author Photo by Nicole Hein

This is a work of fiction. Names, characters, businesses, places, events, and incidents in this book are either the product of the author's imagination or used in a fictitious manner. Any resemblance to actual persons, living or dead, or actual events is purely coincidental.

Visit the author's website at kjerstiaicken.wixsite.com/author

ISBN 978-1-7381748-0-5

First Edition: November 2024
10 9 8 7 6 5 4 3 2 1

This is for you, Bry.

- Chapter One -

April's earliest childhood memory was of the sun-dappled living room floor in her first home. There were a few farm animal puzzle pieces scattered on the brown carpet, framed by a square of afternoon sun that came alive with shadow-dance as the breeze picked up outside. A budding sense of her own existence weighted this ethereal recollection. Why this little moment had been selected to exist within the grasp of consciousness was beyond her. Yet it was a gift; something to hold on to, a remnant from before she was old enough to be at war against herself.

Sometimes, the thought of that first home brought an ache that battled with whatever she was supposed to be focusing on in real time. In other moments, like now, it was grounding. Her mind could conjure up the house in emotional detail, like fingertips recalling the nuances of a favourite toy. There was the worn-carpeted living room with white walls, the orange-and-brown plaid couch that was for everyone, and the black recliner that was only for Dad. If you tried to sit on it while he was home, he would make a big deal of slowly sitting down on you with a loud grunt until your breath was all squished out of you and your mischievous giggle ended on an exhale that couldn't be recovered. Dad always seemed to sense when playfulness morphed into panic, and he'd hop up as if startled, giving you a chance to dart away. If you weren't fast enough, he might grab your arm and yank you back for a tickle-squeeze and a whisker rub. If you were lucky, you escaped from his arm's reach and taunted him from a safe distance, knowing that once he was seated he wasn't inclined to hop up again.

The living room was small. Opposite the recliner was the TV and bookshelf wall (which contained a lot of toys for her younger sister, Britney), and opposite the couch was the large window overlooking a tiny patch of front lawn. The sun only broke through the mature oaks along the street in bits and pieces when they were in full bloom. While April had loved living in a sunnier home after that, in hindsight the overwhelming foliage was cozy.

She peeled her mind away from the flashbacks and took a deep breath. Her white Toyota Tercel turned into an upscale suburb and forced her focus onto the street signs on each side of the main road. She'd never driven through this neighbourhood before, but she had studied the map several times leading up to this hour. It only took a few minutes to make the correct turns and pull up to the curb in front of her destination. Now. It was time to turn off the ignition, take a quick glance in the rear-view mirror; take a deep breath, grab her purse, and open the door. They were probably watching from the bay window beside the recessed front door. Hesitation upon exiting the car would not make for a good start to this interview.

She had chosen a casual outfit for the occasion, after hours of overthinking. A light purple button-down shirt with black capris overtop of simple black flats seemed to strike the note she hoped they were looking for. At five-foot-five, she was used to keeping her head up when she met new people. Moving from the safety of her car and down the walkway, she fought the impulse to cast her face down. A dark-brown bob came down to her chin and framed the circular face that held brown eyes in a perpetual state of wide-eyed observation.

April took quick note of the start of a walking trail to the left of the beige-brick house, and the towering two-storey red-brick home to its right. Seth's home seemed modest in comparison, but the small mobility elevator taking up half of the front steps made it more interesting.

She knocked three times, each rap a little louder than the one before. A glance at her watch told her she was three minutes early; perfect.

The door opened and Mr. Lansing was suddenly there with a friendly smile and wise blue eyes behind rimless rectangle glasses.

"Good morning! You must be April Vale." His handshake was firm and warm. He looked every bit the professional, despite his casual attire of a golf shirt over khaki pants. After two quick pumps, he let go and motioned her inside. "I'm Leonard, Seth's dad. We'll start off with the interview in the kitchen, and after that I'll introduce you to Seth. He's looking at his papers in the living room. Could I grab you a water or coffee?" This he tossed back over his shoulder as he led her down the short hallway and turned left.

Is there a right or wrong answer? "W-water is fine," she replied, coming to a stop once they had rounded the corner. She couldn't help but admire the granite countertops and dark oak cabinets in the tastefully-decorated U-shaped kitchen. She debated whether to put energy into commenting on it, like a normal person probably would. It *was* a very nice kitchen. Leonard took a pitcher from a stainless-steel fridge and poured water into a glass just as April noticed Mrs. Lansing step into the doorway across from her. "Hi April, I'm Vanessa. Seth's stepmom." She closed the gap and shook hands. "Thank you for coming. How are you?"

From down the hall at her back, there came the brisk rustling sound of a page being turned.

"G-good," April replied, following Vanessa's gesture through the doorway into a formal dining room. It wasn't large, but the dark-hued abstract art pieces on the wall made the room feel big and important. She got the sense that many serious conversations took place here.

Vanessa and Leonard took their seats on the other side of the table, and April settled into the chair in front of which her water glass was placed. Several papers were stacked on the table. Leonard picked up the top two sheets and glanced down at them quickly.

"Let's just jump straight into some questions, shall we?" Leonard's smile was kind and knowing. Small talk wasn't going to get very far or be very helpful. April knew she gave off that vibe, and still didn't know whether she liked that about herself.

"Sounds good to me." She forced her hands to stop fiddling with her purse strap under the table.

"Can you tell us about your time volunteering at Maude's Manor?"

Another page was flipped down the hall, slightly muted this time.

April's mind clashed with dozens of possible replies. Her nerves didn't help, but neither did the fact that Maude's Manor had been one of the most significant experiences of her teenage years. When she started volunteering at the local group home to fill a spare class period, she'd had no idea what kind of world would open up inside herself. Summing it up in just a few short words wouldn't do it justice.

"I guess it's…I guess it's hard to nail down an intro to that topic," she laughed nervously. "I mean, the people there were really amazing." *Too much feeling; focus on tasks.* "I mean, I did get some training in assisting with b-basic personal hygiene. I didn't…I didn't physically assist anyone with mobility issues, so I didn't do any lifting, but I helped in other ways. But mostly I helped with recreation. We did games in the home, or outings sometimes. I helped with bowling, going to community events, swimming, going for walks…"

The Lansings allowed the trailing-off to stand for a few awkward moments before Vanessa piped up.

"I'm curious about why you say the people there were amazing. Can you explain?"

Again, April took a moment to order her sudden influx of impressions. "Sure. They...they were so easy to be with. They didn't look down on m- on anyone. To be honest, I—not to get too personal, but I had never met a group of people as accepting as they were. They were nonjudgmental. Spending time with them was like a break from..." *Hit the brakes, hit the brakes!* "I learned so much about the goodness of humanity from my friends there. And I felt like they helped me even more than I helped them." *Way to go, cheese-fest.*

The Lansings both nodded with neutral expressions, April noticed briefly before casting her eyes down to the table.

"And is this what inspired you toward getting a Recreation Therapy diploma?" Leonard asked.

"Yes. I'm open to any job available after graduation, but m-my heart is with people with intellectual disabilities."

"You have one year under your belt now. How have you found the program so far?" Leonard again.

"I love it so far. At least, I find it very interesting."

"And your practicum was at..." Vanessa leaned over to consult the paper in her husband's hand. "St. John's Long Term Care Home. What skills did you develop there?"

"There was quite a bit of training in mobility assistance. I g-got to shadow my supervisor doing an intake assessment for a new resident." April took a deep breath. She didn't want to carry on long enough for the Lansings to catch her unease with this particular topic. She had passed her practicum, but barely. Her supervisor had been rather unimpressed by—well, by her. Being bombarded with dozens of new co-workers had almost completely robbed her ability to speak for many of her shifts.

"Can you tell us why you're interested in this summer

position?"

Her heart rate slowed slightly. "I g-guess it just…your description of Seth sounded…well, he just sounds great. I'd love to get to know him and…well, hopefully anything I've learned so far can help me assist him. And help me gain some more hands-on experience in the field I'm interested in." *Please forgive my speaking skills,* she silently begged while another page flipped in the background of the conversation.

Leonard and Vanessa smiled simultaneously. "We have to agree with you that Seth is great," Vanessa said. "Not that we're biased or anything." An amicable group chuckle broke some of the tension.

"He certainly is a wonderful son, and I'm very proud of him," Leonard continued. "He has this gentle curiosity and strength that most people come to recognize once they get to know him. He knows what he likes and what he doesn't, but he's open to trying new things if the people around him have earned his trust. Overall he leads a very happy, easygoing life. But in the posting we stated that he has a particular challenge that require his caregivers to be calm and direct. I'll explain what that means.

"Seth has a passion for lines of words. It's one of his greatest joys, but can also flip into one of his greatest struggles. He loves books. Books, newspapers, magazines, phone books, anything like that, he will run his finger along every line. Sometimes he'll do it for a few minutes, sometimes for a few hours. That's what he's up to right now. You might notice when you meet him that his fingers are almost permanently ink-stained."

"I like books," April blurted, then mentally kicked herself.

"And so does Seth, but the flip side of that is that screens cause him to get overstimulated. We don't have a TV in the living room, and the computer is down in the basement, where he never goes. Neither of us uses our cell phones when we're in the room with him, and if we're going out somewhere, we have to be mindful of screens anywhere we go."

"Leonard and I are used to working through these moments with Seth," Vanessa said. "At school, they have learned the importance of respecting this particularity of his. But with this being my first year back at work, it's been a long time since we've had a brand-new support person in Seth's life. We don't expect a summer hire to have the full experience of the Education Assistants and other professionals; but the reality is, screens are in lots of places, and we want someone who can help him get through the tough moments *when* they happen."

Leonard nodded along. "What that looks like, for him, is he might run and try to grab the screen. If he gets a hold of it, he usually starts off by running his finger along it, like he does with books. But screens respond and flash and reflect light, and do all sorts of things that escalate him to the point of aggression. He'll get shaky and sometimes he'll yell or cry, and if you're not able to get the device away somehow, he'll usually end up throwing or smashing it. The reality is, he's damaged a number of phones and televisions over the years. One time when he threw a phone, it hit the owner in the chest. I followed up with her and she was okay." He paused and looked directly at April. "Of course, with all of this in mind, we'd have to require his assistant to not have their cell phone visible whenever they're with him."

"This leads to another question," Vanessa said. "If you were walking outside with him and noticed that someone was walking down the sidewalk toward you with a cell phone in their hand, how would you handle that?"

"I would get Seth's attention on something else if I could," April replied. "I'd keep a small book or something in my purse to pull out for a moment like that, or maybe point out something interesting across the street that we should go see."

"And if he was already fixated on the cell phone and running toward it? Keep in mind, he's not a fast runner, so that does help."

"Well, I think…I think I'd first quickly ask the other person to put their phone away. Would Seth keep going for it if he saw it go in someone's pocket?"

The Lansings looked at each other and shrugged. "Sometimes yes, sometimes no," Leonard answered. "But if people catch on to the situation, they often move along quickly. Like I said, Seth can't run fast, so it's not difficult for people to just pick up their pace, and then things settle down."

"If he were to grab the device, what would you do?" Vanessa leaned forward on crossed arms.

"I suppose that's when some of my school training comes in handy," April answered. "I haven't had to apply the aggression-response techniques yet in real life, but I remember the maneuvers for trying to remove items from someone's hands. I place a high value on not causing harm to a person during physical intervention. To be perfectly honest, I'd rather let the device get destroyed than to leave a mark on Seth. Although I guess the risk of throwing it at another person might warrant some tougher physical intervention if I was worried about that." *Slow down.* "I would also never make him feel bad after a moment like that." She looked straight in the Lansings' eyes for the briefest moment, then glanced at the mural on the wall. "I would be his friend before, during, and after a moment like that. That would be my biggest goal."

The formal part of the interview concluded after a few more questions. April tried to get a read on the couple sitting across from her, but they were masters at projecting friendly neutrality. She wondered if that came from years of advocating for a child, then a teenager, who couldn't advocate for himself.

At least, not in the traditional sense, she reminded herself.

"Well then, let's introduce you to Seth," Leonard said, rising from his chair. Vanessa stood after him, smiled reassuringly at April, and the three of them filed out of the formal room into the more welcoming light of the kitchen, then down the hallway toward where the page-turning noise happened again.

As each step drew her nearer toward meeting this new person, April was filled with a familiar doubt.

Will he like me?

Will he accept me?

She rounded the living room corner after Leonard and Vanessa, vaguely aware of a quiet knowledge that her life was about to change.

- Chapter Two -

April did a quick once-over in the bathroom mirror before stepping out toward the front door. She'd done a good job on her makeup this evening—her eyes popped and her lips looked positively kissable. Butterflies had taken flight in her stomach about an hour ago, after a short reprieve from the nervous kind she'd had surrounding this morning's interview.

The front door swung open before she reached it, and there he was. Theo McTeague—*her* Theo McTeague. Dressed in his gray blazer, black t-shirt and black pants, he looked like he'd stepped out of a men's fashion magazine. His wavy black hair suggested just enough boyish charm to offset the maturity of his chiseled face. *April McTeague sounds just perfect, doesn't it?* she thought, not for the first time. Her breath caught in her throat as those probing blue eyes alighted on hers.

"There's a confident smile," Theo remarked, putting his hands on her shoulders. The sensation caused a rush through her entire body, setting her legs to trembling. He was tall enough that she had to tilt her chin almost all the way up in order to meet his eyes from this proximity. "Did you get the job?"

"Well," April replied, "they didn't say so, but they said Seth seemed comfortable with me when I met him, and they were friendlier when I left than when I came in, so I have a good feeling. A hopeful feeling. They said they'd make a decision by Friday."

"That's great!" Theo caught her up in a bear hug and then stepped back, smiling down at her. "They'd be crazy not to hire you anyway. You have more passion for this type of thing than most people have for their own types of things."

A burst of laughter escaped April's lips. It happened so often when Theo was around. "Thanks for the vote of confidence, but I'm pretty sure no one talks about stock markets and investing as much as you do. You're pretty crazy about your type of thing too."

"*You're* my type of thing," Theo said, then laughed. "That sounded weird."

"Just a little bit." April tentatively lifted her fingers toward his and was rewarded with the engulfment of her small hand into his large one. "So, where are we going?"

"That's for me to know and you to find out," Theo said with a teasing grin.

* * *

Fifteen minutes later, they were situated in a booth with a window view overlooking the rolling greenery of an exclusive golf course. Magic-hour shadows accentuated the texture of the perfectly-cut grass, even from this height. April stared in awe, shaking her head slightly.

"Is something wrong?" Theo asked in concern.

"Not at all," April replied. Peeling her eyes away from the view, she sized up the openness in Theo's facial expression. He was fully tuned in to her; his smile was encouraging. She sighed and said, "I still can't shake the feeling that I'm in a reality show where an unsuspecting girl gets the perfect guy who treats her like a princess and all the cameras are aimed at her, waiting until just the right moment to rip everything away and tell her it was all made up."

Theo's laugh was sudden. "And the 'perfect guy,' as you say, would realize that he'd fallen for the girl, so now they're both rich TV stars who also end up happily ever after, right?"

She smiled, a small thrill running through her mind, and picked up the brown leather-bound menu. Everything looked so delicious, but one meal immediately caught her eye and she set the menu down. Theo hadn't even looked at his.

The server came over to get their drink orders. Theo requested the house wine for both of them, addressing her by the name she had given them. April noted that Heidi, who appeared to be about their age, had flawless skin and a wholesome face. She looked like a person with a kind heart, but certainly she must have glanced at this couple and wondered at the mismatch in levels of attractiveness. Not that she'd ever *really* disliked her own looks. Yet sometimes, being with the guy who'd been desired by every eligible girl at their young adults' group served as a reminder of her luck and his magnanimous nature. Or whatever it was about him that had caused him to look her way.

Heidi walked away, and the intimate bubble descended around their table again. April continued. "But going from never being noticed by guys, to being dated by someone who treats me so amazingly well…I don't know. I just feel like—"

"April, I know what you feel like," Theo said softly, reaching across the table for her hands. She realized she'd been fiddling with the cutlery. "I know how hard it was to push through that guard. Trust me, I was there. It wasn't easy." He gave her fingers a reassuring squeeze. "And I could see that even when you realized I was serious about dating you, you weren't going to hand over your heart that easily. But we're getting there, right? Slowly but surely?"

April couldn't discern the source of her smile, but it came to her face automatically. What was a good thing to say next? She chose something safe. "Maybe." She arched an eyebrow at him and he took the flirtatious bait.

"Your heart is like a present I get to slowly unwrap," he replied. "And so far, I'm amazed at what I see. First of all, you love Jesus. Church is very important to you. I love that we have those things in common. Family is integral to your universe, and you're very much loved by mine so far, I can tell you that."

April bit her lip. Their server came back with their drinks and asked if they were ready to order. April's mind hopped back to the blackened chicken dish she'd spotted earlier, but Theo was quick to order pecan-crusted salmon for both of them, with house salads to start. As their server walked away, Theo smiled at April and she momentarily forgot that she didn't even like fish.

"And I don't think you realize how beautiful you are," he continued. "Your eyes are like scared little birds. When you look right into mine, it's like the biggest gift you can give."

April guffawed, then slapped a hand over her mouth and glanced around self-consciously. "Theo, now I'll never make eye contact with you again!"

"Your *laugh*," he pressed on, provoking another, subdued, outburst, "comes out of nowhere and just makes me so happy. It's the best sound in the world. Your spirit shines out of you when you talk about your schooling and Maude's Manor. I tell you, if you get this job with Seth, and any other job you pick up in the future, you are going to change lives just by being who you are."

By now, there were tears forming in the lower lids of April's scared little birds. She blinked them away and stared out the window again, one hand still in Theo's and the other one creating a nest for her chin. Now what? She couldn't talk, even if that was the appropriate thing to do next. Theo's affectionate hold on her fingers seemed to communicate that this silence was okay. At least, that's what she hoped.

He waited about a minute, then set a small box on the table.

"We've only been dating four months, April, but I'm a very happy man and I couldn't be prouder of who I'm with."

April turned her face toward the little box. It was white with a silver ribbon, and although she mostly knew it was too soon, her heart screamed with panic and excitement at the same time.

Theo chuckled. "Don't worry, I'm not rushing things. It's not a diamond in there; it's two." He gently guided her hand toward the gift and she began to untie the ribbon, her breath caught in her throat, until she'd uncovered a white jewelry box and pried it open, the peach-fuzz case sending tingles down her spine. A pair of brilliant solitaire earrings caught the lights of the chandeliers so magically, it was as if they were lit from within.

April gasped. "Theo, I…" she trailed off, shaking her head, pulling the gift closer to examine them. "Are they real?"

"As real as my love for you." She glanced up at him and he laughed. "Okay, that was a bit cheesy, but yes, they're very real. And…yes, I really love you."

"I…" she couldn't say anything more. Taking this all in was too much. A mostly-amazing-too-much with a touch of awkwardness.

"You don't have to say it if you're not ready," Theo said softly. "Only if and when you're ready."

April simply nodded and continued to stare at the earrings. After a few moments, she set the box down and unclasped the ones she'd put on at home, then carefully replaced them with these multifaceted wonders. Theo feigned a backward stumble in his chair with his arm over his eyes as if he'd looked at the sun. Then he righted himself and stared at her with his probing eyes full of adoration and satisfaction. "Perfect."

* * *

Tired hands slid the box of board books, stacking cups, and squeaky animals into its place on the bottom shelf, underneath the early readers that waited patiently for their time to shine in a few years. The woman's shoulder-length brown hair brushed against her face as she pushed herself into a standing position and arched her back, feeling the strain in almost every muscle of her tall, slim frame. She caught a glimpse of her reflection in the decorative mirror across the living room. Dark circles beneath her hazel eyes were accentuated by her pale skin. Basking in the house's silence, she tried to make a choice between having a cup of decaf or heading to bed early when her phone chimed with an incoming text. Her heart kicked up a notch until she saw the sender's name; then her stomach dipped with the disappointment-and-guilt combo that had become her normal resting state in the past few months.

Want me to bring home anything for dinner?

Well, Patrick, maybe some exoneration. Or deliverance. A little clarity on the side, she thought. What she texted back was: Stuffed crust pizza would be great. Any kind.

She resisted throwing her cell onto the couch. What was wrong with her? Why couldn't she stop her mind from going where it shouldn't, longing for what it couldn't have?

Her phone chimed twice in a row, signaling two texts received at once.

Got it. Maybe a movie night if your not too tired?

She noted the error with annoyance, swiped that one over and checked the next one. A smile tugged at the corners of her lips when she saw who the sender was.

Thinking about you today. Hope you're doing well.

- Chapter Three -

Four days later, on Sunday morning, Seth was moving toward the living room when his parents surprised him by already being on the couch beside his magazines. He sat down in the small space left between them and reached across Mom's lap to pick up the first issue and flip it open, where his finger met the lines and began the peaceful dance that brought his world to a point where he could filter out the loud and bright and big things, like the car that just drove past and the ravens bird-yelling in the big trees of the park and the sensation of all his arm hairs standing up because of the coldness of moving from his warm bedroom to the darker living room before the sun made the window brighter. He realized that Mom was talking, and he knew that she used to be only called Vanessa, who had two daughters named Donna and Kristy, but then one day everyone was outside in a park filled with white chairs, and he hated his clothes, but he had a lot of brand-new books to line through which was great, and that day Vanessa and Dad told Seth that Vanessa was Mom, because they got married. Then Seth knew that she was going to stay, and that was great, but Donna and Kristy only stayed for a short time, and then they left, and now they came back to visit sometimes, and sometimes they each took turns having different men with them, but one day David became Donna's only man that came with her because they got married just like Dad and Mom did, and that meant you were in the family. Right now, Mom was saying that April was coming to meet him again, and she was going to see what he liked to do and learn about how to be his friend for the summer since school was almost done and he needed a summer friend, because Mom and Dad still had to go to work even though it was summer. Seth stopped lining and heard that another car was driving, but this one was slowing down outside their house and then it stopped, so April was here. That was okay, because when she sat in the living room last time she didn't talk much and she didn't change the air in the room. There were two other new people who came into the living room at different times last week, and one of them talked too much and the other one didn't, but he changed the feeling in the room, and that made it harder to concentrate on lining.

Dad stood up and Seth went back to lining while April knocked on the door three times, and then it opened and Dad and April talked around the corner first, then they walked into the living room. April said, "Hi Seth," but didn't change the feeling in the room because she didn't care that he wouldn't answer. As he continued lining, Mom and Dad and April did a lot of talking. They talked a long time and he was okay with it until he felt the fullness get heavy deep down inside so he knew he had to go pee, so he set his magazine down and stood up and rubbed his finger on his chin once, because that was how he used to tell Dad that he had to go the bathroom back when Dad needed to help him. He went to the bathroom that smelled like cinnamon, because when Vanessa started to come over, before she was Mom, the house began to change with interesting smells. That was a long time ago, and Seth remembered when the bathroom just smelled like a bathroom—which wasn't as nice as cinnamon, he learned. He went pee, and Vanessa reminded him to wash his hands, and even though he used the towel to dry them, he knew that he would blur the lines in his magazine for the next few minutes, but that was okay because his hands were mostly dry so the blurring wouldn't go very far and then it would soon become dry anyway, and sometimes it was interesting when parts of the pages were crispier than the other parts.

April watched Seth walk back into the living room. His gait was halting, his feet spread apart and knees stiff. His parents had already explained his great dislike of stairs, and she could see now how awkward it must be for him to navigate them. He wasn't a tall guy, only about five-foot-five, but at the age of sixteen there was still a chance he'd grow up or out in the next few years. His sandy hair was short and shaggy, which cast a little-boy charm over his already-youthful face. There wasn't a speck of stubble to be found, nor was there any sign that facial hair was even interested in gaining a foothold. Through the oval lenses of his thinly-rimmed glasses, his brown eyes remained downcast and intent on his internal focus. April's nervousness was firing off as usual with Leonard and Vanessa, but it was rivalled by the way her heart reached out toward Seth. She rejoiced internally when he walked past her and sat down on his couch again and picked up where he'd left off in the magazine. Something about his demeanour spoke to her. They shared an automatic acceptance of one another. Aside from the residents of Maude's Manor, she had never experienced this instant connection with anyone else.

The four of them spent the morning going over Seth's regular daily routine, which included a walk in the park next door. Later, in the kitchen, Vanessa demonstrated the gentle physical maneuvers they used whenever there was an encounter with a screen. This part tied April's stomach up in knots, but the moves lined up with some of the training she had already taken in her college courses, and she trusted she would be able to use them if necessary.

Back in the living room, the four of them went through a description of Seth's communication techniques. Mostly nonspeaking, he relied heavily on a mix of basic sign language, made-up gestures, and simply walking toward whatever he intended to do. April was given a stapled stack of papers that Vanessa had put together, which included diagrams of his most common signs and gestures and what they meant.

During the conversation, Seth moved on from the Good Housekeeping magazine and on to a Sports Illustrated one, but he was willing to raise his hands a few times to show some of the gestures. April had to hide a smile at how his presence shifted slightly in those instances, like an invisible teenage eyeroll.

It was explained to her, although she could tell on her own, that Seth's comprehension of spoken language was average. Academically, he'd never demonstrated the ability to read or write or solve equations, despite numerous attempts in his modified education program. Whatever he internalized at school hadn't translated into skills that he could show, but his engagement with the world had grown alongside his age. As a young boy, Leonard explained, Seth seemed locked away in his own world and became easily overwhelmed by other people and sensory input. But intensive therapies, caring school staff, and the stabilizing of their family unit had enabled Seth to find his confidence.

Since Vanessa's employers at the pharmacy understood her home situation, they had allowed her an ideal schedule that worked within school hours and would remain as nine o'clock to three o'clock, Monday through Friday, throughout the summer as well. April was to arrive at 8:45 each morning and remain with Seth until 3:15, during which time they would mostly be at home, with a short outing each day when possible. The hours were short, but the pay was generous. Leonard was a successful lawyer who had his own law firm, allowing him to pay a lavish wage. April had already surmised that she could afford to forego finding a second part-time job, at least for now. She had no plans to ask for any time off, with home being a three-hour drive away and home being the only place she planned to visit this summer anyway.

After the orientation was over, April drove straight to Theo's house with an overloaded mind and a full notebook. Tomorrow the rubber would meet the road, and she was going to give it all she had. For now, though, she couldn't wait to relax in Theo's arms and ask him how church had gone; to tell him about her day and about her unspoken connection with Seth; to feel Theo's heart racing against her cheek and to know that she was the cause of it. She loved to feel small and encompassed by his presence, to shrink her awareness of the world within the boundaries of their physical tension.

"Hey," greeted the stranger who pulled open the door, his mouth smacking on an oversized wad of gum. He looked like he belonged in a punk rock band, which put his appearance at complete odds with the other guys who lived here. April realized he must be the subletter for Jesse, the roommate who had gotten a summer job as a tree planter in northern BC. The look of complete disinterest in his eyes killed whatever mental momentum she'd built up to formulate the expected greeting. A beat of silence passed, and he said, "So…are you one of the girlfriends?"

"I'm…I'm…I'm April. I'm w-with Theo."

The look of disinterest shifted slightly to menacing as the new guy leaned against the door jamb with his hands in his pockets.

"Theo, hey? Seems like a good guy. Comes from money. Has a lot of money. Going to make a lot of money."

April's small-talk system crashed. Although she knew she was staring just past his shoulder, she couldn't think of a proper reaction.

"He'll be a keeper, I'm sure. Give you the kind of life you dream of. You won't have to work unless you want to. Do your hair and nails and eyelashes and whatever else you want, go to Italy every year, diamond jewelry." He forced himself into her line of vision. "Although you don't look like you're into those kinds of things. Hmm…expensive art supplies, maybe?"

Finally, something clicked out of desperation. "Is…is…is he here?"

"Yes, yes, yes he is." The new guy looked back over his shoulder. "He, he, he's on the phone in his room."

A hard lump blocked her throat. She bit her lip. April contemplated leaving and never coming back. Theo would just have to start coming to her place all the time. As she started to turn away, the gum guy sighed and said, "Come on in." He stepped back and moved out of her way. When she hesitated, he beckoned her in with an exaggerated arm swing, and she hated herself for gliding past as if she had no choice in the matter. Head down, she ambled toward Theo's room and knocked on the door. He pulled it open with a distracted air while listening to the deep voice on the other end, but the second his eyes met hers, he cut in. "Dad, can I call you back?"

A heavy bass beat started up from the next room, where gum guy had taken up residence. April stepped into Theo's room and shut the door, closing her eyes as tears leaked out.

"What happened?" Theo opened his arms and she stepped into them, willing her injured feelings to simmer down before she opened her mouth. After she relayed the story, Theo pulled away from her and reached for the doorknob with such force he almost pushed her out of the way.

"NO!" April cried out, grabbing his arm. "Don't talk to him, don't say anything, please, I don't want—"

"He made you cry," Theo said with a vehemence that stirred her, despite her fear.

"It's my fault! I'm oversensitive, it's not a big deal."

Theo turned the knob and tried to gently shake her off, but she held on tighter and forced herself in front of him. "Theo, please, don't do anything. If I have to get used to him, I don't want him to think I'm a baby. Just please forget about it. I'll be okay, I just wasn't expecting it."

Theo's eyes bored into hers. She could see the rage that was brewing in them, but the protectiveness that radiated off of him made her reach up for his face, pull it down toward hers, and press her lips against his with a passion that surprised even herself. The hard muscles of his jaw slackened under her hands. A few minutes later they broke contact and April walked over to his desk chair on shaky legs.

Theo watched her, his eyes soft and intrigued, and remarked, "I do believe I've just been tamed."

April laughed with a burst of surprise. Still, she didn't fully relax until Theo had moved away from his door and sat down on the edge of the rumpled bed.

"Why don't you ever make your bed?" she asked.

"What's the point if I'm just going to sleep there again the next night?"

"I think they say that successful people always start their day by making their beds."

"Successful at what? Bed-making?"

"Obviously. And, I don't know, impressing their girlfriends?"

Theo raised a brow. "Hmm, and here I thought I'd impress you by beating up Rob."

"Rob?"

"Yeah, the really nice guy Jesse left us as a going-away present."

"Are they friends or something? Jesse is so nice."

Theo shrugged. "I don't think they knew each other before. Anyway, he just moved in today. We all tried to be nice, but he made it pretty clear he's not planning to make friends. I think it's gonna be a long summer in the house."

April snorted. "Yeah, no kidding. Maybe you can just come pick me up every time we want to hang out."

Theo cocked his head and gazed into her eyes. "Are you sure you're okay? I can't believe he made fun of your stutter. That's about the jerkiest move he could have pulled."

"Well, like I said, I'm oversensitive. I need to get a thicker skin anyway. Maybe I can use him as practice, and you'll always be there right afterward to help me feel better."

"That kiss made me feel better," Theo grinned.

April grinned back shyly. "So how's your dad?"

"Weird change in topic, but he's good. They want to have us over for supper on Saturday. Also, how was your day? How did things go at Seth's?"

April filled him in and, as she listened to herself, marvelled at the roller coaster of social experiences she'd had in the past twenty-four hours. Then Theo filled her in on the church service, the message, and the friends he'd spoken to.

"I also talked to the Zhous a bit. Remember how they're starting a small group for whoever's staying around over the summer?"

"Yeah," April said warily.

Theo raised his hands. "Okay, I know what you're thinking, and I know this is a surprise, but they were pretty convincing about how great it would be if we could join, so…I said we would try it out."

"What?!"

"You should have seen them, April, they were practically begging me! I think even their baby was begging me. You should have seen his face looking at mine—"

"Theo McTeague, I love the young adults' group. But this is a *small group.* It's for people who want to get to know each other. You have to talk there. You have to bare your soul. You can't be invisible. It will be us and all these older, wiser people who think we're young and cute and don't know anything."

Theo shrugged. "Or it could be comfortable, and we could learn a lot. And maybe, *maybe* even make new church friends outside of the young adults' group."

"Do we have to?" Even as she whined, April had to concede that this would fall nicely in line with their church's recent teachings on the importance of mentorship. As their pastor had preached on the topic, a longing had slowly begun to unearth in her soul. She loved God and had known him all her life, but in her mid-teens she seemed to hit a plateau in her experience of being in relationship with him. Her yearning to go deeper was a constant undercurrent, but it stayed buried under the big and small things of every day. Every once in a while, she pulled out the yearning like a discarded sweater at the back of her closet, shook it out and tried to figure out what to do about it, then ended up tossing it back. How do you find clarity for something you can't even articulate a question for?

"You have your thinking face on," Theo interjected with a playful smile.

"You think you know me so well." April found an eraser at her elbow and tossed it at him. *Could this be God leading me to the right questions?*

"Ow! Good, now we can show up to the small group and everyone can see the bruise you gave me."

"Yeah, and they'll never want to mess with me." She fiddled with the calculator on his desk and sighed. "Fine. What day is it, and who else is going?"

- Chapter Four -

The young mother checked her cell for the second time in five minutes. She hadn't heard from him in a week. Did something happen? Did he meet someone else? It would be great if he did. As much as it pinched her heart to imagine being cut off from him, fantasizing about the relief of it was almost as enticing as imagining what it would be like to see him in person.

She remembered what it was like to spend those long summer evenings at the lake, racing each other to the ice cream store with the kind of youthful energy that sends sparks into the night sky like fireflies. He was the local and she was the girl-next-door for only two months out of the year, and from as early as she could remember, they had made the most of their time together. Their parents were good friends. Shortly after buying the cabin, her dad had made some kind of connection about mutual church-network friends with his dad, and before they knew it, the two families were having barbecues and campfires together pretty much every weekend. The families' two broods meshed into a conglomerate that went around absorbing other shoreline kids, and days were spent swimming, sunbathing, exploring, fishing, and experiencing the ups and downs of summer camaraderie. There were so many warm memories and fond connections from those years. A few of those relationships were still active today. But the one friendship she had craved the most, yet tried her hardest to pry out of her heart, was the one that had suddenly become the most persistent. Two years of sporadic emails after high school graduation had morphed into eight years of silence, and, suddenly, this spring his name was in her email inbox.

At first, there had only been surprise on her part, which faded as quickly as it came. But when he replied within a day to her response, a small flutter of excitement was fanned deep inside. Frequent emails soon turned to an exchange of numbers, which led to frequent texting. She figured he was aware of her marriage even before he had reached out, and she was madly in love with her husband, so she was shocked to realize how often she thought of him after their first phone call. It was almost enough to cause her to break off all future contact. Almost. But…

"They'll be here soon," Patrick announced loudly from the living room. Robyn winced and bit back her response. How many times did she have to tell him—no yelling when the baby was in bed! Linus was just starting to sleep at night without needing to be held/rocked/bounced/whatever the proprioceptive need-of-the-moment mandated. Robyn couldn't stomach the thought of ruining the progress they had made by riling him up with overtiredness.

"Do you need any help with the snacks?" he called out again.

"Quiet!" Robyn hissed, slamming her serving spoon down as gently as her annoyance would allow. "You'll wake Linus!"

Suddenly Patrick was behind her, whispering, "But he's going to have to get used to sleeping through loud talking anyway, isn't he?" He rested his hands on her hips and kissed her neck. "We won't be able to tell our guests to quiet down."

Robyn moved out of his arms, deftly scooping up the big bowl of snack mix and spinning to face her husband. Of Chinese descent, his handsome and angular face had caught her attention at Bible School several years ago. At the time, he was just one of many eligible guys to notice, but nothing had captured her heart like the way his tender eyes soaked her in; it always skipped a beat when she caught him looking at her like that. Yet now, for the first time ever, she saw that look in his eyes and felt nothing. She masked her realization with a smile.

"Yes," she replied with forced warmth, "but I'd like to have at least a few minutes with everyone at the beginning. If he wakes up too early, you know I'll be busy with him for a while."

As she moved into the living room with the bowl, Patrick followed with plates and napkins. They went back and forth silently a few more times until the juice pitcher, coffee carafe, cups, and store-bought cookies were all sitting in the middle of the coffee table. Robyn glanced around and re-counted the seating availability to ensure there were at least nine spots. It would be cozy, but with the evening sun and the lilac-scented breeze flowing in from the storm door, the room was just the right temperature. Satisfied that everything was ready, and that Linus had slept through his dad's careless yelling, she sighed and glanced over at Patrick before facing the front window.

Does he know something's up?

Patrick smiled at her, took her hand in his, and gave it a squeeze. "It'll be great. I can't wait to do this. Should we say a prayer before they get here?" Robyn nodded and he began, "Dear Lord, thank you for giving us this opportunity to grow closer with you and with some other people who love you too. This is a new thing for us, Lord, to be leading a small group, but we trust you've guided us here and that you've called the right people to come along. Please give us wisdom and insight to lead the group well, and please make this a summer where we all go deeper with you." He paused and squeezed Robyn's hand a second time.

She picked up, "And please show us how to speak truth and love into each other's lives as we all spend time together. And…please help Linus to sleep through most of it. Or all of it.

Please."

The first knock came just then. Robyn started for the door while Patrick announced that they could come on in, and suddenly Myla was bustling into the room and announcing, "I had the *worst* customer come into the salon right at the end of the day. Robyn, you wouldn't believe her! *First* she refused to get her nose out of her phone, even with the cape on, and *then*—"

While Myla carried on, her naturally loud voice dashed any hope Robyn held for a quiet evening. Annoyance flitted across her mind, but she instantly chastised herself and allowed Myla to hook her by the arm and sit her down on the nearest couch so she could finish her story. By the time she had finished describing her rude client, Robyn was laughing in spite of herself. Leave it to Myla to pull her out of her funk.

Myla's husband, Asher, was shooting the breeze with Patrick by the open door. While not as conversationally loud as his wife, his stories were often punctuated with sudden extreme noises. He and Myla were about the same height, Asher being short for a guy and Myla being average height for a woman. He had the stocky build of a rugby player, the casual wardrobe of a teenage boy, and a chinstrap beard around his square face. Myla was black-haired (usually) and voluptuous, in looks and personality. It was rare to see her without jewelry that looked like it was conjured up by her own charismatic energy.

The two couples had been friends for a few years. Before exiting their church's young adults' group scene, Robyn and Patrick had cheered them on through dating and engagement. Then they had stood on either side of the bridal party when they tied the knot last summer. While Asher and Myla Jameson had been very excited for them upon the birth of Linus, their newlywed life and lack of baby experience meant that their support came in the form of impractical advice and illogical gifts. At times, they seemed to resent that the Zhous were no longer as readily available for double-dates as they used to be, but Robyn knew that they would likely understand one day.

The rest of the crew arrived in singles and pairs over the next fifteen minutes. Everyone had found a place to sit, and Robyn caught Patrick's eye from two chairs down. There were two conversations taking place. Yvette was sitting silently between those conversations, and Theo and April were holding hands on the couch across from Robyn. April looked for all the world like she wanted to run away. Robyn hoped it hadn't been a mistake for Patrick to insist so hard that they come. They might be the youngest ones here — only by a few years, she assumed — but she remembered how old the mid-to-late-20's seemed to her back when she was just starting that decade.

"Well, I'm going to cut in here," Patrick announced (with a louder-than-necessary voice, Robyn thought). "First of all, thanks to everyone for coming. I, uh, I don't want to make this out to be like a super formal meeting, but we thought it would be a good idea to start by introducing ourselves, since we only partly know some of you."

"Yeah, strangers," Myla giggled.

"After that, we thought we should go around the group and introduce ourselves, tell the group about what we do or what our hobbies are, anything you'd like to say.

"So, my name is Patrick, and this is my beautiful wife, Robyn." He gestured and she gave a little wave. "I guess most of you know, but for anyone who doesn't, I'm a mechanic at Carson's Garage — going on about six years, I guess. I grew up in Saskatoon and went off to Bible School down in Montana, which is where Robyn and I met." His eyes glowed at her. "She was kind enough to be my girlfriend and follow me up here while I earned my automotive repair certification and got a job. We got married five years ago, and we have a beautiful six-month-old baby boy, Linus. I love what I do, I love our family, and I love Victory Church. And, uh…I'll leave it at that." He looked at the woman beside him, who sat up straighter and introduced herself as Faye.

"I'm a personal trainer at the YMCA, and I grew up in Saskatoon." The first bit wasn't surprising, given her trim athletic poise. Shiny blond hair was pulled back in a ponytail that draped forward over her right shoulder. Her blue eyes were wide-set and seemed to broadcast an inner resolve that she would take no guff from anyone. "I have a 5-year-old son named Aiden, and in my spare time I like to train and run in marathons. I grew up going to a different church, but Victory is my new church family, and I haven't looked back."

Interesting, Robyn thought. In their brief chat before this discussion, Faye had mentioned that her parents were watching Aiden tonight. Did they still go to the church that Faye grew up in?

"Oh, me," Robyn realized. "I guess you all know my name and my family. I'm currently on maternity leave but I'm an elementary teacher at Prince Philip School. I grew up in Wolseley, a small town near Regina, and the rest is—what Patrick said."

Myla took a deep breath and, with a big smile, announced her name and her life story to the group. Within a few seconds she had already garnered a few chuckles—even from April, Robyn noted.

"So after I finished my hairstyling courses I got a job at a studio that I *won't name,* because I'm a good Christian, but it was the worst place to work *ever,* and then I tried another studio that I *won't name,* for the reason stated before, but finally I landed in a really great place that I love downtown—Très Belle—and I'm just saying, if anyone is looking for a fresh 'do…" she lifted both arms and pointed down at herself, "I happen to know a gal."

There was a dramatic pause, and finally she turned to her husband. "Asher, it's your turn!" she stage-whispered.

"I was waiting for you to mention the little detail about marrying me," he stage-whispered back. By now the room was full-on laughing. *Do I hear Linus?* Robyn wondered, not quite willing to stand up and check.

Myla shot him an exaggerated "are-you-serious" look and he

sighed. "My name is Asher. I'm the youth pastor at Victory, and apparently I'm the only one in my marriage who's excited about their spouse." A warm look passed between the two of them before he continued with his brief history.

The next person was as diminutive as she was petite. Her round eyes held no trace of anxiety, but her introduction as "Yvette, from British Columbia, completed my first year of Arts and Sciences at University of Saskatchewan" left no indication that she felt compulsion to expound on the details. Her wavy brown hair fell down to rest upon the shoulders of a classy short-sleeved black cardigan.

"Hi, I'm Samuel," said the next person, raising a large hand in a half-wave. His toothy grin and creased eyes suggested that this was the normal resting state of his circular face. Tall and slender, with skin the colour of dark walnut, he exuded contagious joy. "I'm originally from Eritrea, but my family moved to Toronto when I was fifteen, and then I grew up in this great country. I'm a little jealous of you," he turned and motioned to Asher, "because I also have a special someone who makes me laugh, but she's in Toronto finishing a music degree. Her name is Rachel, and next to Jesus, she's the great love of my life." He put his hand on his heart with a sincerity that quieted the room. "I studied to become a nurse at the University of Toronto and moved here to Saskatoon to work at Royal University Hospital. It is my great privilege to do what I'm doing."

"Are you and Rachel engaged?" Myla blurted.

"No, not yet," Samuel responded. "But, God-willing, that will happen soon. She is planning to move here after school next year. For now, we simply work and wait."

"That must be so hard," Myla offered.

Samuel shrugged. "It is, but with God, even missing someone I love can contain some joy. I dwell often on Psalm 118:24. 'This is the day the Lord has made; let us rejoice and be glad in it.' Because, you see, even the days I miss Rachel terribly are days that the Lord has made. When I choose to rejoice, it colours each moment with hope and strength. Even when I miss her so much it hurts."

"Wow," Myla sighed.

After a few beats, Theo cleared his throat. "Hard to follow up on that. But, uh, my name is Theo. Born and raised in Saskatoon. I grew up with three sisters, so I know a lot about women, and Samuel, you may yet have all the women in this small group comparing us to you after tonight."

Samuel threw back his head and laughed.

Theo continued. "I'm a first-year student at Edwards School of Business, and this summer I'm working at my dad's firm, McTeague Financial. I love to play hockey in the winter, I've been really enjoying the young adults' group at Victory for the past year, and that's where I met April." He looked at her. She briefly met his eyes and smiled, then chewed her lip and looked away. "We started dating in February. And so…that's it for me, I guess."

April opened her mouth, and no sound came out. The briefest hint of panic crossed her eyes, but she blinked hard as if to clear them and opened her mouth again. "I'm…I'm April." Theo was still holding her hand, and now he gave it an obvious squeeze. "M-my…I g-grew up in Edmonton until I was 10, and then we moved to Baylor, just a few hours away from here." She took a deep breath. "I'm….I'm taking a recreation therapy course, and this summer I'm providing daytime support for an autistic teenager." Her tone hinted at an unfinished thought, but after a beat of silence, Theo smiled around at the group and said, "And that's us."

* * *

By the time Myla and Asher left, a full hour after the rest of the group, Robyn could hardly keep her eyes open. When she felt the pressure of Myla pushing herself off the couch, she snapped to full attention and attempted to stand. Myla put a hand on her shoulder and said, "Hey now, I know my way to the door, and you've got your arms full anyway." At that, the weight in her arms registered and Robyn was surprised to realize that she was holding Linus.

In a dreamlike fog, she recalled how he'd woken up halfway through the study, bawled through numerous attempts to settle him in his crib (which she assumed was interrupting the flow of the discussion just down the hall) and finally ended up in the living room because it seemed only his mom's arms were good enough for now. Patrick beamed with pride as the group turned to see them coming in, and Faye offered to hold him for Robyn. "I know how hard that first year is—I let people hold Aiden every chance I had!" Robyn started to hand him over, but the crying started up the second he was halfway between the two women, and it didn't improve despite Faye's bouncing and swaying and back-patting. After a few minutes, she handed him back to Robyn with an apologetic smile, where he promptly started rooting around her t-shirt with an open mouth. Robyn went to his bedroom again to nurse him for the third time in forty-five minutes.

Why do other people's babies fall asleep in strangers' arms?

As a teacher, Robyn knew, to the absolute core of her being, that it wasn't right to compare kids' temperaments to others. Every personality was just as valuable as the next, in all of their strengths and weaknesses. But now, with her own flesh-and-blood, it seemed that comparison was the first lens through which she viewed him. Obviously, he was her most favourite baby in the universe. But when she saw other mothers with their babies, she wondered why they looked so natural when she felt so off-balance. Was there a motherhood gene possessed by these women who popped out babies that didn't make strange; babies who slept through the night with no trouble; babies who allowed their mothers a chance to put on makeup before heading out in public? Did that same motherhood gene allow them to think clearly and calmly when their babies cried, instead of spiraling into brain fog and a racing heart? Was Robyn's anxiety about her own mothering being absorbed by him osmotically while he nursed and slept against her chest? Was he born anxious himself, and was that why he couldn't handle being away from her?

And now, on top of it all, she felt guilty that Faye hadn't been able to have a nice moment with Linus. Was Faye embarrassed that she hadn't been able to settle him?

This time, Robyn's lolling head jerked up because of a gentle touch on her cheek.

"Let's get you both to bed," Patrick was saying softly. "Everyone's gone."

Robyn's heavy lids raised up just enough to take in the cups, napkins, and crumbs scattered around the living room. What if mice were enticed to come in overnight? What if they climbed into Linus' crib?

"Don't worry about the mess, I'll get it in the morning," Patrick reassured her, reaching down to pull Linus off her lap.

"No!" she hissed sharply. "I'll take him. If he wakes up again, I'll lose it."

Patrick stepped back with a bemused look on his face. "Okay…how can I help?"

"Nothing," she replied as she edged forward and stood up slowly, careful not to jostle her ticking time bomb. She stepped past her husband and edged around the coffee table, then turned back and said, "Actually, yeah, don't leave this mess for tomorrow morning, or I'm going to worry about it all night."

As she stepped into the bedroom, she heard Patrick stacking the cups with bone-jarring *clinks* and hurried to swing the door shut with a little backward kick. Linus stirred slightly in her arms, causing her to jolt. He then released a series of airy toots that turned her heart into a puddle of mush.

She slowly lowered him into his crib, pulled out her hands with a slow deliberation that she prayed he wouldn't notice, and watched him for an exhausted moment.

He was heartbreakingly beautiful. That silky black hair had a texture she could feel in the depths of her soul, unlike anything she'd ever touched before. He had hazel eyes, warm and almond-shaped like his dad's, and cheeks that went in forever whenever she smooshed them with kisses. It was impossible to reconcile the fact that this little human plumbed the greatest depths of her joy while simultaneously invoking the greatest bouts of her fear.

How is it possible that you're wrecking me and filling my heart at the same time?

The sudden buzz against her hip might as well have been a lightning strike. Robyn nearly leapt to the ceiling, and her chest physically hurt as she whipped out her phone to press the "off" button, but the sender's name registered before she could act.

Devon!

Sorry it's been a while. I was really busy helping Carly with something. Anyway, it's late and I hope you're sleeping and that you'll get this message in the morning. When are you free for a phone chat again soon? Just let me know.

Robyn released a breath she hadn't realized she'd been holding. She stepped backward until she was leaning against the wall, staring at the small screen, a wave of profound relief washing over her. So he hadn't decided to cut her off after all!

Patrick's footsteps sounded just outside the door. Robyn turned her phone off instantly, even though he carried on toward the bathroom at the end of the hall. She felt a little guilty, but she was so weary of feeling guilty that she stuffed the feeling down and savored the way her spirits had lifted when she saw that name.

How is it possible that you're wrecking me and filling my heart at the same time?

- Chapter Five -

She should have offered to clean up.

April lay awake, her mind doing all the tossing and turning while her body remained still. The ceiling was such a great place to fix her eyes—fuzzy as it was without her contacts in—while she berated herself for such a poor performance tonight.

Her stutter had been even worse than usual. Also, her opening act left her feeling so off-kilter that she didn't open her mouth at all for the rest of the evening. Patrick's introduction to the study of Ephesians sounded great, and there was a lot of good discussion around the book itself and the format the study would take. It seemed that everyone had something to add to the conversation. Sure, Yvette had only spoken up two or three times, but that was still something. April, though? She sat there like a scared little bump, adding layer upon layer of self-consciousness until she was sure that the discomfort emanated from her strongly enough to stifle the whole room.

Then Patrick had read the whole book aloud. It took about twenty minutes, but it was the first time April had listened to an entire book of the Bible in one sitting. There was something intriguing about listening to it according to its original purpose of being a letter, not just a collection of separate ideas compiled into one chunk. The rest of the summer would be spent focusing on each chapter one at a time, but this first overview was a good reminder that each segment was part of a whole.

Shortly after the reading, the baby started to cry. While more discussions carried on throughout the whole ordeal of Robyn going in and out with him, April was completely focused on whether she should offer to help in some way. Leave it to strong, self-assured Faye to offer up help without hesitation. What must it be like to automatically jump into any social situation like that?

Right before prayer time, while Robyn's eyelids were growing droopy, Patrick laid out a few ground rules. The first one was, confidentiality was a must. April was impressed by how plainly it was stated. If anyone talked about anyone else's prayer requests outside of this small group, it would be gossip and a breach of trust. The second one was, bringing in prayer requests about people outside the group was encouraged so long as they were prayed about but not discussed at length. The slippery slope into gossip must be avoided as much as possible. The third ground rule was that no one would ever be asked to pray out loud. Patrick or Robyn would always lead and close, and in between that, people could pray out loud as they wanted to.

Since the group was just starting to gel, nobody brought up prayer requests about anything very personal. Myla talked about her grandma, who was moving from her lifelong home into a seniors' complex. Asher requested a general prayer for the youth of the church, Faye asked for parenting wisdom, and Samuel wanted to pray blessings over the Zhou family for opening their home. Theo said he wanted prayer for patience in dealing with his new roommate, adding, "I've kind of wanted to strangle him ever since he made fun of April's stutter." Heat rushed to April's face so fast she thought her cheeks would ignite.

It was nine-thirty when the prayers finished up. April glanced around at the mess, noted the half-asleep young mom on the couch, and was working up the courage to stand up and start collecting cups and napkins when Theo suddenly stood up and announced that they would be on their way.

"Really looking forward to next Thursday," he said.

"Us too," Patrick replied. "Remember to read Ephesians 1. I'll email out those questions tomorrow, and next time I'll try not to lose the hard copies again. 'Bye, April."

She looked down in a sort-of nod as she followed Theo out the door and into the cool evening air. The relief of escaping the small crowd was short-lived.

I'll bet they're sorry they invited you.

There's an exhausted new mom in there, and you didn't lift a finger to help.

Your personality was absolutely shining *tonight. You positively* dazzled *them with your wit and charm.*

As Theo drove, he carried on about how much he had enjoyed the evening. April half-listened, biding her time until she could fall into bed.

She realized Theo was waiting for a reply to something.

"Oh," she said, "um…I'm sorry, what was that?"

"I was asking if you wanted to do our homework together on Sunday afternoon," he repeated. "You know, read it out loud together and go through the questions together."

"S-sure."

Theo glanced at her as they waited behind another vehicle in the left-hand turning lane, the red light of its signal illuminating his face in a staccato rhythm. "April, are you okay?"

"Theo…why did you have to bring up my stutter?"

"But…I mean…I'm sorry. I didn't…oh look, now I'm doing it." He chuckled. April shook her head and looked out the passenger-side window.

"No, babe, seriously." His fingers brushed her cheek, but then it was time to make his turn. "I wasn't thinking. It just kind of slipped out. I just figured since…you know…everyone there heard you stutter at the beginning, it wouldn't be a big secret or anything."

"Thanks for the reminder of the awesome first impression I made."

"April, what is with you and all your worries about how you come across to people?" There was a slight edge to his tone. "I'm *proud* of you, you're an *amazing* person, people *like* you! Nobody cares about a little stutter. Well, people like Rob do, but there aren't any Robs in our small group. Didn't you think everyone there seemed nice?"

April felt like she had backed so far into a tunnel that she could barely see. "It's…it's not about that."

"What's not about what?"

"You're asking me too many questions and saying too many things, and I'm tired and just need to go home and shut out the world for a while!" She squeezed her hands over her ears and forced out a laugh that was meant to break the tension, but the inauthenticity only made things worse.

"Oh, come on! I thought we were past all this!" Theo ran a hand through his hair. They pulled up in front of her house. He rested his forearms on the steering wheel. "April, I thought I was *in.* I thought you'd finally let me all the way into your inner world. I worked so hard to get you to trust me, I…"

April had already pushed her door open and her legs, with minds of their own, were taking her away.

She loved Theo. She was sure she did. She thought she did. But she was done with absolutely everyone for tonight. He must have figured that out, because she heard his car disappear down the road as soon as she shut the front door.

Half an hour later she was staring at the ceiling with a hard lump in her throat. "God," she whispered, "What is *wrong* with me?" She turned onto her side, curled into a ball, and wept.

The indefinable feelings overtook her for a few minutes until she was forced to get up and blow her nose. *You can't even cry in a pretty way*, she mocked herself. A torrent of destructive thoughts was gearing up for a full-fledged assault. Something inside of her salivated for the masochistic release.

You're pathetic, you know that?

You're worthless.

No one likes you.

No one wants you.

No one cares what you think.

What you think doesn't matter anyway.

Why are you even here?

She glanced over at her cell. It was turned off. She wondered if Theo had tried phoning her. He had her landline number as well, the one she shared with her roommates, but that hadn't rung. Maybe he was too annoyed with her to even bother. Maybe he was finally realizing she wasn't worth it.

Might as well throw a pity party on top of everything else.

Calling it that didn't stop it from happening, though. It only made things worse. Which somehow made things better, as far as the dark energy swirling inside of her was concerned.

She turned on the lamp and swung her feet over the edge of the bed. So what if it was late? A walk around the neighbourhood would burn off some of this mental muck. Fumbling for her glasses, she found herself happily anticipating the smooth silk of the summer evening air against her bare arms. The world always made more sense when all the people were tucked nicely inside their homes and April could walk amongst them without the risk of interaction.

Her mom would kill her, she knew. More than once she had talked to April about the dangers to avoid in the city. April crept out the front door, although the need for quiet wasn't necessary. Dara was working nights at the hospital, and Nancy hadn't come home yet from whatever she was doing. Not that they would have been concerned about her going out right now, anyway. Becoming a third roommate in response to an online ad didn't automatically turn you into the type of person to make friends easily, even under the same roof.

She lived in an alright neighbourhood. Sure, there were more reports of property damage and vehicle theft around here than there were in other parts of Saskatoon, but violent crimes were few and far between. As she descended the three concrete steps and heard the sounds of traffic on Thirty-Third Street a few blocks away, she fought down the question about why she didn't care to examine the risk factor of being a lone woman in a dark city neighbourhood.

The first time she'd felt this particular thrill of—what? Freedom? Defiance?—had come after living in Baylor for almost three years. Good ol' Cosette. How was she even doing these days? As always, when her thoughts turned to her former friend, April felt pangs of loneliness and angst in equal measure. Cosette had opened her eyes to the world in astounding ways. She had also shattered April's confidence in the safety of friendship.

And here I am. I fell for it again. Her feet seemed to be trying to keep pace with her racing heart. *They reach out…you lean in…it feels right…then WHAM.*

It was time to stop this train of thought. April imagined herself back in the living room in her first home and took a deep, jagged breath. Home. The feel of the brown Berber carpet on her bare feet as she read an Archie comic in Dad's chair. The warmth of the sun. The presence of her mother just on the other side of the wall, humming while she cooked supper. Britney, on her stomach a few feet away, playing with the doll that she'd gotten for her fourth birthday. Dad walking through the door in his electrician's overalls, Britney squealing and running into his arms while April herself noted his arrival somewhere behind her awareness of Jughead's latest food antics.

She knew life hadn't been perfect back then. It took effort to recall the loneliness she'd felt in the elementary school down the block, and there were the occasional tense moments where Mom or Dad had punished her or been unreasonably grumpy toward her —but overall, life in that tiny house had been uncomplicated and safe. If only it were possible to go back to that state of bliss. Was it possible? It often felt like that with Theo, but then there were times like tonight that tripped her up painfully. Was it possible to be fully at-home with Theo if she pushed through the fraught dance of going deeper with him?

Maybe Theo will be my new/old house someday. The thought brought a smile to her lips for the first time in hours.

She'd rounded three corners already and was heading back toward home. Sleep suddenly seemed much more possible, and she couldn't wait to get back under the sheets. Maybe there was hope that she could become a better girlfriend and enable herself to fall freely in love with Theo.

The sound of footsteps resonated from a little way behind her, and April picked up her pace, suddenly caring about being a lone woman in a dark city neighborhood much too late at night. She arrived home and settled into bed for a second try at getting some sleep.

- Chapter Six -

April was there, and she was warmth and comfort projecting onto him from her spot on the couch, silent and present. This was not such a new thing anymore, but it wasn't all the way old yet, but it was enough and *she* was enough that this was good and right.

Her fingertips were there at the edge of the page, and that was okay but not great, but okay enough to not be bad. Then her fingertips were gone and that was a better kind of okay. His heart had started beating a little faster, but now it was slowing down to normal again. He did not like to share his lining with anyone, but sometimes Dad or Mom or the teachers at school shared it with him just for short times, and that was okay because they were not taking the book away, they were just trying to share because they loved him or wanted to be with him, that's what they sometimes said. April's little bit of sharing seemed like love too. He didn't like to share, but he liked the love.

It was only her fifth day spending time with Seth, but already April felt they had developed a familiar groove. He didn't look in her direction very often, but whenever he did, she wondered what it would be like—and if it would ever be possible—for him to look her directly in the eyes. Even just for a moment. She had considered asking Vanessa about this, but it didn't seem right to discuss it where Seth could hear.

"I really like sitting here with you, Seth," April said quietly. He continued his task while she smiled at him. "I can hear the birds singing outside. Can you? They must be happy about the sunshine. Maybe they're finding a lot of bugs to eat."

Normally her inner voice would be speaking up right about now, giving its negative evaluation on her social performance. But there was no inner voice, and this was not a social performance. This was just *being* with someone.

Seth shot his head up and glanced out the window, wrinkling his nose as his glasses started to slide down. He quickly looked back down at the book and carried on.

"I hope we can go for a walk again today," April continued. "Yesterday was a lot of fun. Can we go for a walk right after lunch?"

There was no response from the occupied boy, but an hour later, after having noodles and peeled apple slices in the dining room, the duo found themselves descending in the creaky mechanical lift beside the front door. It wasn't so very different from the one at Maude's Manor, but it was a new dynamic to be riding it beside someone who wasn't in a wheelchair.

Seth wasn't big on touch, but in the two walks they had taken so far, he had reached out to April several times whenever the ground was uneven. Vanessa had reassured her that Seth fell very rarely. Apparently, his confidence hadn't gotten the memo. Regardless, April loved the chance to hold his hand, to feel the thrill of his trust run through her veins.

At the end of the front walkway they turned right, April commenting on the sunshine and the birds. The little dog from across the street was at the storm door again, barking and making a fuss. Seth recoiled slightly, but continued moving forward.

"Do you like that dog, Seth?" she asked. "I wonder what its name is. I like dogs, but I've never had one. I wonder if I'll ever get one."

By now they were turning onto the path toward the park. Yesterday they had walked the entire perimeter of the pond before heading home.

Before this week, April had never appreciated the importance of smooth, well-maintained sidewalks. Perhaps it was a sign of privilege in a prosperous new neighbourhood, or maybe it was just a blessing for Seth that didn't need to be overthought.

"Would you ever like to have a dog? Or maybe a cat would be better. A cat wouldn't be so loud and jumpy." She glanced over at Seth's face. All she could read there was concentration as he put one foot in front of the other, but the vibe of receptive listening was real. Their shared presence was open.

"Or a lizard in a glass cage, maybe. A chameleon, or a gecko that jumps around." April noted a break in the reeds up ahead, where sunlight glimmered on the pond's surface. The quiet hissing of the fountain at its center beckoned them to draw nearer.

"Do you like going to pet stores?" she continued cheerfully. "I like going just to look around. I enjoy watching the fish. Someday I'd like a fish tank of my own."

The sun was warming her skin. A mosquito whined somewhere around her head and the pattering of their feet reached her ears in a satisfying, off-beat rhythm. Up ahead, two middle-aged women speed-walked toward them, talking about a Harold and a Mark and some other people in their worlds. As they got closer, they smiled and one of them said, "It's nice to see you, Seth. Do you have a new friend?"

April gave her name and slowed her pace ever-so-slightly. When she could tell that Seth wasn't gearing down with her, she matched his speed again. "N-nice to meet you!" she added over her shoulder on her way by. The women chuckled and waved.

When she was sure they were out of earshot, April piped up.

"They seem nice, Seth. They must live in your neighbourhood, right? You're lucky to have kind neighbours who know your name. I don't even know my neighbours. I barely even know my roommates."

And whose fault is that?

Ignoring the inner question, she offered her hand as Seth's shot toward her. A tree root was waging war against the underside of this section of concrete, raising a slight ridge all the way across the path. One day the root would win, she knew. Underground things seemed to have that way about them.

They walked in silence for the remainder of the route.

Rounding the corner at the park's exit, April realized she was smiling. What a beautiful walk it had been, and what a wonderful togetherness she shared with Seth. To think—this was only the beginning of an entire summer with him!

* * *

Later that day, while buzzing on the lightheartedness of the afternoon, April texted Theo: wanna hang?

He didn't reply immediately, but she knew he was at work for another hour. Having put the olive branch out there gave her some semblance of peace. She knew she was oversensitive and difficult at times, and Theo deserved better. Tonight, she would try to more clearly explain her social anxieties so that he'd understand and not feel so frustrated with her.

He did indeed wanna hang. When he showed up at her door after work, tie loosened at the neck and an insecure look on his face, Theo held out his arms without saying a word.

"Last night sucked," April whispered into his bicep.

"Which part?" he whispered back.

They held each other for a few silent beats, then April stepped back. She shot her eyes to his, then looked away and took his hand. "I'm making spaghetti for supper if you want to stay. I want to tell you a bit more about my first year in Baylor."

While discussing her early years in Edmonton came easily, sharing details from her early years in Baylor required a push past some inner resistance as she moved the spaghetti around her plate. Theo was safe—when he was in a listening mood, which he seemed to be right now—and this was how people did relationships, right? They shared the things that shaped them, even their humiliations?

The move from Edmonton was a huge blow, but it was softened by all the time they could now spend with her grandparents. For how frequently they'd visited the farm over the years, their place had been like a second home all along.

There was nothing like the openness all around her on the farm. At home—her first home—the horizon was hidden by buildings and trees. Here the horizon hemmed you in with so many miles of open space in every direction, that you couldn't sense the boundaries of your own existence. One of April's favourite farm pastimes was to stand on the hill on the other side of the old barn and just slowly look around, feeling her soul expand toward the edge of the earth. A familiar ache would always rise up from within. She didn't know what exactly it meant. It felt like longing and curiosity, and she pressed into the feeling because it was life. To feel deep things was as essential as eating or breathing, even when it hurt.

Now, as a resident of Baylor who spent plenty of time on the hill, those big feelings were almost too much even for her to bear. She missed home. Her new house was bigger, and she had her own bedroom now, but while all of their possessions had arrived and were slowly being unboxed over the past few weeks, April's sense of belonging had gotten lost in transit. Everything in her screamed that Edmonton, the little house, was home—but the logical side of her (that her parents worked *so* hard to coax out lately) knew that *this* was home. That it would eventually start to feel like home. That someone else had the little house in Edmonton, and that it was *their* home now; not hers anymore. Her heart might not understand yet, but there was no going back. Her brain made painstaking efforts to remind her heart of that, but it was a stubborn thing.

Despite all of this, one of April's optimistic focal points had been the possibility of making friends. Would starting fresh in a new school allow her to shed whatever had stopped her from making friends in Edmonton?

The box still contained her. This realization slapped her in the face on the very first day, when she started toward the school doors and a nearby group of girls swarmed her without warning.

"Hi, I'm Cassandra," said a dark-haired girl with crooked front teeth and neat cat-eye framed glasses.

"I'm Aimee," said another girl, this one with cropped blonde hair and a few freckles.

And so it went, until eight girls had shared their names as they surrounded April in a circle of enthusiasm. Her mind buzzed so loudly with adrenaline and overwhelming feelings, both good and bad, that she squeezed her backpack tighter to her chest and kept her eyes on their feet. She opened her mouth. Nothing came out. By now a few of the girls had already started having side conversations. Only a couple of them were looking at her expectantly. She knew what was expected, but it was stuck. Her mind was blank, and her words were lost somewhere behind the flood that had overtaken her brain.

One by one, or in pairs, the girls hopped away with little welcome greetings, then hurried their way toward the main doors. At the end, only Cassandra and Aimee were left. They had endured the awkward silence with no indicator that it was a problem.

They're probably nicer than I deserve.

"So…can't you speak?" Aimee asked curiously. There was no rudeness in her tone at all, but April's ears burned even hotter than before.

"Your name's April, right?" Cassandra offered. "My parents

know your grandparents. I'm surprised we've never met before. You used to come visit your grandparents a lot, right?"

April managed a small nod. The thing was, she *did* recognize a few faces from going to church with Grandma and Grandpa over the years. But without the knowledge that one day she'd be living among them, she had never been all that curious about the strangers on the fringes of her family time.

"Well anyway, you can come to class with us. Do you know where our room is?"

April fell in step with the two girls. Without glancing back, she knew her mom had been watching the whole thing from the schoolyard gate. If only she could walk back home with her right now. She was already exhausted.

Since that time, she managed a few words here and there with her peers. She was able to respond to her teachers, often past a bit of stuttering, but enough to convey that she understood what was being taught. They seemed to like her and often praised her work, which was enormously satisfying. Yet she had noticed that her classmates—even Cassandra and Aimee—slowly backed out of trying to engage with her. They were happy enough to have her tag along and watch their games at recess, but it seemed like the silent hole she had dug for herself was finally getting over her head. It was both comforting and painful.

Midway through October, the family was having Sunday lunch at the farm. It was a new weekly ritual. Grandma's cooking, once considered a treat, was now becoming a norm, which soothed some of the pain of homesickness. But on this Sunday, April's stomach churned and her mind raced. Her mom had tasked her with a nearly impossible feat for the next day. There had been fights. There had been tears. There had been begging, threatening, and even bribery attempts. Not even offering to wash dishes for the entire rest of the school year had gotten her off the hook—tomorrow, she would be handing out invitations to her birthday party.

"So I hear you're turning eleven in a few days!" Grandma now remarked with a smile, buttering her bun. "How is the planning coming along?"

"Well, I really only wanted it to be a family party," April muttered.

Grandpa waved his arm. "We won't be as fun as a whole crew of kids your own age. One day your parents won't be able to keep all your chums out of the house, just you wait and see." He lowered his face toward Britney's. "And I bet you'll be having a big party in the spring, won't you?"

"Yes!" Britney replied, pleased as punch. "With horses and a Ferris wheel and everything!"

April rolled her eyes while the grown-ups laughed. They all thought Britney was so cute. Little did she know, the poor thing, that her imaginary friends weren't going to be acceptable as guests. Mom was going to end up forcing her to invite real people too. Although, maybe by then Britney would actually have friends. Her shyness hadn't inhibited her to the same degree as April's had. She already had one or two classmates whose names came up in frequent conversations.

As soon as dessert was served, April excused herself and brought her dishes to the sink. Each week they took turns helping Grandma with the dishes, and today would be Dad's turn. Mom and Grandpa would go to the living room to talk about whatever it was grown-ups talked about, and Britney would either want to tag along with April or play with the old-fashioned dolls that used to belong to their aunties. April disappeared into the yard before she had a chance to find out what her little sister would choose.

There was a double line of evergreen trees at the far back of the yard. Zipping up her fall jacket while she ran, April dodged through the familiar route, moving her hips at precisely the right moments to dodge branches on her way to the other side of the tree boundary. The sun was warm and the air was crisp. Relishing the sharpness at each intake of breath, she tried to outrun the threat of tears until she was safely ascending the hill. Aware that no one could see her from the house—she had checked many times over the years, just to be sure—she allowed herself to collapse at the top and roll up to face the sky, breathing hard.

God, she prayed, knowing he heard but never sure if he cared, *why did you make it so hard for me to do things? Why can't I be like everyone else? And why do I even* want *to have friends anyway? Why can't I just be happy being someone who doesn't make friends? Why can't I just be one of those people who is happy being alone?*

She cried and cried on the hill that day, but she had to stop when she heard her mom calling her to come back for Britney.

At home the next day, she had to put the invitations into her backpack.

On her way to school, however, she had a startling realization: she didn't have to *actually* hand them out.

All throughout the day, despite the presence of those invitations burning a hole in her concentration, April's resolve was set. As much as she loved her parents and didn't normally have a problem following their rules, this was just too much. At her birthday parties in Edmonton, her mom always did the phoning, and then the other moms came with their kids. April still wasn't sure what the adults assumed was going on, but during those parties, she could feel her own discomfort like an extra person in the room. The moms drank coffee upstairs and only later gathered around with the kids for the cake and presents, but all the playtime leading up to that was mostly just a small gaggle of kids playing with April's toys while she hovered around the edges and tried her best to respond whenever someone was kind enough to speak to her. She certainly didn't mind eating cake and enjoying the gifts, but the relief after her guests left sometimes made her fall asleep.

So ten-year-old April, with the invitations hiding in her backpack all week, found herself deliberately lying to her mom for the first time she could remember. It was the only way to avoid the social unknown.

Friday evening came. April returned from school to find that her mom, fresh from the grocery store, had already begun decorating the house. April's stomach turned when her mom's beaming face alighted on hers. Streamers in various shades of blue were spiralled from the center light over the table toward the corners of the dining room. A "Happy 11th Birthday April!" banner stretched across the entire length of the wall above the backyard-facing window. On the counter between the kitchen and dining room, several large bowls were covered with tea towels.

The invitations had said, "You're invited to April's house for a make-your-own-pizza night in honour of her 11th birthday! Date: Friday, October 16. Time: 5:30–9:00. Address: 138 2nd Ave."

Every day after school, April's mom had asked if anyone said they were coming. Every time, April had said that no one said anything, but that she assumed they were, because they had all been happy about the invitations.

Britney was shipped off to Grandma and Grandpa's for the night.

Board games, nail polish, and snack bowls were set up on the coffee table in the living room.

Dad was coming home early so he could help out with the festivities.

April offered her mom a weak smile and said, "It looks great."

And now she was stuck. Having successfully hung onto a cliff edge all week, she now realized that she had set herself up to fall anyway. And to take others down with her.

At 5:30, there were personal-pan-sized circles of dough scattered all over the kitchen counters. Tomato sauce, cheese, and various meats and veggies were all laid out in serving dishes, spoons and tongs standing at attention.

At 5:45, Mom and Dad morphed from joking about Baylor taking the "slow, laid-back rural thing too seriously" to shooting poorly-masked glances of concern at each other. April was sitting at the table, trying her best to figure out how to make this whole thing go away.

At 6:00, Mom cast April a too-bright smile and asked, again, if she was sure people were planning to come. "I'm going to call some of them," she said, reaching for the phone. "Maybe they lost the information."

Without warning, April heard the words burst out of her mouth. "Don't call anyone, Mom!" Her parents turned to look at her, shocked at the panic in her voice.

There was no going back now.

"I didn't hand out the invitations. I was too scared. No one is coming. No one even knows about it. *Please* don't call anyone."

April knew she would remember the looks on her parents' faces for the rest of her life.

Sitting across from Theo now, she tried to convey what she had seen.

"It was like…well, first of all they looked surprised. They didn't say anything at first. I remember staring at them because part of me was begging for their understanding and I so *desperately* wanted to see that, but all I saw was their shock change into disappointment and anger and pity all at once. I couldn't look at them after that. I was so embarrassed. I couldn't believe what my shyness had done to them. All that work…" She trailed off and glanced up at Theo, who was chewing slowly and regarding her with an unreadable expression. "And yet, even though I knew I had done something wrong by lying to them all week, I was also angry at them for not listening before all of that, when I'd told them I didn't want to invite anyone over. It was like they thought if they pushed me into it, somehow I would become the outgoing daughter they wanted me to be. That somehow, I would magically have friends—*real* friends—for the first time ever."

Theo swallowed and offered a cheeky grin. "But the most important question is: What happened to all of that food?"

April laughed, relieved by the humour, yet irritated. "Well, my parents and I had our own pizzas that night, and they tried to be nice. We played a couple of games, but then I went to bed early. They froze the leftovers. We ended up eating a lot of pizza over the next few months until they were used up, but it sucked because every time we ate some I just felt more guilty and embarrassed."

"Did you ever end up having a party that year?"

"Well, no. We didn't talk about it after that night. But…I do remember that when I was in bed that evening, lying awake just hating myself, I heard Mom crying. I didn't hear what she and Dad were saying, but I knew it was my fault. But it was also their fault. Anyway, it was a complicated mess, and I still don't know exactly how to feel about it, but something good did come out of that night."

"Besides all the pizzas?"

April shot him a look. "Stuff the jokes, McTeague. One was enough. I'm baring my heart here. Isn't this what you wanted?"

"Hey, hey, guys make jokes. I'm sorry, we can't help it. But yes, I love that you're sharing this with me. What good thing came out of that night?"

After ensuring the amused sparkle in his eyes had simmered down, she continued. "I remember lying there and thinking of how the Bible talks about putting others ahead of ourselves. About treating others as if they're more important than we are. And I realized that my shyness was getting in the way of that." She shrugged and took her first bite of spaghetti, which was now lukewarm. "And I guess that kind of put a new motivation in me. Selfishly, I never wanted to feel like such a failure and disappointment ever again. But unselfishly, I think, I decided it was time to forget myself and try my best to be whatever another person needed me to be. Because it would take my focus off my own fears and make it so that I could actually *be* a friend, instead of just waiting for people to try harder according to my needs. And maybe I would actually start to feel that God was happy with me.

At that point I didn't trust that he could love me, and I was always trying to figure out how to make myself feel better about that. This new resolve seemed like it could tick a lot of major boxes for me."

"And did it work?" Theo asked, leaning forward on folded arms.

April ate a few more bites, enjoying the distraction of his sculpted arms beneath the thin fabric of his sleeves.

"Kind of. Sometimes. I think. Maybe. At least, it helped me make my first friend when Cosette moved to town. But I think I'll just finish eating my poor, neglected spaghetti and talk about her some other time." She took a deep breath through her nose and relaxed her tight shoulders. "Do you want to watch a movie tonight?"

"Sounds great to me." Theo stretched back and flexed his arms with great exaggeration. "What would you like to watch?"

With a shrug, April said, "You pick." She had once suggested *The Lion King*, her favourite childhood movie, but his incredulous laughter had put that opinion firmly in its place. "You pick" was always the best answer. She wondered if Theo had noticed how often she replied that way. If he did, she hoped he knew it meant that he was more important than her—and she hoped that God was pleased, too.

- Chapter Seven -

Linus was trying his best to break her down. She was sure of it. One moment her sleep exhaustion had her questioning her own sanity, and in the next moment he was burbling those little bubbles with eyes that shone with such contagious joy she couldn't help but laugh.

Her mom, mother-in-law, and other mom friends had reassured her countless times that this was all normal. "Babies break you and fix you all day and all night long, especially for the first year," her mom had told her once.

So far, that was proving to be true. This was *so* much harder than her younger self would have ever imagined. She had expected just the right amount of hard—the kind that makes you sweat and press against your own limits. What she hadn't anticipated was how often she would be pressed *beyond* her limits, coming face-to-face with sides of herself she hadn't known existed.

Back when she was pregnant, her doctor had often talked to her about the importance of setting the baby down and walking away when she was overwhelmed. In those days, cradling her round belly with all the affection in the universe funnelling through her hands into her unborn child, she logged those comments away as irrelevant for her situation. Probably something doctors just have to say to every pregnant person.

Reality check: she was no less human than everyone who'd cared for tiny humans since the beginning of time. It hadn't happened for a few months, but Robyn clearly remembered a handful of times when sheer force of will led her to set a screaming Linus down in his crib while she walked away, so much exhausted angst buzzing through her body that she knew she couldn't trust herself to be gentle with him.

On this Sunday afternoon, she reflected with gratitude on her doctor's directives. They had guided her through some of her toughest times.

At the moment, she and Patrick were going through the first chapter of Ephesians together. Yet it was hard to keep her mind on the passage when Linus was squealing and babbling on his tummy at her feet, stretching his dimpled arm toward plastic cups that she'd placed just an inch out of his reach. She glanced from him to her husband, whose brow was furrowed in concentration.

He was so handsome. Staring at his face, she revelled in the affection that unexpectedly called out from a distant place in her heart. Willing it to grow, she thought about the way she'd felt when she first caught him looking at her at Bible School. He had been eating at a separate table during lunch, shortly before Christmas break, and she had been chatting with the group at her table when she felt pulled to glance in his direction. She saw the softness in his eyes before he smiled and held her gaze for an extra beat, causing her to turn away with butterflies in her stomach. She'd had a crush on someone else all semester, but when he began dating another girl a few weeks back, she'd nursed her minor heart wounds and then suddenly become aware of Patrick. Quiet, confident, unassuming Patrick. Seeing him notice her was the clincher. She fell fast after that.

Without warning, thoughts of Devon invaded with a weakly-resisted force. Now Robyn's stomach filled with new butterflies even as her heart wrenched uncomfortably.

The texting was getting more frequent. In the past few days, she was often taking her phone into the bathroom so she could carry on their never-ending conversation behind the only lockable door in the house. She kept her phone on silent and would only check it in those moments. The texts had begun as information-sharing, getting to know the details of one another's current lives. The infrequent phone calls—four so far—had been brief and simple. But lately they had begun reminiscing on their lake days, and it felt like a burst of new life whenever he shared something that she assumed hadn't been a big deal to him—like when he tackled her in the sand during beach football, or the time they got caught in a downpour on their way back from a friend's cabin. She remembered how she felt when the two of them had glanced at each other mid-run, laughing. There had been a yearning jolt inside of her when she noticed the way the water dripped off the ends of his ragged blond hair, running in rivulets down his carefree face.

Still. Devon lived in Stony Plain, just outside of Edmonton. She would never have reason to go there, just as he would have no reason to come to Saskatoon. One day this would slide away. In the meantime, it was just the right amount of fun to brighten her period of adjustment into motherhood. Maybe one day she'd even tell Patrick about re-connecting with Devon. Patrick already knew about him, from the early weeks of dating as they got to know about each other's growing-up years. Given that Patrick was aware of her former feelings for Devon, it hadn't seemed appropriate to mention yet that they were back in touch. There was no sense in making him feel funny about the whole thing.

Maybe if Devon found someone to love, they would all be able to visit each other. Then Patrick could roll his eyes, along with Devon's wife, as their spouses exchanged corny inside jokes from their teenage years at the lake.

* * *

Thursday night rolled around. April once again found her adrenaline spiking as she and Theo walked up to the Zhous' front door, but her recent recounting of her childhood resolve was fresh in her mind. Tonight, she would do her best to put the others first. She would take her focus off of how uncomfortable she was, and hone in on what the others were saying. If she could help Robyn in any way, she would make herself do it.

Even if she was shaking.

Myla's chatter could be heard even before they were on the doorstep. Theo shot April an amused face before knocking. She tried to return a smile, but it felt more like a grimace.

"Hi, you guys!" Patrick greeted with great enthusiasm. He and Theo exchanged a few pleasantries while April noticed Myla and Robyn chatting on the couch beyond them. Should she squeeze past the guys and join them? Didn't women usually gravitate toward other women in these group situations?

What's the normal thing to do here?

She didn't have time to decide. Faye was rapping on the open door behind them, holding a tray of veggies and dip with her free hand.

"Hi, thanks Faye. That looks great!" Patrick said.

Theo pulled April into the room so Faye could walk past. Without letting go of her hand, he sat in a chair beside the couch so that April could sit on the end of the couch beside Myla.

"Well, hi there, girl!" Myla chirped, turning fully to face her. "How was your week?"

"Is this…is this Asher's spot?" April managed to ask.

Myla waved her hand. "Nope, it's yours. Hey, can you tell me more about this autistic guy you hang out with? Or is there, you know, confidentiality?"

April's eyes shot up to hers briefly. "Okay, well, I think I love him!" *Now where in the WORLD did that come from?* "I mean…" a nervous giggle escaped. "I mean, I guess I can say a few things, but yeah, I should keep some things con-confidential."

She told Myla and Robyn about Seth's quiet demeanour. She explained that he loved books and why, and that he had the most interesting presence. All of a sudden, she realized that the room had gone silent. Everyone was listening. She also realized that her hand was no longer in Theo's, and that she had been waving her arms as she talked. Ducking her head down, she squeezed her hands together.

"Wow," Myla said. "I've never heard anyone describe someone as having an interesting presence before. That's different. I mean, I love how simply you explained something that's, like, pretty deep."

Theo gave her knee a little squeeze. April managed a small smile in Myla's general direction.

"I hope she likes my presence too," Theo piped up, eliciting a few polite chuckles. April turned to him with a wrinkled nose, but as she turned her head toward him, she briefly skimmed Robyn's expression. Her lips were smiling, but her eyes were not. As the group conversation carried on, she couldn't drop what her mind had snagged on: Robyn was tense. Why was that?

One by one, the rest of the group arrived, and the official Bible study commenced. After opening in prayer, Patrick launched into the agenda.

"Now we thought we'd go around and read the chapter out loud—everyone who's comfortable can take two or three verses, and we can just go around until it's done. Anyone who's not okay with reading out loud can just say 'pass' or something."

No one was looking at April, but the group's collective knowledge felt heavy to her.

Robyn cleared her throat and started off. She read with a tired, neutral but not unpleasant tone. After her came Myla, whose normally loud voice had gone strangely airy as she read. All April had to do was glance at Theo, and he took over from there with his confident air. Next was Yvette, whose quiet voice and crystal-clear diction reminded April of the crisp tinging of a triangle in band. That contrasted with Samuel, whose accent dragged out some of the consonant sounds while his voice rose and fell with great passion. In some people it would seem over-the-top, but his authenticity breathed life into the words. April thought she could listen to him read the phone book and be riveted. Faye read in a clipped, firm way. Asher mispronounced a few words, but with unassuming confidence, and that brought them to the final words, "which is his body, the fullness of him who fills all in all."

There was a list of questions that everyone had answered for themselves throughout the week. Patrick read the first one and left the floor open for anyone who wanted to discuss.

Immediately Samuel jumped in, listing off the spiritual blessings mentioned in the first half of the chapter. April silently read her own list as Samuel spoke. Things like grace, redemption, and forgiveness were there. These were words that April had heard all of her life, as normal as hearing "toast" or "school" or "sun." She knew there was great meaning behind each word, and occasionally she had seen people weep over the concepts. Even now, hearing Samuel say each word as if it was life itself, she wondered why there was such a disconnect in her own emotional response. It was like looking at a brick—yes, important for building things and providing structure. Yes, good to notice and be thankful for what it quietly does in the background of everyday life. But to draw so much of a reaction from some people? She just didn't get it.

"And we have an *inheritance,"* Samuel was saying, his hand reaching out as if to receive something. "It is *so amazing* to me that I have an inheritance from the God who created everything all around me, the whole universe, and yet *he* gives *me* an inheritance. As if I am a *son!* Because of Jesus, I *am* a son, but it is just too much to comprehend. I can not wrap my mind around it."

A few heads were bobbing up and down enthusiastically. Asher blurted out, "I know, man, right?"

While April pondered her inability to feel the group's

enthusiasm, she noted the start of a small infant cry from the back of the house. Robyn pushed herself off the couch as quietly as she could and slipped out of the room.

Patrick lovingly touched her hand on her way past him before he turned to the next question. "Verse eight says that he lavished the riches of his grace on us. What does 'lavished' mean? Could you share a story from your own life that illustrates this point?"

The group remained quiet for a beat or two. Then Faye cleared her throat.

"I'll share my response. So…it's not easy being a single mom, and sometimes the hardest place for that is church," she began. Her confident demeanour faltered briefly before she took a deep breath and sat up straight.

"In my old church," she continued, "when I started attending again after a few years away, I could tell that people were running both me and Aiden through a filter. There was, like, a subtle coldness that wasn't there when I was growing up. I wasn't ready to be open and honest about some of the things I'd recently gone through, but there was no room given for the possibility that I was desperately looking to re-connect with God and my church family. I felt like I'd been put on trial behind my back, and was living out a sentence that no one bothered to tell me about."

Compassionate silence met the gap as she took another deep breath before continuing. "I couldn't stand it after a while, so I decided to try Victory Church. I knew they had a preschool program, so I thought it might be worth plugging in and checking it out. On my first Sunday there, everyone was so warm and friendly. They were excited about Aiden, and kind to me without those unspoken questions in their eyes. It seemed like, in the place of assumptions, there was only love.

"That's what I thought of when I read verse eight this week." A smile reached her eyes, and her confident voice returned without effort. "Victory Church lavished love on me and my son. Their welcome opened up my understanding of how God lavishes his love and grace on us too. That experience was a major springboard for bringing me closer to God, and for helping me come to terms with a lot of stuff that I'd gone through. The best part is, partly because of this church community, now I don't just know that God loves me. I *know* God loves me."

* * *

Two hours later, April was drinking iced tea on the couch in her small living room. The late June heat was slowly being carried out through the open window.

This living room was one of her favourite places. Its size reminded her of the Edmonton house, although the hardwood floor and eclectic mix of thrift store furniture could hardly compare to what she'd known before. Still, when she sat in here there was a cozy longing that pressed down like a weighted blanket in her mind. Sometimes she watched TV or movies, but often she preferred to read, or to just sit and think.

Faye said she *knew* God loved her. It seemed to be that way, didn't it? God's love was truly felt by those who had gone through something big and dramatic and life-altering. In Faye's case, it was by becoming a single mom and being ostracized by her former faith community. April was always thankful for her healthy upbringing and simple life, but sometimes she wondered if it was a barrier to knowing God more intimately. She'd never heard a testimony of someone with an uncomplicated existence like hers. Over the course of her teen years, she had been to many youth events and church services where former drug addicts, gang members, abused people, or crime victims shared about the redeeming power of God in their lives. It seemed to be a universal truth that a major life crisis was a prerequisite to experiencing God. Half-jokingly, April had often wondered if she should go break a law or do something extreme to see what came out the other side. But wasn't making good choices the best way to honour God in the first place?

She could relate to the older brother in the Prodigal Son story, watching while the returning struggler was celebrated and given all their father's riches while she stood back watching from her place of continuous, unnoticed labour.

Another popular Biblical image resonated strongly with her, but not in the way that redeemed wayward souls often spoke about.

Would she always feel like one of the ninety-nine that the Shepherd left to go in search of the lost sheep?

- Chapter Eight -

On the evening of Canada Day, Theo and April parked near the Exhibition grounds and walked to Diefenbaker Park. The live music could be heard from several blocks away. As they drew nearer, hand-in-hand, the scent of burgers lured them ever closer.

April could hardly wait for the fireworks to begin. Although her younger self had loved watching the shows that Baylor put on every year, the small town's budget clearly couldn't compare with what the city was able to afford. Last year had been her first time seeing the big event, although back then she was watching alone and wondering how it would feel to share the moment with someone else. Now, as she and Theo made their way through the clusters of people sitting on blankets and wandering around with food in their hands, she glanced at him and noted the stirring in her chest. Would the fireworks seem as romantic as she'd imagined they could be? It seemed cliché to expect that, but April didn't mind dealing in clichés. She'd been waiting for them ever since she'd understood the concept of falling in love.

"Hey, Jason!" Theo called out to someone in a large group nearby. It seemed like Theo knew everyone in Saskatoon, but that was to be expected for someone who grew up here. April smiled her way through the introductions and the small talk, and then they moved on toward the center of the park.

Theo's parents soon came into view at one of the picnic tables. According to Theo, they came early every year so they could snag one of them. His father, Grant, was standing at one end of the table, a camp barbecue under his watchful eye, while his mother held her grandbaby, Lila, on one hip. Isabelle gesticulated gracefully toward her beautifully-dressed daughter, Felicia, with her free hand. That was one thing April had noticed right away upon meeting the family—none of the women did anything in a clumsy way. Every movement either had purpose or poetry behind it. April wondered, not for the first time, how much secret judgment they harbored toward this girlfriend who was clearly not on the same level of class as the McTeagues.

"Theo, hello!" Isabelle crooned, pulling her son's arm so she could plant a gentle kiss on his cheek. "And April, how was Seth this week?"

"Really good! He let me keep my hand on his book for a bit longer than usual yesterday. I think we're making progress in the trust department."

"Well, that's wonderful! I'm sure he's delighted whenever you walk in the door."

Felicia, Theo's oldest sister, took a squirming Lila from her mother's arms. "Would you like to see Uncle?" she purred, handing the 6-month-old over to her brother's waiting arms. Theo kissed the baby's feather-soft hair as she reached up to pat his face.

"Well, hello to you too, darlin'!" he said, touching his forehead against hers.

April loved watching these two interact. Theo was a devoted uncle; she could only imagine what kind of father he would be one day.

Isabelle opened a large cooler and began to pull out Tupperware bowls, prompting April to wonder if she should have brought something. Should she offer to help now? If she were with her own family, her mom would tell her what she wanted her to do, and if she didn't say anything, April figured she wasn't needed. What kind of assumptions did Theo's family have about the proper way to interact while setting up a picnic?

While she debated what she should do, Theo's arm suddenly came around her middle and rested on her hip, pausing all thoughts. He smiled at her in a way that put her mind at ease. Whether or not he had sensed her inner struggle, he certainly seemed happy to be with her.

The evening passed in a semi-comfortable way. The McTeagues were good at telling stories on each other, and April found herself laughing along with them. Her lack of conversational initiative didn't seem to be a bother to anyone. Theo seemed quite proud of her, in spite of the fact she felt she didn't shine.

Felicia, her husband Tom, and little Lila had to leave shortly after supper. Theo's other sisters, Suzanna and Carissa, bounced around visiting other people they knew but always gravitated back to the family table. Suzanna's husband, Craig, was the other quiet family addition who made April feel less conspicuous for her reserved nature amongst the bubbly clan.

If only the two of them knew how to engage each other in conversation.

April excused herself to use the restroom just as the sky was edging over into darkness. The current band, a raucous metal group, played so loudly she could hardly hear a thing. So when she stepped outside of the squat concrete building and started back toward the table, she didn't notice that someone was trying to get her attention until her peripheral vision caught an arm waving wildly. She turned to look, and her jaw dropped.

The young woman was about twenty feet away, but April would recognize that beautiful, confident, heavily-pierced face anywhere. Throughout high school her hair had worn several different colours and styles, and now it nestled against her head in a purple buzz-cut. A low-cut maple leaf-adorned tank top hugged all the curves of her short but charismatic frame. Cosette was practically bouncing, and she ran over before April even had a chance to know what she was feeling.

"April, April, how in the world are you? Oh my gosh, I can't believe I ran into you here! What are the chances? I don't even live here, I'm just visiting some friends for the week, and oh my gosh, what are the chances of running into you? Hey, you've got to meet my friends! Guys! Guys!" Cosette motioned to the cluster of people she'd just burst away from, pulling on April's arm. April's stomach alerted her to the fact that this was not her favourite situation to find herself in, but there was no choice where Cosette was concerned. There never had been.

"Hey, this is my friend April! She and I were best friends for what, like, five years in Baylor? We did so much together, didn't we? Oh man, those were fun times. Do you remember climbing the grain elevator on the weekends? You guys, she's the one I told you about, the one that broke into the pool with me at like, three in the morning to go skinny-dipping, and no one ever found out!"

"Wow, April, I had no-no-no idea you had such a wild side!"

The deep voice made April's eyes shoot up toward a familiar face curtained by uncut brown hair, and her already-unsettled stomach jumped in distress.

"What? Rob, you know her?" Cosette asked.

"She's dating my roommate," Rob replied, dropping a cigarette butt to the grass and stubbing it out with his toe.

"What—you have a *boyfriend*?" Cosette squeezed April's arm even tighter. "You were such a total romantic back then, but you couldn't even talk to anyone! I'm so happy you have a boyfriend! Can I meet him? What's his name?"

"It's Theo," Rob cut in. "And she can still barely talk, at least not to me."

"Rob, you can be such a jerk sometimes." Cosette glowered at him, but then she laughed like it was actually quite funny. "Come on, April, let's leave these losers and find somewhere else to talk. Is Theo here? Can I meet him?"

Tears were pressing against the backs of April's eyes; she hated herself for it. It was a little easier to breathe as Cosette walked her away from the group, but only by a small margin.

There was a loud pop and a crackling sound. Both girls whipped their heads around to see the first sparkling trail making its way up the navy-blue sky before exploding in a cascade of white glitter.

"Ooh, I love fireworks," Cosette spoke loudly over the din. "So anyway, April, what are you up to these days? Are you in university, or what?"

"I'm…um..." April glanced around, trying frantically to find her bearings. She was pretty sure Cosette had pulled her in the opposite direction of Theo's family, but her spinning mind made physical orientation nearly impossible. "I'm…I'm taking a course for Rec Therapy. For working with people, like in nursing homes or care homes or community organizations."

"Oh, like working at that place in Baylor? Mary's Manor?" Cosette gasped. "Oh my gosh, that is right up your alley!"

"Maude's Manor," April replied. "And I'm supporting an autistic guy this summer. I get to hang out with him while his parents are at work." The sooner she got this conversation over with, the better. The last place she wanted to spend her first romantic-fireworks experience was away from her boyfriend, and with someone who made her feel smaller than she normally did.

"And what's this boyfriend of yours like?" Cosette asked between the loud sky-pops. "His name is Theo, right? That's what Rob said?"

April nodded, scanning the silhouetted crowd. Surely the man in question was out looking for her right now.

"Well, that's great, that's really great, April! Me, I'm between jobs right now. I was at a few restaurants in Regina for a bit, but I didn't like that work very much, and after this week I'm going to be moving to Calgary to stay with my cousin and try it out there. I think I'm destined for a bigger city, you know?"

"Back to Calgary?" April asked. Cosette had moved from there to Baylor in Grade Seven. She had complained incessantly about life in that city. Then again, she complained incessantly about life in Baylor too.

"Yeah, I figure I should give it another chance, now that I'm an adult and can make my own life choices." She suddenly burst out laughing. "Wow, these fireworks are lame. Calgary's were so much better growing up. Maybe you should visit me there next Canada Day and see what a real city is capable of."

"I should really find Theo." The pronouncement exploded out of April. "He's probably wondering where I am. I told him I was going to the bathroom, like, fifteen minutes ago."

"He probably just thinks you ate something rotten," Cosette guffawed. "Come on, I want to meet this guy who won over your carefully guarded heart!"

"He's with his family," April countered.

"The more the merrier! I can scope them out, make sure they're all good enough to be your in-laws one day! Come on, let's meet this fabulous guy."

April looked around, trying to think her way out of this situation, when a series of staccato booms exploded bright light over the whole park. In that brief moment, she spotted Suzanna looking right in her direction from quite a way off. Suzanna raised her hand before the darkness dropped back over everything.

Cosette had noticed her too. April found herself being pulled along so fast she almost tripped over a mound of grass or a blanket or something. She hoped it wasn't someone's leg.

"Hey, April, Theo went looking for you. Did you see him?" Suzanna ask-yelled over the next collection of pops.

"N-no," April replied. "Um…I guess he'll just come back?"

Cosette stuck out her hand. "Hi, I'm April's friend, Cosette. You must be Theo's family?"

The ladies of the family introduced themselves and asked polite questions of this friend, while April felt Cosette's grip loosen enough that she could pull her arm free. She drowned out the conversation for a few moments while craning her neck in all directions, but then she heard something that yanked her attention right back.

"…so then I heard this loud 'rip' and there was April, on the ground but with this huge hole in the back of her jeans, so after all of that I had to boost her back in the window so she could change before-"

"I don't think they need to hear the whole story, Cosette," April blurted out, her ears burning. "Come on, let's-"

"There you are!" Theo announced, putting his arm around April's shoulders. "I was getting worried."

"Oh, don't worry about her, she just ran into an old friend," Cosette positively bubbled, grabbing his free hand to shake it. "I'm Cosette! She must have told you about me?"

April was thankful the fireworks dimmed at that second, because Cosette turned to her with wide eyes and mouthed the words *he's hot!* with far too much enthusiasm.

"I recognize your name," he replied, oblivious to her nonverbal assessment.

"Oh, and it's funny—I introduced her to my friends just now, and one of my friends is your new roommate, Rob! What a small world!"

"Ah, the nicest person in the world. How do you know each other?"

"He and I dated last year. It didn't work out, but we're still friends. He's an idiot, but he can be fun too. Anyway, we should totally get together sometime, all of us! I'm in town for a few more days. Theo, I can tell you about sides of your girlfriend you probably didn't even know existed, oh my gosh!" She threw back her head and laughed. "Let's just say I was a bad influence, but she wasn't exactly timid about going along with me, you know what

I'm saying?" She poked her elbow in April's ribs, eliciting a plastic smile. "Okay, so what's your number?" She pulled her phone from her purse. In horror, April heard herself recite the landline to her house. At least it was one degree removed from sharing her personal cell number. Cosette shot Theo a mischievous grin before yanking April into a side hug. Then just like that, she bounded away into the night. "We'll talk later!" she hollered over her shoulder.

"Your friend sure has a lot of energy," Isabelle stated.

"She…she does," April replied, wondering how she might go about erasing the past ten minutes from everyone's minds.

"I'm going to take April for a walk closer to the river," Theo told his family. He took her hand in his, and they made their way through the clusters of people toward the back of the park. April could feel her heart rate slowing down, but she didn't know what Theo's tighter-than-usual hold on her hand meant.

There was an old swing set just off of a small parking lot by the riverbank. A group of people was hanging around there, the smell of cigarette smoke overlaying the subtle burnt scent from the fireworks. Theo and April walked past them, toward a bench that was surprisingly unoccupied. Here they sat, facing the show in the sky, Theo's arm stretched along the back of the bench while April leaned into him. Neither of them spoke up for a while.

In a perfect world, being here with Theo while watching the fireworks display was supposed to be the culmination of years of waiting for a moment like this. She had imagined they would share a few kisses, hold hands, say sweet things to each other. While not fully comfortable with his family yet, she thought the evening had gone well and would naturally slide into a delightfully romantic interlude before saying good-night with a full heart.

But then Cosette had thrown a brick through the window of her expectations.

"I'm…I'm sorry you couldn't find me," she offered.

"That's fine, April. I was just surprised. You're not usually the one to bump into someone you know and start chatting up a storm."

"*Me* chatting up a storm? Did you just *meet* Cosette? I can hardly even get a word in!"

"Then listening up a storm. Is that a thing?"

"With the right person, I guess it is. So…about what she said…"

"Oh, you mean about the wild side. Yeah, you don't talk much about your teen years, besides your family and Maude's Manor. What's this other stuff Cosette was talking about?" Theo turned to face her fully, his hand now kneading her shoulder. She couldn't tell if it was a massage or a coping mechanism for some kind of inner tension.

"It's…it's really not much. Like, I didn't sleep around. I didn't drink or go to parties. Really, Cosette's blowing it out of proportion because that's the way she's always been. I mean, for a goody-two-shoes like me, breaking any rules felt like a huge deal, but compared to a lot of people, I was basically an angel."

"So what exactly is she talking about?"

"Just a bunch of dumb stuff that your family knows about now. Stunts that I didn't really want to pull, but I felt like I had to go along with her."

"Why did you feel that way?"

The night was already wrecked. Might as well shovel some dirt on it, April figured.

"You know how I didn't have friends and was still super shy for the first little bit in Baylor? I mean, I stayed super shy the whole time, but in Grade Seven, Cosette and her mom moved to town. I watched her try to make friends in her first few weeks at school, but even the nice kids couldn't handle being around her for too long. She was extremely overbearing. The thing is, she was like that with me too, but I kind of liked it. She didn't seem to care that I hardly talked, or that when I did talk, I had a stutter. She gave me an automatic person to go to at recess and lunch, instead of inviting myself to always be on the edge of everyone else's action. On the other hand, I also felt sorry for her because I could see that the other kids didn't like her, so I felt good about being her friend. Maybe even a little proud."

"It sounds like you were being a good friend," Theo said with a nod. "That was your good heart in action."

"Well, yes and no. I tend to try to categorize things and figure out whether they were good or bad, and this…that whole time, all those years of being friends with her…I can't pin it down anywhere. I think the beginning felt all good, and I felt more comfortable in my skin with her. But…I almost wonder if I was just more comfortable hiding behind her and escaping myself for a while. You know what I mean?"

"Not exactly." Theo shook his head. "Can you explain it another way?"

"It's kind of like…I guess when you already feel small in the world, it's easy to get sucked into someone else's shadow. And that feels like a relief, at least for a bit. It felt like I was becoming free in some ways, but over time I realized that I was hating myself more and more. I felt like I was becoming a normal person, but at the same time I felt more and more trapped."

"Girls are so confusing," Theo sighed with mock exaggeration.

"Yeah, well, deal with it if you want to be with one. Especially this one."

"Why do you think you felt so small in the world to begin with, anyway, April? I've never even thought about how I feel in the world. I've always just been…I don't know, *me.* There's me in the world, but it's like saying there's oxygen in the air. It's there, but you don't overthink it or have feelings about it; it's just there. I'm here, you're here, everyone else is here, why overthink your size in the world? Doesn't that just take away from actually *living* in this world, and keep you stuck?"

"Ding ding ding, we have a winner!" April could hardly disguise the irritation in her voice. "Theo, why do you think I hated myself so much? Sometimes still do? In fact, *often* still do! Don't you think I'm fully aware that I'm stuck, and that I hate being stuck, and that I feel like a loser just for the fact that I'm not actually *living,* as you say?"

"Okay, I didn't mean it like that. Come on, April, you *are* living! You've got this program and job that are perfect for you, and they make a difference in the world. You have a family that loves you. You're involved in a church and small group with people who care about you. You have a bumbling but attentive boyfriend who doesn't fully understand you, but wants to, and you are a hard worker with goals and dreams. What about your life isn't fully living? Being shy doesn't take that away from you."

"It's…it's deeper than all that," April sighed. "I don't know, sometimes I've wondered if talking to a therapist or counsellor would help, because I agree with you—there is a lot of good in my life. I have no right to feel so small and disconnected from most of it. I mean, literally, the only time I feel truly connected with anything these days is when I'm with Seth." The thought of frantically adding "and you" came a little too late, and by the time she almost voiced it, Theo had already stiffened up.

"Well then." Theo gave her shoulder a final squeeze and removed his arm from the back of the bench. "It's nice to know where I stand."

April put her hand on his arm. "Theo, I didn't mean it like that. I usually feel connected to you too. I do! It's just…I don't know how to explain myself. I'm way more complicated than I wish I was. The thing is, I like you a lot. I'm *crazy* about you."

"But not crazy enough to feel comfortable with me?" The hurt in his voice made her grit her teeth in self-directed anger.

"I *do* feel comfortable with you. It's just different somehow. It's like, with Seth…I don't know," she swished her hand around while frantically searching for a description. "I don't worry about what he thinks of me. I don't wonder if I'm 'being' right, or 'doing' the right thing. It's effortless. Right off the bat, it was clear that neither of us felt expectations oozing out of each other. But it seems like, with everyone else, I'm always on edge even when I'm not. Like now. Look at this, right here. I'm 'doing' this wrong. Look at what a mess I've made of our night. Instead of enjoying the fireworks with my amazing boyfriend, I've accidentally hurt him by trying to explain myself and botching it so badly. When the real me tries to poke out, I lose control of the outcome." She looked sadly at her lap. "I never meant to imply we're not connected, Theo."

"But you did." He sat up straight.

"No. You're reading too much into my words. It's not as simple as that." April stood up and began to pace in front of the bench. "I'm trying to think of how to explain it to you better, but I don't even understand it myself."

She stopped pacing and stared hard at the dark ground as if it would give her the right words to say. Nothing was coming. The silence stretched on between them while the sounds around them illuminated the invisible wedge.

The thing is, I do *understand it. I understand that I don't feel like I can always let my guard down around Theo. But I didn't want him to know that, and now I can't take the words back. Way to go, you nervous rambler.*

"This has been a fun night," Theo said dryly. "But I think I'll have to go home and lick my wounds for now."

"Theo—"

"No, try not to feel bad. I'm trying to understand. I just don't know what to say right now." He stood up and held out his hand. April took it. They walked together as the crowd cheered. The grand finale of the fireworks show had come and gone, and they hadn't even noticed.

After passing the McTeagues and saying their good-byes, Theo and April carried on toward his car. They turned the first corner out of sight of Diefenbaker Park. Theo quietly released April's hand for the remainder of their walk.

- Chapter Nine -

Even though her heart was a little tender—maybe even because of it, she couldn't tell—April's resolve to level up with Seth became stronger. On Friday she had stated her intent when his stepmom arrived home from work, and Vanessa agreed that it was a good goal for the next week.

Monday morning dawned mild and sunny. The plan was to take Seth for his first car ride with her and go for a walk at a different park in the city. It would be a break in the routine they had established—being in the house all morning, eating lunch, then going for a walk in the park by Seth's house—but not such a big leap that Seth couldn't handle it. With his family, Seth was often going to different places in the city and trying new things, but they had the obvious benefit of a lifetime together. April knew it would be a healthy stretch for Seth to experience a new thing with a new friend.

Seth was content that April was here and lunch was almost finished, but when she said it was time for a car ride, he didn't like that idea at first, but then April said that she had a new book to share with Seth in the car and that he could line it while they went for a drive to Rotary Park. Seth knew that Rotary Park was beside the river, and he went there sometimes with Dad and Mom, and one time a frisbee fell on the path in front of them, which was unexpected but funny because of the sound it made, like a miniature clap of thunder, and it was delightfully red. The new book was sitting in April's car, which was white but had red-orange rust spots above the wheels. Sometimes car rides made his tummy feel calm but his eyes feel full of too many quick lights, especially if there were lots of trees making the sun blink too fast through the window, but that usually didn't last too long and anyway it was interesting as well. Seth knew that it was important to go to the bathroom first, so he did that and April reminded him to wash his hands, and now his hands smelled like flowers as he and April walked out the front door and went down the metal elevator.

It seemed like they should walk past her car like they usually did on their way to the park, but then she turned toward the car and said, "The new book is back there, in the backseat. My seats are gray and soft, and the book is called *Moby Dick*. It's about a whale." Mom and Dad had cars too, but theirs didn't have red-orange rust spots and Seth was interested in riding in a car with red-orange rust spots, so even though the seats felt different and his knees had to bend even more than normal when he sat down really low to get in, he was happy. He hardly even noticed when April reached around him to put on the seatbelt because he had picked up the new book and was lining it as soon as he flipped it open.

April noticed her hands were shaking, but in a good way. She glanced in the rear-view mirror at Seth, whose head was bent over the book. Vanessa had told her that Seth rode in the backseat in order to stay consistent from vehicle-to-vehicle, since some had screens in the console.

So far this seemed too easy. Maybe it really would be smoother than she'd expected? Vanessa had talked like it was a big step, yet in a relaxed manner that now made April wonder if the insinuation of the big step was more for her sake or Seth's. Maybe Seth would have been ready on day one, yet his parents knew that they had hired someone who needed more time to break routine? Either way, she supposed it didn't matter. She had quickly become his friend, and she knew that being his friend meant that he was also being *her* friend, and since it was a relationship, they both had to be genuine. If that meant he made allowances for her to be the scaredy-cat one, so be it.

It was a fifteen-minute drive to Rotary Park. Seth was silently lining the whole time. The radio was tuned into a country station, quiet enough to be background noise but loud enough for her to recognize the songs. *Bless the Broken Road* by Rascal Flatts came on. She wondered if she and Theo would have a broken road on their way to long-term love, but that thought did nothing to assist with her triumphant state of mind, so she turned it off. Shoving aside the image of Theo's pained expression on the weekend, she turned into the parking lot of their destination.

He knew the car stopped and the engine was turned off, but also he didn't really notice all that much because he was still lining. He was aware that the buzzing in his head was growing louder—he liked April and he liked Rotary Park and he now knew that he liked riding in her car, but he didn't know yet if he liked all of it together. The sun's heat against his leg lessened when April opened his door and her shadow fell across the backseat where he was sitting.

"We're going to walk here, Seth, but you can let me know when you're ready."

She was still standing there a few pages later, and her shadow had darkened the pages so that they weren't as bright to look at, which made his eyes more comfortable, so it was nice that she was standing there.

This new book was not only thick and full of great lines, but it was extra-helpful because of the buzzing in his head being louder than usual in this exact circumstance, so Seth was lining even faster than normal. April's shadow came and went a number of times—he didn't know exactly how many—and even though the sun's warmth was pleasing, his back was becoming a bit damp. He noticed loud music from other cars a few times, but it always stopped abruptly when the cars parked nearby. A baby was crying somewhere farther away, and April talked quite a few times, but as the buzzing in his head continued to grow, he couldn't pay attention to her words very much. One time she put her hand on his book, but he pulled it away because in that moment the buzzing got especially loud, like it did the first time she touched his book at home.

At some point, without even noticing exactly how it happened, his door was closed and the engine was running again and they were driving away from the parking lot. He lined and lined and lined and the next time he looked up was when the car stopped and the engine turned off, and they were in front of his house. The buzzing immediately started to go down, but then Seth remembered that April had said that they were going to walk at Rotary Park, but they hadn't done that, and now they were home, and he was very happy to be home, but he knew he had missed his chance to see if a red frisbee would land on the path again. April opened his door and told him that Moby Dick would stay in the car for the next time they drove somewhere, and that he could go inside and go back to the newspaper from this morning.

He lined a few more pages and realized that the buzzing was going down, but some deep, sad feeling was rising up. He was soon able to set down the new book because April said it would be there next time, and anyway, he wanted to get back to the newspaper on his couch. The sad feeling made him look down at the sidewalk very hard as he held April's arm on the way inside, and she stayed beside him the whole way to the couch. Then she sat beside him and she gave him his newspaper and told him that he was a great person and she was *very* pleased that they got to spend time together in her car today. She said that they would go to Rotary Park another day. The sad feeling inside of him began to fade after she said that, and when she put her hand on the other page of the newspaper and traced a few lines while he traced his lines on the other page, it was right and good, and he was so happy to be with her.

- Chapter Ten -

It was pure, unadulterated pleasure to be pushing Linus' stroller along the path while he smiled and babbled at her from under his blue-brimmed hat. She knew that one day he'd start facing forward in the stroller. While that would be fun in its own way, Robyn wondered if she would miss the amount of eye contact they had on their outings now. Someday, the world around him would become more interesting than his mom's face.

If I'm this sappy now, what will I be like when he starts daycare?

It was mid-July, which meant that maternity leave was officially at the halfway mark. Part of her thrilled at the idea of returning to the job she loved. She missed the classroom—the challenge of engaging a multitude of personalities at once, the creative outlets of decorating the room and coming up with art activities for each new theme. There was also the matter of the paycheque, which she knew would be mostly eaten up by childcare costs, but that little extra on top would make a difference in paying down their mortgage and reducing her student loan debt.

Patrick had insisted that the decision to stay home or return to work was completely up to her. She had wrestled through that choice all the way through pregnancy and then in the first few months of external motherhood. Her mom had stayed home full-time, but her mother-in-law had returned to work after each of her children were born, and both extolled the virtues of their decision. In the same way, reading opinion pieces online and in magazines left her with no objective hard lines, other than to realize that her decision would be heavily praised and criticized either way, possibly even by Linus himself one day. Her heart belonged with Linus, and to a lesser degree with teaching. Yet as her energy returned, her mind and ideas belonged more heavily with teaching, and with easing the family's financial burdens.

On the evening of recognizing this gravitational pull, the simultaneous weight and release of recognizing her final decision had made her cry in bed. Patrick had held her as she tried to express herself, but while the hug felt nice, it heaped guilt on top of the turmoil that she was already shedding tears over.

God, why is even a simple life so complicated? She prayed silently now, before catching herself and remembering that she had something to hide from her maker. Of course, she knew that he knew about the thing that really wasn't actually a thing, but still…

Robyn lifted her gaze away from her son's face to take in the river on her left.

Rotary Park was one of her favourite places. The riverbank was shallow, bringing the water views closer to eye level when you took the paved path parallel to it. There were often canoes or kayaks coasting downstream, and all sorts of people basking in the wide-open green space between the path and the parking lot. Robyn loved for Linus to experience the joys of fresh air and nature, as well as the communal joy of being amongst other people who were enjoying it in their own ways. She was already looking forward to his future experiences of field trips with classmates, learning about the world around him and making memories with his friends. He likely wouldn't grow up with a cabin as a second home the way she did, but she would love to take him to her lake at least once and show him all the places she used to play, maybe even knock on the door of the family that had purchased her parents' cabin and ask for a tour…and possibly walk the paths between her cabin and Devon's, just for old times' sake.

As she was about to veer off the trail to pull out a bottle for Linus, Robyn heard somebody call her name. It was hard to shake that out-of-context vagueness when she saw the couple making their way down the path in her direction, but the young man's awkward gait and the lovely dark bob on the woman beside him made her gasp with delight.

"April! Hi!" she called back with a wave. "Is this Seth?"

They were about fifteen feet away. Robyn decided to wait instead of walking toward them. She recognized that Seth had a very pointed focus on his steps and likely wouldn't appreciate being stopped suddenly.

"Yes, we've been coming here a couple of times a week for the past little while," April called back. "The first few times he didn't want to leave the car, but now we walk around the park like a couple of pros, don't we, Seth?"

Robyn noted the pride and warmth in April's voice, as well as the lack of stutter. Small group had met together three or four times, and April had never initiated a conversation before, let alone with such volume and confidence.

"That's great! Hi Seth. I'm April's friend, Robyn, and this is my baby, Linus."

They were about five feet away now. Seth glanced up and back down, not breaking stride.

"How's your day going so far?" April asked, just as Robyn felt a vibration in her back pocket. It could be the pediatrician finally getting back to her. She nodded and held up an apologetic finger while pulling out her phone, saying, "I'm so sorry, this might be something I need to take."

As she attempted to make out what was on call display, April cried out, "Seth, no!" Robyn had barely registered Dr. Chan's name on the screen before the phone was snatched away. April's arm flung out in front of her, momentarily coming between her and the stroller. The sudden surge of tension and movement right in front of Linus caused Robyn's protective instincts to shove past April's arm and run away with the stroller for a few feet before she came to her senses and turned around. Seth had her phone and was squeezing it a few inches from his face with one hand, while jabbing a finger against the screen in a display of aggression she hadn't realized his boyish demeanour was capable of. April was pleading with him to trade out the phone for a book that she held open in front of him, trying to maneuver it between his face and the phone, but there was no yielding. With a cry that sounded equal parts angry and afraid, Seth threw the device like a shot put. It narrowly missed April's head and landed in the grass behind her.

Robyn watched as April slid the book into Seth's now-empty hands with a quivery "sorry" mumbled over her shoulder. Seth appeared to be dazed as he took the book and moved his finger along the lines robotically. He was breathing hard, and so was April, but it seemed clear that the struggle was over.

Robyn started toward the phone, then stopped herself. Maybe it was best not to draw attention to it at all until Seth was gone. She took a deep breath to slough off the leftover buzzing from the adrenaline rush. Linus was kicking his pudgy feet in the air—when had he pulled off his socks?—and Robyn gave his button nose a playful little poke, which set him to laughing and telling her a story with all sorts of noises.

"It's okay," she replied to April, just quietly enough to not interrupt Seth's calming-down ritual.

"Seth, let's go a little bit farther," April said. "We're almost at our turn-around spot."

Robyn watched as Seth glanced up. April slipped the book out of his hands and offered her arm, which Seth took before they carried on. They passed the spot where the phone had landed, but a tree's shadow helped to conceal it. As soon as they were past it, Robyn quietly slipped over to it and, without even checking the display, shoved it back in her pocket. She pushed the stroller a little farther into the grass, then stopped and remembered the bottle. Pulling it out of the side pocket of the diaper bag, she handed it to Linus, then watched as April and Seth stopped beside a park bench. They were far enough away that Robyn couldn't hear, but she saw that April was in front of Seth and looking directly at his downcast face, apparently trying to make eye contact. The gentleness in her face was clear, even from this distance; yet Seth's shoulders were slumped in a universal display that made Robyn's heart ache for him. After a beat or two, the duo turned around and started to walk back the way they'd come.

Robyn pushed the stroller through the grass toward the parking lot while Linus enjoyed his bottle. She took her time detaching the bucket seat from the stroller and clicking it into the backseat, then folding up the stroller and lifting it into the trunk. Those tasks completed, she waited by her open door as April and Seth made their way toward a rusty white car just a few vehicles down.

Robyn smiled at them, but neither of them looked up to notice. She checked to see that the bottle was empty, then took it from Linus and replaced it with a duck-shaped teething toy which he promptly jammed into his mouth. Robyn closed the door and hit command start so the air conditioning could flow, watching as April assisted Seth into her car. Then she walked over and said, "Hey."

April looked up and offered a sheepish grimace. "I'm…I'm so sorry, Robyn. I can pay for-"

"Not even a question," Robyn cut her off. "I'm sure my phone is fine. I just came over to tell Seth how nice it was to finally meet him."

She knelt to be at the same level as the young man in the backseat who was buckled up, finger-tracing the lines in his book and wearing shame like a cloak.

"I hope I see you here again sometime, Seth. It's a beautiful park. I'm glad I met you at one of my favourite places."

His demeanour didn't change, but when Robyn stood up, she saw that April's had. The younger woman's eyes shimmered with gratitude. April mouthed, "Thank you" and stepped forward as if to hug Robyn, then bolted herself into place.

"Anytime," Robyn said, starting back toward her own car. "See you on Thursday!"

Once seated behind the steering wheel, she checked her phone, which was intact. She called Dr. Chan's office back and thought about the young man with the boyish face, and her small group member whom she'd finally seen with her guard down. Shoving aside that she was not fully facing God these days, Robyn tossed up a quick prayer for Seth and April before Dr. Chan's assistant picked up the line.

* * *

Twenty minutes later, after depositing himself on the couch with his magazines, Seth's shoulders continued to slump. April gave him as many reassurances as possible that he was a good person and that no one was mad, but the lump in her throat probably made her sound like a liar. Really, when was the last time she had a good cry? *I need to watch a sad movie tonight,* she thought to herself. Time for some cathartic release.

On top of today's experience, the situation with Theo sat like an undigested lump deep inside of her. She tried to remind her stressed-out heart that they had found each other again in the few weeks since the Canada Day fiasco. In fact, a couple of days ago they'd managed to address that elephant in the room.

It had begun with Theo asking, while they sat across from each other at a diner on Broadway Avenue, if she was doing okay.

Too many thoughts hit her at once. She had asked, "What do you mean?"

"I mean…" he shrugged. "I mean, are we okay? Are you

happy with me?"

"Yes, of course I am," she replied without hesitation. "I mean…yeah, I'm sorry again about that conversation on Canada Day. I was just thrown off by Cosette. Seeing her kicked up a lot of weird feelings, and I got weird with you." His silence lingered long enough that she wondered if he expected more from her. "I think it's okay if we just forget about the whole thing, Theo."

"That works for me," Theo responded. "We all have our off-moments. But there's no one else I'd rather fight with than you."

April put her hand on top of his, shoving aside the notion of unfinished business. Theo was happy with her again. They'd had a real fight, but it hadn't been too bad, all things considered. Still, it had been unpleasant enough that she wondered how to avoid such problems in the future.

April brought to mind her resolve to regard others as more important than herself just as Theo said, "I love you."

Knowing he deserved to hear it back this time, she pushed out a whispered response: "I love you too."

He hopped up from his side of the table and squeezed in next to her. The enthusiastic kiss he planted on her right after that seemed to linger for days.

Even now, sitting beside Seth, that moment came back to her with surprising force and she smiled. Things weren't perfect, but she was going to continue working on being what Theo deserved for her to be.

Seth was still lining, but when April brought her attention back to the present circumstance, she realized that his hand was going much slower than usual. She looked into his face and saw a sheen of moisture that she'd never seen before. Her heart cracked open, and she turned completely sideways on the couch.

"Oh, Seth," she murmured softly, resisting the urge to hug him. "You know you are *so* loved and you have *such* a good heart, right? What happened at the park today is finished. My friend Robyn isn't upset. She knows you're more important than her phone."

Seth was still lining slowly. The wetness in his eyes swelled until one tiny tear trickled down his cheek. He lifted his head with surprise.

April instinctively reached up to wipe it, then stopped herself and asked if she could. Seth indicated nothing, but held his face still.

Gingerly, April touched her thumb tip to the bottom of his cheek to reach the end of the tiny rivulet. When he didn't flinch or pull away, April allowed the touch to linger for just a few seconds, then pressed in gently to wipe upwards and then pull her hand away.

It was so subtle that April wondered if she imagined it, but Seth's eyes darted toward hers for a split second before he turned back to his magazine and began lining in his normal way.

Oh Seth, if only you understood that you are worth more than your weakest moments, April thought. Carried by the momentum of the gift he had just given her, she prayed that God would help him realize how loved he was. She thought of verse eighteen from last week's small group study on the third chapter of Ephesians: "I pray that you, being rooted and established in love, may have power, together with all the Lord's holy people, to grasp how wide and long and high and deep is the love of Christ."

God, give him strength in his inner being to trust in how much you love him. And how much I love him too.

- Chapter Eleven -

It was Sunday afternoon, and Linus was napping. His sleep independence had grown exponentially over the course of the past few weeks; therefore, Robyn's hope for a smooth transition to daycare was growing. Not only was he on a semi-regular schedule, but he was also becoming less insistent on nursing. He seemed just as content with a bottle of her expressed milk. He was gumming soft foods very easily, and he loved to roll sideways across the living room floor, looking for the next item to investigate. His dependence on her was easing up to the point that Patrick's recurring advice seemed more and more plausible. Maybe a weekend away with friends was on the docket? When Patrick first suggested it back in the spring, Robyn appreciated the sentiment but balked at the ridiculous impossibility of it, both for her sake and Linus'.

It's not just about me, she realized. *Patrick wants some one-on-one time with his son, too.*

Or maybe he wants you out of the house because he needs a break from you.

The notion seemed unlikely, but it was followed up with *don't* I *need a break from* him? *From feeling guilty whenever I look at him? Maybe a little time away will make me miss him enough to put him back in first place…*

An incoming text jolted her from her thoughts. Robyn read it and burst out laughing from her perch on the edge of the empty tub, then slapped her hand over her mouth and cursed herself. How could she be so careless? Quickly, she glanced at the closed bathroom door as if to discern whether Patrick might have heard her from where she'd left him, sitting alone in the living room.

Stop being so funny! she tapped into her phone.

His response was quick: I can't help it! I sure would like to actually hear your laugh again sometime, though. Snorts and all. I'll have to be funnier next time I call you.

I didn't snort this time. I think that was part of my youth. Now I'm an old married mom.

There was no reply for a minute. Suddenly Robyn's awareness of time kicked into gear. She stood up from the edge of the tub, flushed the toilet and washed her hands. She itched for a response, but it wasn't coming, and now her time was up. Turning off her phone's notifications, she exited the bathroom and strode into the living room with feigned nonchalance. Patrick watched her enter, amusement beaming from his face.

"Sounds like you're enjoying a little bathroom humour," he remarked.

"Ha ha, very funny! I don't comment on the loud noises I hear from you in there," she answered with a playful shoulder jab. His eyes sparked with delight. Robyn tried to ignore the surprise that registered there as well. He clearly wasn't used to this lightheartedness from her lately. Little did he know, it wasn't even because of him.

Patrick gave her shoulder a gentle counter-jab while he told her to put up her dukes. This was how they used to flirt. This was how they used to play. Robyn forced a smile and begged her eyes not to reveal too much as she responded by gently shadowboxing with her husband, just like they used to do when things were easy.

Like in the old days, they ended up in a heap on the nearest couch.

Patrick kissed her passionately. Robyn went through the motions of reciprocating, trying but repeatedly failing to push Devon's face out of her mind.

Patrick slowed down and pulled back, looking intently into her eyes. Robyn tried to hold his gaze, but shame and fear turned her face away.

"Robyn," Patrick said softly, touching her cheek. She shook her head and felt her throat tighten up. He turned her face toward his, but she couldn't look. She ducked her head and pulled away, standing up and pulling down the hem of her shirt.

"Robyn," he tried again. "What's wrong?"

She finally made herself look at him, and the love that emanated from his face nearly broke her.

I could stop all contact at any time, she thought. *Patrick doesn't even need to know. Not that there's anything wrong happening.*

But Devon's going through a hard time supporting his sister. He needs me right now. Maybe after Carly is settled…

"I'm just really hormonal," Robyn whispered. "I'm sorry."

Patrick stood up and started to put his arms out just as Linus wailed from down the hall.

"I'd better go get him," Robyn said hoarsely, offering up a little smile in her husband's direction as she walked away.

* * *

Across the city, in April's cozy living room, she and Theo were comparing notes on their study of Ephesians 4. Two cups of iced tea sat on the floor, thin circles of condensation marking the hardwood around them. The blinds were pulled down over the picture window and a fan blew quietly in the corner, but April could still feel the stickiness under her shirt and she assumed it was even less comfortable for Theo. At present, he was flipping a few pages back in his Bible to Galatians while looking irresistibly handsome in his royal blue polo shirt and khaki shorts.

"Okay," he said, sticking his finger on the page. "So the list of the 'Fruits of the Spirit' says, 'love, joy, peace, patience, kindness, goodness, faithfulness, gentleness and self-control.'" He said it in a slightly sing-song voice from a familiar childhood Sunday School tune, evoking an affectionate smirk from April. "And Ephesians 4:1-3 says," he flipped back to where another finger had kept the spot, "As a prisoner of the Lord, then, I urge you to live a life worthy of the calling you have received. Be completely humble and gentle; be patient, bearing with one another in love. Make every effort to keep the unity of the Spirit through the bond of peace.'"

April looked at the notes she had already written. "I wrote down that both lists include love, peace, patience, and gentleness," she said, in response to the study's first question. In response to the second question, the source of the fruit in Galatians, she read aloud, "The source of the fruit in Galatians is the Holy Spirit. It makes sense that the Holy Spirit is also the source of the characteristics listed in Ephesians 4:1-3, because most of them are the same. Ephesians 4:3 also calls us to 'make every effort to keep the unity of the Spirit through the bond of peace,' which also seems to say that the Holy Spirit is necessary for the kind of unity and peace Paul is describing."

Theo nodded along. "Yep, that's pretty much what I got out of it too," he said. As he expounded his thoughts on the role of the Holy Spirit in the life of a believer, April tried to focus on his words, but she was too distracted by her impressions.

He is such a good guy, and he takes the Bible so seriously. How could I be so lucky? A sense of unworthiness shimmered on the horizon, just enough to make her wonder why she would ever question whether Theo was the right fit for her.

Theo finished speaking and pressed the cool glass to his forehead. "I'm glad I wrote these things down yesterday, because I don't think I'd be able to think clearly today with this heat."

"Well, you sounded really wise. So, good job on that," April said, fanning his face with her study papers. "Do you want to finish at your place? You have air conditioning."

"Yes, but I also have Rob. He was there when I left, and I don't think he has work today." He frowned, then said, "In light of the Bible study, I've been trying to be nicer to him. Since I've been reminded that I'm supposed to care about his needs, not just my own. You know?"

Yes, I know very well. April nodded, taking a long drink.

"He's basically the last person I want to be nice to, but the other day I decided to try having an actual conversation with him."

"Really? How did it go?"

"Not too bad. All I did was mention that I was grabbing some pizza for supper and I asked if he wanted any, and he said sure, and then we talked for a few minutes about the best pizza places. Not exactly deep and meaningful, but it's the first time we've been civil to each other."

"Maybe you should have called it 'peace-za.'"

Theo stared at her. "Lame."

"I don't know, I think I could give your dad a run for his money."

"And you two can share jokes back and forth while the rest of us watch on in horror and I try to pretend I don't even know you."

April whacked his arm. "Yeah right. You'd be so proud, and you'd try to join in, but then you'd be embarrassed because you can't keep up."

"So, backing up," Theo said with a grin. "I'm trying to be better about Rob, but I'm still not sure it's a good idea to hang out there today. If he's rude it'll set back my progress in wanting to actually try with him."

"Fair enough. So, overheating at April's house it is."

They continued their study while April gave in to the sense of their connectedness today.

He is such a good guy, she thought again. *Satan must be working overtime to try and convince me that something's wrong here. This is obviously what God wants for me.*

Her constantly clenched stomach didn't get the memo, but it was a sturdy enough shelf to rest her thoughts on for now.

* * *

That same day, the late afternoon offered up a refreshing breeze through the Zhous' open front door as the couple wrapped up their own personal discussion on Ephesians 4 in preparation for Thursday. What had started out as a stilted, overly polite question-and-answer session had gradually morphed into normal conversational tones.

Linus was playing with his toys on the floor while his dad asked, in a silly voice meant to provoke the belly laugh that Linus was famous for, "Verse 29 says, 'Do not let any unwholesome talk come out of your mouths, but only what is helpful for building others up according to their needs, that it may benefit those who listen.' What are some examples of unwholesome talk?"

Robyn smiled at her son's raucous laughter. Patrick scooped him up and nuzzled his face into Linus' belly, which intensified the happy reaction. As she sat across from them and watched the scene, a quietly clear answer to the study question dropped into her heart with a blindsiding impact: *unwholesome talk can be any kind of talking—or texting—that makes your heart unfaithful.*

She thought of the phone, silently waiting in her pocket for the next bathroom break. For the first time, she admitted to herself that the slippery slope she'd been trying to ignore was passing the 45-degree-angle mark and she was already losing her footing.

Whether or not she was willing to stop the decline was a whole other matter.

* * *

When Thursday night rolled around, everyone was there

except Yvette, who had told them the previous week that she was going to visit her family. As the rest of the group chatted amongst themselves, catching each other up on how their weeks had gone, April couldn't help but notice how pale Myla appeared to be. She was still her usual chatty self, but with slightly decreased volume and speed. April also noted Robyn's constant avoidance of her husband's attention. Whenever he looked her way, she made a point of paying closer attention to the conversation on her other side. When he put a hand on her back, she was suddenly inspired to go fetch more napkins from the kitchen.

For her part, April was enjoying the feel of Theo's arm along the back of her chair. He was chatting with Samuel on the other side of her, and she was half-listening, half-observing the two distressed ladies across the room. A memory flashed across her mind, transporting her momentarily to the Grade Nine classroom during lunch hour one day.

She and Cosette were eating together in one corner of the room. As usual, there was a general din of chatter punctuated by the occasional adolescent noise burst. On the other side of the room sat Aimee and Cassandra and a few of the other girls, while the boys mostly took up the middle rows.

"Do you see how mad Aimee looks?" Cosette said to April, being careful not to glance in the given direction. "She keeps looking at Jackson while she's talking, and Jackson doesn't even notice. She looks super ragey. I wonder if they're going to break up again. They can't seem to make it stick more than a week at a time."

"I didn't know they were dating again," April said even more quietly, forcing Cosette to lean in.

"I think they got tired of keeping everyone updated," Cosette said with a laugh. "Anyway, if you want to know what a girl looks like when she's given her heart away to a guy who doesn't care anymore, that's it."

"How do you know he doesn't care? It just looks like he hasn't noticed. He's not even facing her right now."

"Do you see him looking at her, or trying to talk to her in the hallway anymore? Guys aren't as clueless as people say they are. They just stop caring. They want the girls who are easy to keep happy, and when happy goes out the window, they stop trying. When girls become too much work, guys move on."

Cosette suddenly turned all her attention on April, boring a look deep into her eyes.

"I know you want to get married someday, so trust me, if you want it to last, don't show your husband your troubles," she said with her trademark confidence. "Save them for me. I'll be like the third wheel in your marriage, maintaining your emotions so he'll keep you, but I'll still be free to do whatever I want whenever I want, and then we'll all be happy." She laughed again, and April laughed along with her but felt a sense of dread drop into her stomach at the way Cosette's words had cast her formless suspicions into something concrete. Happy marriages were the union of a happy wife with a husband who didn't have to work to keep her that way. Hadn't Cosette as much as told her that her mom's neediness is what had driven her dad into another woman's arms, effectively ending their marriage? In contrast, April's parents had a successful long-term marriage, in which April had rarely seen her mom cry, or her dad ever act like he wanted to avoid her. It seemed like the Bible and Cosette were in agreement about at least one thing: putting other people first was the best way. Apparently, it helped you keep them around, and it made God happy.

But what about your own needs? Was it possible to share your needs without it becoming a problem, or was it best to ignore them until they went away? Was putting others first like a muscle you exercised until you didn't have the weakness of your own needs anymore?

April supposed that marriage would be a good place to apply this exercise one day. Until then, continuing to practice it with family members and friends would do. That way, when the right guy came along, she would be ready to jump right in. In some ways, Cosette was an ideal training ground for this. Her big personality showed April how to put someone else first, simply because there was no choice to do otherwise. Hopefully April's future husband would be like Cosette in that way. That would be rather helpful.

The memory came to a stop as Patrick called the group to attention. He himself was acting normal, and if he noticed Robyn's refusal to engage in non-verbal reciprocity, he didn't let it show.

Was Robyn making the mistake of forgetting to put her husband first? Being with Theo, a man who had a strong character yet was easily hurt by her fumbled explanations of herself, had taught her that romantic relationships were far more complicated than she had expected them to be. Perhaps she and Robyn could talk someday and help encourage each other in their respective journeys.

After the way Robyn interacted with Seth in the park that one day, the idea of reaching out to her in friendship didn't seem impossible.

Robyn didn't have a lot to say throughout the discussions that evening. Her inner world was momentarily soothed by the distraction of a lively exchange on the Person of the Holy Spirit. Theo had brought up the topic of baptism, which garnered a mix of reactions from around the room. Faye had been baptized as a baby in her parents' church. Myla and Asher had both been baptized in their teens and were adamant that it was the only way.

"Baptizing an infant means it's not the person's choice, so why would their parents do that to them? Either they're following a tradition that's based on fear of their baby dying before they have a chance to consciously choose faith in God, or they don't know any different," Asher said confidently.

Faye had been sliding closer to the edge of her seat and shaking her head slightly, and with a clipped tone she replied, "I'd invite you not to assume anything about my parents' faith or what drove their decision." She sat back in her chair and threw up her hands. "See, this is what drives me crazy. When believers don't understand why other denominations do things differently, the belief is that they're ignorant or inferior. Paul talks about the importance of unity in the church. How can we reach for that if we start by making assumptions about our brothers and sisters just because we don't understand the things they do?"

The conversation carried on, at times with an edge of tension. Robyn saw that Patrick was leaning forward in the ready position, prepared to facilitate if things got out of hand, but they never did.

By the end of that topic, it seemed like no one had changed their minds, but maybe some greater mutual understandings had been gained. She was curious about how Myla and Asher might talk about "those infant baptizers" in the future; it was a topic that, when amongst fellow believer baptists, they had both allowed themselves to express their opinions without restraint. It was easy to let a judgmental stance run unchecked when you were always preaching to the choir.

Near the end of the evening, Patrick read aloud the final study question: "Verses 26-27 say, '"In your anger do not sin": Do not let the sun go down while you are still angry, and do not give the devil a foothold.' What does this passage tell us about the role that anger plays in our lives, and what are some ways that anger gives the devil a foothold?"

"I think tonight is a great example of this," Samuel said after a beat of silence. "Was there some anger? Yes. It was small, but it was there. Was the anger wrong? I do not believe so, because anger is just an emotion that we cannot help. The question is, did the anger go underground and become a playground for the devil in anyone's mind after these conflicting views were discussed? Only each of us can answer that before God, because that is where we nip it in the bud. If we leave here tonight harbouring any ill will toward our neighbours in this group, or thinking they are all wrong and we are all right, then this will start a process of driving a wedge between brothers and sisters. Even small wedges are to be managed before they become big wedges."

Patrick was nodding his head.

Robyn glanced at him and wondered what he thought about the wedge in their marriage. Was he thinking about it, or simply trying to wait it out?

A few minutes later, prayer requests were being shared. Samuel shared the praise item that he was going out to visit his girlfriend in Toronto in two weeks.

"Are you going to propose?" Myla asked, clasping her hands together. Despite her smile, it was shocking to see how much paler she had gotten since the start of the evening.

Samuel just grinned and said, "When it is time for me to propose, besides God, she will be the first to know."

A retching sound erupted from Myla. She clasped her hand over her mouth and shot off the couch, making a beeline for the bathroom. Robyn hopped up after her, passing Asher, who had a surprised, resigned smirk on his face.

Myla barely made it. She fell to her knees before the toilet and emptied her guts into the bowl, then leaned her forehead against her forearm and panted a few times. Robyn closed the door and sat on the edge of the tub beside her, then swept Myla's hair behind her ear and rubbed her back. Her friend suffered through a bout of heaving, then a little more splashing resonated from the ceramic surround-sound.

"I'm…so glad…you keep a clean toilet," Myla sputtered. "It's…much nicer to puke in…than some."

"Do you feel better now?" Robyn asked. Myla nodded and straightened up. She flushed the toilet and sat back so she was leaning against the wall, completely spent.

"I'm going to get you a glass of water," Robyn said, pushing herself up.

"Thank you," Myla answered, then grabbed her hand. "You know what this means, right?"

Robyn, whose mind had flitted on the possibility, couldn't help the bubble of excitement that rose inside of her.

"You mean…" she started.

Myla nodded.

"You mean—don't make me say it. You say it. Are you serious?"

Myla chuckled and said, "I want to hear you say it. I don't think either of us would be this happy if we both suspected food poisoning."

Forgetting her sleeping son on the other side of the wall, Robyn screamed with delight and dove down to hug her friend, who laughed uproariously. From down the hall, the group broke into cheers and laughter, and the bursts of "Congratulations!" and "Praise God!" filled the air.

"I guess Asher gets to take some credit, too," Myla said with a laugh. "Oh man, Robyn, morning sickness is a joke. Why don't they call it all-day sickness?"

"I don't know, but I don't think I've ever been happier to watch a friend feel so rotten. Oh Myla, this is the best! I can't believe it! Our kids are going to be so close in age! Linus can be like a big cousin to yours!"

After a few moments of enjoying this revelation in the intimacy of the bathroom, the two friends emerged. They entered the living room, where everyone was standing and talking excitedly. As one, they all turned to congratulate Myla. Faye came forward to give her a hug. Even April stepped forward to tentatively place her arms around her for half a second.

"Here's the glorious bearer of my progeny," Asher said, reaching out to pull Myla back to his side. "Guys, it's really tough listening to puking and dry heaving all day long. You don't know how hard it is."

Myla gave him a gentle push to the stomach. "You're lucky I still find you charming."

Robyn met Patrick's eyes and they smiled at each other,

remembering the early days of her pregnancy.

The group finally settled down enough to close in prayer and thanksgiving, and then the disbanding began. Myla and Asher were the first to leave, Myla nibbling on a few slices of cheese that she had requested for the ride home. Samuel and Faye followed soon after. Theo was busy talking to Patrick about his experiences with Rob, which left April and Robyn alone.

Robyn started to collect dishes. When she noted April's hesitation, she asked her to help. Relief washed over April's guarded face as she started to reach for the nearest cups. She followed Robyn into the kitchen. After going back and forth between the rooms a couple of times, everything was stacked on the counter.

"Well, that was an exciting night," April offered quietly, watching as Robyn pulled the dishwasher door open.

"No kidding! I didn't expect them to become parents so soon after getting married. She's my first close friend to have a baby, so I'm *really* excited to have a fellow struggler like me."

"Struggler?" April asked. "It…it doesn't look like that from the outside."

Robyn's laugh caught April by surprise, and she didn't know whether she was supposed to join in, so she just watched with a blank face.

"Sorry, I'm not laughing at you," Robyn said, stacking the dishes in the machine. "It's just that, if you knew what was going on inside my head most of the time, you'd know how much I don't actually have it together."

"Well, at least you can let your struggle show only when you want it to," April said quietly. "Some of us wear ours all the time for the world to see."

"Hey." Robyn stopped stacking and stood up tall, looking at April across her small kitchen. "I don't think you're seeing the full picture of how you present yourself to the world."

April was looking at Robyn's chin. "I'm very aware that first impressions matter the most. And the first impression I give everyone is that I don't talk. Or that when I do, I stutter."

"You're not stuttering now," Robyn offered. "Not that I care when you do, but it's not like it happens all the time."

"Yeah, well, for some reason it doesn't follow me everywhere. Just when I'm either nervous or can't organize what I'm trying to say."

"And as for the first impressions thing. Why do you think that matters most?"

April shrugged. "I don't know. It seems like I've read that in a lot of places, or that it's talked about a lot. Like, first impressions can make or break a job interview. Thankfully not the one I just had this summer—"

"And could that be because your first impression, to Seth's family, wasn't your stutter or your nerves, but your heart? That they saw what really mattered, and saw that Seth was responding to your heart as well? To the *real* you, just below the surface?"

"Maybe," April conceded.

"And that Theo obviously saw something in you worth pursuing, and still does?"

"I suppose so." April chewed her lip while Robyn finished loading the dishwasher, added soap, and closed the door. She pressed a few buttons and then the soothing hum kicked in.

"April…" Robyn began, leaning back against the counter with her arms crossed. "Would you like to go for a walk sometime? Maybe some evening I can leave Linus with Patrick and we could grab some coffees or whatever you like, and just pick a trail?"

April's eyes met hers briefly. "Y-yes, I'd love that! What night works for you?"

- Chapter Twelve -

They were at Riversdale Park with the playground and swimming pool in the middle, and children were making lots of loud noises, and there was a lot of splashing, which he knew he wouldn't like if he was close to the pool, but April was just staying on the path with him and she said they were going for a walk instead of a swim, so that was okay. This sidewalk was bumpier than most, but he knew where some of the biggest bumps were, so he knew when to slow down and lift his feet even higher, and whenever he did this April said, "lift," but he knew she wasn't telling him what to do—he knew she was just saying what he was already doing, because April knew that he knew what he was doing and she never talked to him like he didn't know what he was doing.

"I'm going to visit my mom and dad this weekend, Seth," April said. "I've told them all about you, but I'm excited for them to see the pictures I took of you last week. Then they can see how handsome you are."

Mom and Dad and Donna and Kristy always told him that he was handsome, and so did the teachers at school, and now April told him that almost every day too, especially on the day she brought her camera and took pictures of him standing beside a tree at Meewasin Park. That was the day he saw the person on a blanket looking at their cell phone, but they were far away, and while the buzzing in his head was growing, April put a book in his hands and turned him so they were walking the other way, and even though the buzzing wanted to pull his body back that other way, the lining was right there and his finger lined and began to pull his ideas away from the cell phone until after some time he had forgotten about it. When they were back at the car, April told him he did an "awesome job." He knew she said that after any time like that where he didn't run toward a reading screen or a cell phone, and then he remembered turning away from that one earlier, and even though the buzzing bounced up a little at the memory of it, there was also that warm feeling that lifted his chest from the inside.

They were getting closer to the parking lot, and there was April's white car with the orange-red spots, but his toe caught and suddenly he was down, his knees bursting into fire as whiteness exploded behind his eyes. Something touched his arm and he screamed and flung his arm back to push it away. He screamed some more and the knee pain burned, burned, burned…

April moved off to the side and sat close by as Seth shrieked in pain, his knees still pressed into the gravelly concrete. The stares of passers-by felt heavy to her, even as she tried to push them out of her awareness and focus solely on being present with Seth while he expressed his surprise and pain. She had never seen him get hurt before. Was this normal? She would have to ask Vanessa later. What if he needed stitches? She would have to call his stepmom if there was a bad cut. But if it was minor, would he allow her to treat it back home?

"Excuse me, do you need help?" asked a nearby woman with a large tote and a purse over her arm, two young swim-suited kids standing a ways behind her with terrified expressions.

"Um…no…no thanks, I'll just wait with him a bit," April replied. "Thanks, though."

The woman reached into her purse and pulled out a small handful of Band-Aids, then stepped forward quickly and handed them to April. "Just in case," she said, offering a shrug and a kind little smile in Seth's direction. "I hope he's okay."

"Thank you," April said again, watching as the woman stepped back toward her kids and spoke in hushed tones, coaxing them past the scene and on toward their afternoon of fun.

The wailing continued. April stared up at the clouds, focusing on how one of them looked like a dragon. There was even a little fluff-patch just a short distance away from the gap that looked like its mouth—

"Can you help him out already?"

The clipped voice came from behind her. April glanced back to see an older woman with a novel in one hand, her other hand shielding her eyes from the glaring sun.

"I can hear him all the way from the pool deck."

It took a moment for the woman's words to register, the confrontational tone hitting April like a minor shock.

"I'm…I'm…I need to give him space to c…to calm down first," she pushed out, her heart thudding.

"While you're waiting for him to calm down, the children in the pool are getting more and more scared," the woman snorted, moving her hand to her hip. "Is there someone you can call, at least? Since you're not able to keep him quiet?"

In a flash, April battened down the hatches. It was rare for her to feel the hot lava of explosive anger rise up from the depths of her being, but she instinctively knew that her response wouldn't be healthy. She made a point of looking away and training her eyes on Seth, paying attention to the rise and fall of his back as he breathed heavily between cries, which were slowly ebbing. Twin puddles had formed on the ground underneath his down-turned face, and more tears continued to drip. She had no control over the woman behind her, but she wished to high heavens that she could say just the right thing to put her in her place. Her mind was a loud mess of protective rage.

The silence seemed to register as the woman muttered, “Finally. Get him home, and maybe choose a different park next time. One with fewer people to disrupt.” The sound of her retreating footsteps eased the atmosphere.

About a minute passed while Seth’s crying completely abated. April waited another beat or two, and then she approached him in a crouch from the front.

“Seth?” she tried, putting her hand on his arm. His head jerked up and he pushed her away. She landed on her rear end and stayed in front of him, silently willing him to allow her into his tightened circle of safety. He was in self-preservation mode. She knew it couldn’t last forever.

A check of her watch told her it was two o’clock. Surely they would be able to resolve this and get home before three, right? She didn’t relish the idea of having to sneak a call on her cell phone without leaving his side. If it came to that, she might have to ask a stranger to make the call for her from a very safe distance.

Maybe that very helpful old hag would be the one she’d have to ask. April chuckled without amusement at that thought.

“Seth, I have the book in my purse,” April said, the idea dawning on her now that the adrenaline was wearing off. She pulled out the tattered copy of Moby Dick that had accompanied them to almost every city park in the past few weeks, and slowly slid it underneath where Seth was still looking down. When it covered the rapidly evaporating tear puddles, he reached for it and settled onto his hip, curling his legs underneath himself so he could sit up straight and do his lining. April’s eyes shot to his exposed knees, the flesh embedded with tiny stones and dirt, the damage contained to two small patches of already-drying blood. Ideally, he would allow her to disinfect them once they got home, but that was a separate issue for a separate moment.

She gave him ten minutes with the book before she gently put her finger on the page. He pulled it away with an irritated grunt, so she gave him another five minutes and tried again. Same response. On her third try there was no resistance, so April mustered up as much peaceful cheeriness as she could and touched Seth's arm, telling him it was time to drive home. She stood up and held onto his forearms, both of his hands still occupied with the book, and gave a gentle upward tug. He started to put his knees under again to hoist himself up, but then cried out in alarm and collapsed back down. April's heart raced as she willed him not to react the same way as before, but he remained quiet and instead doubled-down on his lining ferocity.

April huffed out a sigh. "Seth, I'm proud of you for distracting yourself from the pain," she said softly. "I'm going to try and get the dirt off of your knees and put something soft there for you to kneel on, okay?"

He flinched when she gingerly brushed the areas around the minor wounds, and the ferocious lining increased in intensity so that the book was shaking in his hands. Then April took the handful of Band-Aids from the ground beside her and placed them right beside his knees. At her next attempt to prompt him upward with a tug on his forearms, his knees rolled onto the thin but effective shields, allowing for slightly less painful pressure as he exerted himself into standing up. April sighed again, with relief this time, and waited a minute for him to get his bearings. He limped slightly as they made their way to the car, Seth leaning harder on April than usual, and once he was gingerly settled onto the backseat, April jogged back to the spot to collect the Band-Aids and throw away the soiled ones.

It was two-thirty-five. She sat in the car to turn on the ignition, then stepped out and leaned against the back door, inhaling and exhaling deeply a few times.

God, thank you for helping me help him, she prayed. *And I don't know if this is a good thing to ask for, but please make that old woman feel really guilty. And bless the one who gave us the Band-Aids.*

As usual, her words seemed to hit the empty air and fly out

into a vacuum, but acknowledging the God she wanted to know always felt right, even if she didn't sense he cared. He certainly must care about Seth, anyway. How could anyone not?

As they drove toward Seth's house, April's racing thoughts grounded themselves on the warm sunbeam on the living room floor of her Edmonton home. Her heart rate began to settle at the peaceful, secure emotions that were conjured up. That moment in time was before everything. Before the move, before the awareness that her shyness was going to remain a major issue throughout her whole life, before she knew that her stutter was called a stutter and that it was a nervous trait, before the birthday party fiasco, before Cosette, before feeling like a failure as a girlfriend and as a Christian and as a general human being, before that horrible old lady today…

And yet my life has been so easy compared to most people's, she thought to herself. *Why does being myself feel so hard? Am I just weaker and more pathetic than everyone else?*

She re-focused her thoughts onto the sunbeam, and onto the teenage boy in the backseat who was still lining his book, and an impression dropped into her from out of the blue.

You are a sunbeam for him.

The depth and truth of the statement pressed down into her with irrevocable authority. A sense of love permeated the car, charging the atmosphere and pulling a strangled whisper from deep inside, where unmet needs pretend that they don't exist until they feel hope for the first time.

"God?"

- Chapter Thirteen -

"Carly is moving to Edmonton this week."

"Really?" Robyn fiddled with the kitchen window latch, enjoying the birdsong that floated in alongside the shrieks of childish laughter from the park down the street. She was also enjoying the sound of Devon's voice on the phone: self-assured and a little gravelly, like Bryan Adams. The singer's music had always brought Devon to mind, even back when she was too freshly in love with Patrick to take note of any deviant heart jolts that accompanied those songs.

"Yes, we finally found a place that works for her. It's close to the mall she works at, and way across the city from Ty."

"That's awesome, Dev. I assume Ty isn't being a problem?"

"No, he gave up after I called him regarding his last text to Carly."

Robyn remembered. Devon had fed her the details all along this months-long saga of Carly leaving her new husband after his drug abuse came to light within two weeks of their marriage. Devon and Carly's parents had moved to Ontario many years back and were able to provide financial and emotional support, but the practical and immediate care fell on Devon's shoulders.

Poor little Carly. Robyn remembered the young girl with

blond ringlets, but she had only been twelve when Robyn spent her final summer at the lake. She had belonged to the younger posse, and never crossed Robyn's mind much in the ensuing years. Yet now, after shouldering some of Devon's anguish when he had called or texted with the struggles and details of helping her get away from this toxic situation, she felt a mantle of protectiveness for the young woman. Or was it protectiveness for Devon? Was the soft spot for Carly, or for the big brother whose heart was hurting and angry and needing a soft place of its own to land on?

"I'm glad to hear that. I hope Carly can find joy in being single again. It's not what she planned, but compared to what she could be living with, it's *so* much better."

"Yes, it is. I never fully trusted Ty. I just wish I'd known why that off-vibe was there. Maybe I could have warned her away from him with more than just 'I don't like the guy.' I think that actually pushed her harder toward him in the first place."

"That could be. Especially since you couldn't pin down anything concrete to warn her about. She might have thought you were being unreasonably overprotective or something."

"Yeah. Probably. I guess you would know what it's like to be in that zone where you just know you're going to marry a guy, right?" he chuckled nervously. "Not…I'm not saying *you* shouldn't have gotten married. I'm just making a stupid joke."

"Yeah, no, Patrick's a great guy. No secret drug use with him." Robyn bit her lip and glanced over her shoulder, despite the early-afternoon hour in which Patrick was one-hundred-per-cent definitely at work instead of home. The sledgehammer that struck her heart with this change in topic was too complicated to discern.

"I'm sorry, Robyn, that was a dumb joke," he repeated. "I think I'm just fried after all of this. And I'm *very* relieved that Carly will be living on her own soon. She's been fine to live with, but you know…there's only so long a guy can share his one-bedroom apartment and sleep on his couch." That nervous chuckle again. "But you know, I…"

The trailed-off sentence hung for what felt like five minutes. Robyn's hand had stilled on the window latch and her heart was pounding in her throat. She thought of Patrick, who was out working at a job to support his family, and who poured his love on them constantly but never asked for anything back from her—and she thought of Devon, whose need for her support had breathed life into something inside of her that she hadn't recognized was there.

She thought of the shared memories of magical childhood summers that had always left her pining for more.

And she pondered the recognition that Devon was actively pulling more from her now…that he had maybe wanted more from her for longer than she knew.

"What I'm trying to say is," Devon exhaled deeply, a slight rattle in his voice. "What I mean is, I appreciate your friendship. More than you know. I feel like God must have prompted me to reach out to you right before this all began. Your listening ear and your support have given me strength and something to be happy about through all of this. No matter how crappy Ty was being to Carly, or how emotional she was, or how hard it was to focus at work, I always knew I could count on you bringing a smile to my face. I just…thank you. You mean…you mean a lot to me."

"Oh, Dev, you mean so much to me too," Robyn said softly, her voice thickening. "If only you knew how much I wanted to stay friends after those summers at the lake, but you were unavailable. I love that we're talking now, but…why those silent years?"

"Shoot, Robyn, I just realized my lunch break is almost over," Devon replied, a heaviness in his tone. "And I'm guessing your little guy will be up soon."

Disappointment rang like an anvil-drop clear down to her feet. "Well, yes."

"Can we talk again soon?"

"Of course." Robyn turned to face the doorway toward her

living room, swallowing hard.

"Okay. Well then—talk to you later, Birdie."

She smiled at the resurrection of an affectionate childhood nickname. "You bet. Good-bye, Dev."

* * *

On Saturday morning, April's fingers brushed against the solid wood headboard of her childhood bed as she stretched. The grooves were as familiar as they'd always been, momentarily pinching the past and present together. It was moments like this that gave her pause and put her back in touch with her inner self—the one that felt too much and sensed too deeply and would be more comfortable enjoying the presence of her own mind than extending energy on trying to be whatever the people around her expected her to be.

Letting people down was the worst possible offense. It was a harsh world when everyone was so easily disappointed.

God, I remember when I used to lie awake, afraid that you were going to send me to hell if I made just one bad mistake, she prayed now. Her teenage memories were inextricably linked with that sense of impending doom, especially during the years of breaking rules with Cosette. Over time, that sense of God's anger had morphed into a sense of God's disinterest. Even now, she knew he loved her, but it was a head knowledge that didn't line up with her heart response. She was waiting, though. She held out hope that one day she would actually feel the supposed truth, instead of having to convince her mind of it whenever she wanted to give up on God or cower from him.

The sun had risen some time ago and was shining through the slats of her old, discoloured blinds. The smells of coffee and bacon were wafting into her room. She could hear Theo and Dad talking in the living room down the hall. Pretty soon she would have to get up.

It was a relief to have already gotten past the beginning stages of her family meeting Theo. She and Theo had come to Baylor a few weeks after they started dating. Of course, he got comfortable right away and made himself at home. In their subsequent visit, her mom even remembered to buy peaches—something April hadn't grown up on, but that Theo had once mentioned were his favourite fruit. Both sides of the equation seemed to be making adequate space for each other.

I am so *thankful for that moment in my car with Seth,* she continued her prayer to God, grabbing her glasses and sitting up so that the lightweight blanket slipped off her torso. Her spaghetti-strap tank top fit snug against the natural rolls of her stomach, and in the full-length mirror facing her from across the room, she could see that her messy hair and bare shoulders looked kind of sexy. Despite her uncertainties about how to go deeper with Theo without botching the process, she looked forward to marriage and all the new, intimate stuff that would come along with it.

Okay, sorry, God, was that an inappropriate thought in the middle of praying? I don't know. Anyway…thank you again for letting me feel your love in that moment. I love you, too. I always have. But I want that feeling to last. I'm tired of forcing myself to believe that you love me without actually feeling the experience of it in my heart. But that moment, it gave me hope. And I'm going to trust in that hope. I'm trusting that it was a sign of the truth, and maybe even a sign of things to come between me and you?

Before getting all the way up, April reached over for the Bible on her nightstand and flipped it open to the bookmarked page. She liked to keep it simple and just follow the reading plan suggested on its back pages. Lately she had been reading through the book of Job. She was near the end now, where God was proclaiming his might and power and greatness to remind Job and his friends that he was on the throne, no matter what they were going through and no matter what they thought about what they were going through. It was a comfort to be reminded that God was bigger than everything that existed, but she was mostly looking forward to the next book—Psalms. The poetic and heartfelt expressions of the writers made her feel normal. Like it was okay to tell God exactly how she felt. Even though her prayers seemed like they went skyward and didn't land anywhere, she'd always maintained a trust that nothing was off-limits in her communication with God. The Psalms were evidence that at least a few other believers had lived that same way, too.

Twenty minutes later, April was padding down the hallway in a t-shirt and shorts. She stopped outside of Britney's closed door and smiled, then pounded thunderously as fast as she could and ran into the living room. Theo gave her a bemused look, hardly succeeding in his attempt not to check out her legs, while her father just shook his head and continued talking to Theo about whatever topic she had walked in on.

"April!" her mother chided from the kitchen.

Britney stormed out of her room, tousled hair sticking all around her head like a halo and eyes with a hard glint that were set to kill.

"It was Theo!" April shouted, jumping behind him and pushing him toward the angry teenager. "It was his idea!"

"Wait, no! What?" Theo exclaimed in confusion, while Britney stormed past him and glared at her sister.

"No, I don't think he'd be that much of a *jerk*," Britney retorted.

April tried not to giggle as Britney attempted to stare her down.

Theo disentangled himself from being April's shield, then turned a mock glare on her and pursed his lips. "You're right, he wouldn't. Unless it was to my own sister. Britney is too nice and sweet to be mean to."

The corners of Britney's lips twitched, but she maintained her laser glare at her big sister.

"Just you wait until tomorrow morning," she said in a menacing voice.

"Breakfast is ready!" their mom called from the kitchen.

April gave Britney a Cheshire cat grin and looped her arm through Theo's, traipsing past her toward the kitchen. Britney shot a cat-like hiss in her direction, then fell in line beside her dad.

"Just like the old days, hey Melissa?" Max asked the girls' mom as they all settled around the table.

"It's so refreshing to hear the joyous sounds of bickering once again," Melissa said, setting a steaming bowl of cheesy scrambled eggs on a hot plate in the center.

Everyone else laughed amidst the scraping of chairs, and after their dad said grace, the meal was enjoyed with easy banter all around.

April's heart was full. It wasn't hard to imagine a world where she and Theo came here together frequently throughout the years, eventually as husband and wife, then with babies in tow.

* * *

After everyone had eaten, April's parents cleaned up while the two girls disappeared to get ready for the day. Theo was left to browse photos on the living room wall, having been shooed away from assisting in the kitchen.

He had been given the official "tour" back on his first visit. There were black-and-white pictures of four sets of great-grandparents in traditional sombre poses on their wedding days, set in a collage frame near one corner of the room. Kitty-corner to that were Max and Melissa's wedding picture, and lining up the side were two baby portraits of April and Britney. He could see the slight resemblance in the shape of April's eyes. Even as a baby, there appeared to be a hint of guardedness in her face.

As the wall continued, there was a mix of candid photos. Most of them were from different vacations the family had gone on. In one of them, April was twelve years old and beaming a goofy, eyes-squished-shut grin as she held up an average-sized rainbow trout—

the first fish she had ever caught—and Theo thought about how much he loved that side of her. The side that let her hair down and lost all the self-consciousness that plagued her daily. It was one of the reasons he had been so intrigued by her at the young adults' group back in the fall of last year.

He had joined Victory Church after graduating high school and moving away from home. He had no problem with the church he'd grown up in, but there was a strong compulsion to establish himself outside of being Grant and Isabelle's son. Combined with that was the pull toward an active social life with other believers his own age. The renowned Victory Church young adults' group fit the bill.

Of course, the first few weeks of attending the Friday night gatherings were solely for the purpose of discerning which young women were available. One of the perks of living in a small city with a few post-secondary institutions was that there were going to be a lot of girls moving through over the next many years, meaning that there were going to be plenty of opportunities to meet the right one.

Theo had casually dated a few girls in high school, and he'd given the "let-down talk" to a number of others who had made their unreciprocated interest known, but he wasn't interested in dating just for the fun of it. He intended to build a life with a forever partner, one who loved the Lord as much as he did, and who wanted to buy a house and have kids and grow old with him. He figured that if people were attending a church's social group, chances were high they would already have a lot of foundational things in common.

There were the obvious stand-out girls, the ones who commanded the crowd and moved about with confidence. It was easy to get to know them, as they were easy to talk to and seemed to have gravitated toward him as well. Theo wasn't immune to the knowledge that girls considered him a great catch, but usually it wasn't something he considered on any significant level. His challenge wasn't finding someone who wanted to test the waters with him; his challenge was keeping his head on straight so he could find the one that *he* wanted to pursue, and not the other way around.

Within the first little while, he had taken note of all the regulars, and had fallen into easy rapport with many of them. He had noted a few of them who gave him that wide-eyed, hopeful look during their conversations that always made him consider: would she be someone to encourage? Physical attraction was undeniable toward pretty much every one of them, and the admirable personalities and character traits were a huge draw as well. Yet Theo wasn't fooled by the automatic pull toward everyone who looked at him that way. If he was, he could string along any number of girls at the same time and leave a mess of broken hearts behind. He had zero interest in playing that game. High school had taught him the difference between dating because you like someone's attention, and dating because you actually want to get to know the other person better. His hope and prayer were that he wouldn't fall into the first category ever again.

As he considered his options among the confident girls who had openly flirted with him and dropped obvious hints, his mind wandered over to some of the quieter ones who hadn't paid him any attention at all. Considering a pool of uninterested women provided a surprising amount of appeal. He was so used to being chased and simply having to choose with whom to respond in kind; now, he wondered, what would it be like to go after someone that he would have to work for?

He tried not to be too obvious about it, but after making this determination, Theo spent the next couple of Friday nights trying to strike up conversations with the girls who interacted quietly among the margins of the larger crew. It was an enjoyable, yet sometimes awkward, social experiment. He was chatting with a duo of shy girls one time when one of his popular acquaintances pressed up against his side and tried to join in the conversation, laughing a little too hard at Theo's comments and effectively pushing the other ladies out. He hid his annoyance, but he became keenly aware that this particular outgoing girl had knocked herself hard off of his "maybe" list.

One of the quiet girls his mind circled back to was April Vale. She always came alone and left alone, and rarely seemed to initiate conversations with anyone, but something about her took root in his mind. Maybe it was her air of vulnerability. Her looks didn't jump out and grab attention, but the more he pondered her, the prettier she became. He began to notice not just the full picture of her looks, but the smaller details. Like the way the lights played off her dark hair, and the way her haircut framed her face like a heart. Her eyes were slightly round, with a darkness that was both warm and mysterious. The way her hips moved when she walked began to draw his attention. She didn't have a confident stride, but her curves began to stir something in him whenever he chanced to glance over while she was on the move. And in the occasional moments when a smile lit up her face, even a nervous one, he was drawn to the small dimple in her cheek.

What did she think of him? *Did* she think of him? If so, what had she observed, and what did she feel?

It got to the point where he was thinking of her all throughout the week. He wondered what was locked away inside of her, and what it would take for someone to get to know her. What would it be like to see those lovely, mysterious eyes sparkle with pure delight?

Now here they were, five months into their relationship, and he still had to wonder what it was that set off those random moments of unadulterated ease. What he had just observed over brunch with her family, and the energetic teasing of her sister right before, filled him with pleasure and longing. It was obvious why she would be like that with her family, but why wasn't she like that with him all the time? By now, shouldn't she have recognized how safe she was to be fully herself with him?

He thought of those moments of flirtatious connection. Whenever she called him "McTeague" and looked at him with that coy expression, he felt like he had made the winning goal in a playoff game. It made him want to grab her face between his hands and kiss all his affections and longings into her until she had to catch her breath, but at this point he didn't trust that his passion wouldn't frighten her away.

The sound of clinking dishes and muffled conversation drifted into his awareness as he pulled himself away from his thoughts. Time to ponder something else before he thought too long and hard about their kisses, both the ones they had and the ones he wanted to have.

"Hey." April's voice came from behind him. He turned toward her with a grin.

"Hey," he replied. April's hair was wet and wavy, practically shimmering in the late-morning sunlight that beamed through the window, and the effect was unnervingly strong. She sidled up beside him and looked up at the pictures he'd stopped in front of.

"Ah, the famous Christmas pageant of '97," she murmured. Thirteen-year-old April was wearing a faded blue terry-cloth robe with a dishtowel draped over her head, a shepherd's crook nestled against her chest behind crossed arms, and seven-year-old Britney was mid-"baa," on her hands and knees while covered in bunches of cotton batting.

"I remember you telling me about Britney crying from stage fright, but then you promised to stand beside her the whole time," Theo remarked.

"Yeah, I guess I'm not always a jerk to my sister," April responded. "I mean, back when she was little and cute and all."

"I have a feeling you still get that protective urge every once in awhile," he said, turning to find the nearest couch to sit on.

"I suppose so," April replied, bouncing onto the couch cushion beside him.

This was definitely a delightfully unguarded moment. Theo

put his arm around the back of the couch and pulled her closer, pressing his lips lightly into the top of her head. He glanced back to see that Britney had just entered the room with a cup of something steaming in her hands.

"Ew, gross," she muttered, setting the coffee on the end table beside Theo. "Mom asked me to bring this to you."

"Thanks!" Theo loved how many details April's mom remembered each time he visited. April hadn't succumbed to coffee's cultural hold yet, but Theo had long since learned the benefits of caffeine during study times and much-too-early morning times, and now it was a daily pleasure.

April asked Britney about a friend of hers, and the two girls began a lengthy conversation about mutual acquaintances. Theo tried to follow the conversation, and April tried to explain the connections and keep him in the loop, but his mind was mostly stuck on the rather distracting fact that his girl—his April—was so deeply in her element that she'd begun waving her hands animatedly. How often did that happen when he was alone with her? It happened every time she talked about Seth, but otherwise she pretty much kept her hands in her lap, or she fidgeted with something, like a cup or a piece of jewelry. Her voice rarely raised to this level of inflection.

With a start, Theo realized that he himself was more relaxed right now than he had been in ages, and he knew that April's own comfort was the reason. He'd dated self-conscious girls before, but never had he fallen so hard that his own sense of wellbeing had become completely tied up in someone else's. He felt betrayed by his mind, like it had attached itself to her tumultuous journey behind his back. As much as he loved this moment, he was uncomfortable with the recognition that his happiness had become so recklessly attached to hers. As far as he knew, he had never been a moody person—but was this just a normal part of love that he hadn't expected?

* * *

"I want to take you somewhere," April said, tugging on Theo's hand. It was late afternoon at the farm. They had just enjoyed coffee around her grandparents' kitchen table, along with Max and Melissa. When her grandma announced she was going to start on supper, Melissa offered to help and she suggested April show Theo around the farmyard. The young couple meandered around the familiar nooks and crannies of April's childhood. April found herself lost in thought much of the time. Theo had to repeat a few of his questions until finally April realized it was time.

"Okay," Theo replied, allowing himself to be pulled along through a double-line of trees. "Where is this 'somewhere' you speak of?"

April heard the lightheartedness in his voice and hoped this wasn't a mistake. The depth of meaning she felt in her heart was a mismatch for the tone he'd read into the situation, but maybe he would understand in a minute. Her legs were spirited along by the childlike call to run up the hill. She dropped Theo's hand, allowing the energy to propel her upward until she had reached the summit. Theo was running right alongside her until he caught her around the waist at the top, spinning her around playfully and yelling, "I won!"

April couldn't help laughing, but she didn't want to laugh.

"We're on the hill!" she declared once Theo had set her down, as if that explanation meant anything to him.

"Yes, I can see that, and I'm with the most beautiful girl on the planet." He kept his hands on her hips and looked into her eyes.

April looked down, leaning the top of her head into his chest to avoid searing in the intensity of his gaze. She loved seeing his affection up close, but in certain moments there was a hint of a need that unnerved her and made her feel unsafe. She wrapped her arms around Theo, pretending to soak in the hug while hoping that his look would be more settled once they stepped apart.

"This is the *hill*, Theo," she murmured into his shirt. "The one

I've told you about, where I used to do all my thinking and feeling and praying. It's one of my most favourite places in the world."

Theo held on like that for a few minutes. April turned her head sideways and listened to his fast-beating heart while she surveyed the view. There was the faithful old red barn. The farmhouse beyond it was concealed, but just past the barn roof she could see the front lawn, bordered by lilac bushes whose blossoms had already faded for the summer. Lilac season was never long enough.

Theo's hand stroked April's back.

"What are you thinking about right now?" he asked softly into her hair.

"I'm thinking…I'm thinking, why do even beautiful things feel like they hurt a little?"

I'm thinking, I've been dreaming about showing you this place ever since we started dating.

They stood there like that for a few minutes, April feeling insecure about his lack of response.

I'm thinking, what I just said was too sentimental for you and now you're annoyed with me and trying to figure out what to say.

She knew it was probably a confusing statement for a concrete thinker like him, but sometimes things just slipped out. She blamed being home, and being on the hill, and the sensation of his racing heart that she knew was beating with excitement about her. Too many things were taking down the guard that she needed to have in place so that she could filter her words and actions according to Theo, not according to her own random whims.

I'm thinking, how do I make you comfortable again since I wasn't speaking your language? How do I make it better for you?

Theo released her so that he was looking down at her. "I think I know what you mean," he said. The assessment in his gaze spoke of both satisfaction and hunger. "No one can see us from the house, right?"

April thought about lying, but she nodded her head, and he

kissed her hard. Swallowing her unsettledness, she poured as much energy into her kissing as she could muster until they were both breathless. *No more no more no more* her thoughts whispered, but Theo was still fully engaged in the act, so April continued to kiss back until Theo pulled away, turned and walked a few steps back.

April stared at his heaving shoulders. Should she have ended the kissing sooner? Did he appreciate this, or would he have preferred her to be the one to put a boundary on how far they went physically? What did he expect of her?

Finally, she broke the silence. "That was a lot of passion, McTeague."

Too much passion for me. I didn't want it. But you did, and that's what matters, right?

He glanced back at her and shook his head with a laugh. "You have a way about you, Vale."

* * *

Shortly afterward, around the supper table, April's grandma asked about Seth.

"Oh!" April gasped in delight. "I almost forgot—I have some pictures of him in my purse!" She ran to retrieve them, then passed them around the table. She launched into story after story about him, answering questions and expounding on details that brought out a lot of appreciative smiles.

"You know, April," her grandpa said, "this is exactly how excited you used to get when you worked at Maude's Manor. I remember how much you talked and talked about the retarded people you used to work with there. You seem to have found a calling."

April flinched inwardly at the outdated term. She knew her grandpa meant no harm and she didn't want to embarrass him, but should she correct him, or—?

"I think she was almost talking as fast as Cosette," her dad remarked. "By the way, do you keep in touch with her?"

Warmth flooded April's face as she responded, "No, not really. But we did bump into her randomly on Canada Day."

"Hmm, what's she been up to?"

April recounted those details, noticing how her mom had begun to watch her with an unreadable expression.

"It must have been fun to see her again, but I'm surprised you fell off each other's radars so quickly after she moved away. You two were like peas in a pod." Max took another nonchalant bite of roast.

"Lightning in a bucket," her grandpa agreed.

It was true. Cosette's mom had found a job down in Moose Jaw right before the girls went into Grade 12. That last year had been lonely for April again, but she'd been surprised at how much easier it was to breathe. There had been a small handful of emails and phone calls from Cosette for the first few months. April found herself needing a lot of time to recover her emotional equilibrium after each one, not understanding why. Yet it seemed like her lack of reply and initiative must have matched up nicely with Cosette's ability to immerse herself fully into new situations. At some point, the last contact came and went without her knowing it would be the last one.

"She and I—we are very different people. And I have better friends now." April flashed Theo a smile.

"No doubt about that. Some friends are just for a season, I suppose. That girl came from a troubled home life, didn't she? I bet you were as good for her as she was for you."

Because I was disappointingly antisocial before she came along, right? April thought behind a fake smile.

"Do you remember that time you both got caught trying to skip school? Remember that, Melissa? We knew we had to ground you as a punishment, but really, I was happy to see that you were coming out of your shell. It's healthy to have a little teenage rebellion. All that energy has to go somewhere."

"Yeah, Dad, and what were your teenage rebellions?" Britney asked with a laugh.

"Yes, Max, do tell," Grandma jumped in, then promptly cut him off with her own story of the time she started to notice the smell of cigarettes in his dirty laundry.

Yeah, my natural rebel spirit just awaiting release. The less disappointing version of me. Sure thing. April's thoughts were derailed by her mom asking her to come help get dessert.

"You bet," April replied quickly, her knees almost hitting the table as she backed up with greater force than necessary.

With the backdrop of the resuming table conversation behind them, the two ladies glided through the swinging door to the adjoining room. The smell of apple pie provided a balm to April's frazzled nerves.

"Could you grab the whipped cream?" Mom asked as she opened the oven door. Placing the pie on the counter, she offered her daughter a little smile. "I thought you could use an escape from that conversation," she said. "Was I right?"

April nodded. "Yes. To be honest, I really don't like talking about Cosette. Everyone seems to think she was, like, this saviour for me. It gets really annoying."

Mom had pulled a knife out of the block, but stopped and looked fully at April before continuing with her task.

"I know, honey," she said quietly. "At the start, I thought she was good for you, too. I couldn't put my finger on why I was growing concerned—not right away, anyway. And your dad, well, he was fully convinced that this friendship was a pure gift. I tried to see it that way, too, and your dad was so optimistic about it. Every time I tried to bring up my worries, he had this way of convincing me that I was worrying too much."

Relief, surprise, and extreme discomfort rooted April to the spot for a moment. She had never heard her mom express doubts over the greatness of Cosette's influence.

You have no right to go here with me, she thought, watching her own hand pull open the utensil drawer and start collecting forks and a big spoon. How her body knew to do all of this without her mind intentionally telling it to, she didn't know.

"This doesn't seem like the best time," her mom continued. "I can see that. And I'm sorry to be bringing it up so abruptly like this. I've been wanting to talk to you about this for a little while now, but I didn't know how to start the conversation."

April was nodding, but words were tangled up too deep inside.

Slices of pie were placed on seven plates in silence. April dolloped a large spoonful of whipped cream on each one. Laughter emanated from the dining room.

"It's not like Cosette was the worst person on earth," April finally murmured into the thick air. "She was fun and exciting, and I have some good memories of being with her."

Mom set down the plates she had just picked up and waited while April paused thoughtfully.

"I just found it interesting that when she and I moved our separate ways, I thought I would miss her. But mostly what I felt was relief. And when I ran into her on Canada Day, I felt...almost devastated. And then guilty, because how can I feel that way about someone who used to be my best friend?"

"I think," her mom suggested, "it's because she wasn't actually 'bringing you out of your shell' like so many of us thought. I think—correct me if I'm wrong—but I think it was because she was so powerful that the only way to maintain your own identity would be to stand firm in who you were without her. And I wonder if, at the time, you didn't know the answer to who you really were. So instead of being set free by her lack of inhibitions, you were boxed into the persona that suited her best. Deep down inside, you were aware of that. That's where the devastation came from when you saw her again; from the part that knows."

April swallowed hard and shook her head. "What kind of a wimp lets someone else take control of her like that?"

It took a moment for April to realize she'd voiced the question out loud. *Filter, for goodness' sakes, where have you gone this weekend?*

Her mom's fingers wrapped around her wrist for the briefest of seconds.

"Not a wimp," she said with gentle firmness. "Someone who wants to love others so much that she hasn't made space to love herself yet. I see that your desire to love others sacrificially can be a strength. But if that strength isn't being fed from a healthy source, it won't stay pure. It can turn back on you with destruction."

April wanted to lean into the hope that peeked out ever-so-slightly along with her mom's words, but the question was stuck in her throat: *The Bible only talks about putting others above ourselves—so how can it be right to focus on loving myself?*

- Chapter Fourteen -

At church the next day, April was pleased to notice how many people smiled at her and Theo together. He had already met most of the people there in prior visits, and she still couldn't help but feel some pride that her hometown crowd was aware that shy little April had somehow managed to snag a most attractive mate.

After a quick lunch, April and Theo packed up the car and said their good-byes. April felt a bit like cardboard while hugging her mom, in spite of the head knowledge that yesterday's kitchen conversation had been exactly what she needed to hear.

It was a silent drive back to the city. The radio was turned up and Theo's hand rested on April's leg. She was grateful for the silence while her thoughts kneaded themselves over and over.

"I want to go to Edmonton," she blurted out, surprising herself.

"Edmonton?" Theo laughed. "Okay, I'll just start heading there now."

"No, I'm serious, Theo. I want to go there. But obviously in a planned way. I've been dreaming about seeing my childhood home ever since we moved away from there. Why have I never just, like, *gone* there? I can totally do it now, on my own. I'm going."

Theo glanced over at her with mild amusement. "I love how spontaneous this is. But are you serious? Because if you are, I'm up for a road trip too. When do you want to go?"

"Next weekend."

"I can't do it then. Remember? I've got that fishing trip with my dad."

April looked out her window. Love would mean choosing a different weekend so that Theo could join her, as he so clearly wanted to. But right now, she didn't have the energy to be loving about this. She needed to get away—from him, from the intrusion of this unexpected truth-laced intimacy from her mom, from all the everyday stuff that reminded her of just how inadequate she was at managing her confusion about her life—and see with her eyes, maybe even feel with her hands, the safe place that had been calming her racing heart down for years. She needed it with an urgency that couldn't be repressed.

"Yes, I know, but I'm sorry Theo. I can't wait that long. I need to go as soon as possible. I need to get away and—something. I don't even know what. Maybe I'll figure it out when I'm there."

His disappointment seemed to fill the small space in the car. April tried not to hate herself for making him upset again. She really sucked at this putting-others-first stuff. Hopefully God would forgive her and help her sort out her junk so she could get back in the saddle with trying to put Theo first.

Just...after Edmonton.

* * *

It was always nice to be with April, and when her arm leaned against his arm on the couch it was okay because it was warm and just the right pressure. She was sharing the lining again but that was okay because it was good to be doing things with April after two days of her not being here. She was telling him about her mom and dad and grandma and grandpa and Britney and Baylor and Theo and the hill and church. It was okay because there was no weight in the air when she talked and her voice made him feel good. She said she was proud to tell her family about him and he knew that his mom and dad were also proud of him and that meant he was good. Like sometimes some teachers or other kids at school or even other people he didn't know were not proud of him, because the air was heavy when he was close to them or they made his stomach hurt with unsafe feelings, or sometimes he used to get grabbed or pushed by some of the other kids and it was scary when that happened, and he knew they definitely weren't proud of him when they did that.

When April said it was time for a car ride, Seth's legs started moving, and he was so happy he laughed before he went to the toilet and washed his hands with soap and then walked out to the car with April. The sun was warm on his skin and hair, and April was proud of him and he was holding her arm, which was still warm but now the sun's heat was making her skin feel even warmer to touch.

When he sat inside her car, he saw that there was a new book for lining. April started driving and asked him if he liked it and she said that it was called *Little Women,* and it was her book when she was younger and she wanted him to have it for their car rides. The lines in the book were on pages that seemed a little bit yellow but the lining worked no problem, and it smelled like new and old at the same time, and the sun was warm through the window, and the lights were flashing through the window across the book as they drove, and he knew it was from tree shadows as they passed. It made the lining even more fun, and that made him laugh again, and the air in the car became even lighter than normal. He thought that must be because April's proud feelings for him were so strong.

* * *

April filled her week with Seth, soul-searching, an evening stroll with Robyn, and lots of journaling.

Normally a catalyst for clarity, her journal entries seemed to be driving her anxiety up several notches. By the end of most writing sessions, her heart was racing and she had the urge to throw her journal across the room.

Something was off, but she couldn't put her finger on it. Sometime during that short conversation with her mom, something had clicked and then gone fuzzy again. She couldn't go back to only wondering *if* something was misaligned in her world. It was like she'd been alerted to a thin veil of fog that didn't destroy her ability to see where she was going, but cast its subtle effect over every detail of her life. Aggravated and troubled, she found that her prayers were hitting the ceiling at twice the rate as she cried out to God again and again for wisdom to understand what she was missing.

I am trying SO hard, God! Yet I'm even more confused about my relationship with Theo and my relationship with you. Why won't you help me?

* * *

Meanwhile, Robyn found herself in a different kind of blur. The guilt that nagged at her whenever Patrick was around started to get cancelled out by the growing resentments she felt toward him. Going through the motions of the mornings, including a peck on the lips before he left for work, drained her almost completely. As soon as he left for work, she turned on her cell phone and greedily awaited the barrage of texts she knew would be forthcoming. This always re-energized her.

She and Linus laughed and played and bounced around the house throughout the days. If Patrick had the gall to text at any time, she suppressed a flash of anger at the intrusion. If his text included a typo, which it often did, she felt something akin to disgust. At the beginning of their relationship, she had thought it was a cute quirk of his. But compared to Devon's satisfying grammatical accuracy, it now struck her as grating and immature.

One night, she rolled over and stared at Patrick's broad back as he slept. She still loved him. She couldn't deny that, no matter how much Devon had grabbed hold of her heart; no matter how much he felt like a familiar pair of shoes that fit just right.

Patrick had felt like that once, too. She supposed that sense of perfect belonging was still there, but was it slightly less natural than what she sensed with Devon? Or was her memory skewed by this crush?

Robyn hated the impact of thinking that word so concretely, but she also couldn't deny it anymore. Still, it was just a crush. One day things would change. Maybe if she had a chance to talk to Devon in person, she would see for herself that their dynamic was truly better suited as friends, which would put her butterflies at ease in future texting conversations. This would all be an episode to put in the rear-view mirror, and Patrick would never have to know. He didn't deserve the hurt feelings of knowing about this, since it was objectively harmless anyway.

What if I had waited longer for Devon and not married Patrick?

The thought came unbidden while she washed lunch dishes one day. She mentally slapped it away, but not before shock and regret coursed through her with an intensity she knew would be impossible to wash away on her own.

- Chapter Fifteen -

It felt like more than a week had passed since the previous small group gathering took place. April felt the lack of preparedness press down harder than usual on her social abilities. She and Theo hadn't had their usual Sunday afternoon session due to their drive home from Baylor and subsequent busyness, and she had completely forgotten to read Ephesians 5. Now, as she sat and listened to the group take turns reading through the verses, the familiarity of some of them grounded her. At least, that's how she stated it to herself as both pride and despair rose up in agreement with verses 1 and 2: "Follow God's example, therefore, as dearly loved children and walk in the way of love, just as Christ loved us and gave himself up for us as a fragrant offering and sacrifice to God." And then later, in verse 21, "…submit to one another out of reverence for Christ."

I already think others matter more than I do, she prayed silently as Asher started in on the passage about wives submitting to their husbands. *And I want to do that, too, when I'm a wife,* she continued. *But I'm struggling so much lately with the sinful desire to put myself first. Please help me to stay submissive, like Jesus was. I want to be more like him and less like me.*

Samuel was the last one to read, his voice doing its regular crescendo. He finished the final verse and shook his head in amazement. "I tell you, that is a lot of instruction for a man. To love his wife as Christ loves the church? That is a high calling. It is a beautiful imagery."

Asher was returning from the kitchen with a plate of crackers and a glass of ginger ale, which he placed in his pale wife's outstretched hands. Myla barely concealed a dry heave into her arm, then tucked into the snack with silent desperation.

"Does anyone else think that the church has a history of over-emphasizing the part about a wife's submission?" Faye asked, looking around at the group. "I'm not sure what everyone else's experiences have been, but I know I've absorbed the message about submitting to my husband in spades. Meanwhile, husbands who dominate their households are often given a free pass," she finished.

A moment of silence passed. April mentally chewed on the observation, wondering if she could say the same for herself.

Theo and Patrick spoke up at the same time. Patrick closed his mouth and motioned his hand toward Theo.

"You might be right about that part being emphasized a lot," Theo said. "I'll be honest, I haven't been as aware of the passage for husbands. But it could be that God knew that women wouldn't realize the power they have over men. A reckless woman can take a husband out at the knees, but one who submits can help a man step into the roles that God has for him. She can be his helper, like God designed Eve to be for Adam."

Faye pinched her mouth shut but her eyes had darkened considerably. It felt like the start of the baptism conversation all over again.

"If I may," Patrick spoke gently, "I would like to suggest that the world is full of examples of women who submit to their husbands, yet the husbands do *not* become godlier for it. In fact, I personally believe that this passage, applied improperly, has done a *lot* of harm. Not just toward women, but toward all of society."

"But how can you apply Scripture incorrectly?" Theo asked. "It tells us what to do, so we should do it. No matter how we feel about it, we do it out of obedience. If a woman submits to a man, and he doesn't take that opportunity to step up and *be* a godly man, that's on him. But at least the wife has honoured God. If she's not rewarded in this lifetime, she will have a great reward in the next one. What matters is her obedience, not the result of it. She has no control over the result."

"But you just said that a woman has more power over a man than she realizes," Faye replied. "So, does she have that power, or doesn't she? Which is it?"

"Just because she has power doesn't mean every man is going to respond properly," Theo retorted, growing rigid. April fiddled with the corner of her opened Bible, running her thumb down the sides of the feathery pages over and over.

"So, in other words, women don't actually have automatic power over men. Men are more in control of their own actions than they want to admit."

"Of course they're in control, but a woman can make it easier for them to be loving and godly by doing what the Bible says."

"But if a man is taught *only* that when he's growing up—without being taught about developing his own character and integrity and dependence on Christ—he lays his own personal accountability at the feet of his wife, and then it's her fault if he's treating her poorly."

"That's not what I was saying!"

Faye looked down at her hands, which had started trembling. She tucked them under her legs. Even Theo seemed to have noticed. The tension in the room shifted toward compassion and surprise as Faye pulled out one of her hands and wiped a tear away from her eye.

Robyn moved beside her and put an arm around her shoulders.

"I'm sorry," Faye whispered in a quivery voice. "It's just that, this topic is extremely personal to me."

"No apology needed," Robyn assured her. The other group members murmured in agreement.

Faye took a deep breath and sat up straight. Robyn withdrew her arm and Faye began to speak.

"I moved to Regina several years ago to be with my boyfriend. We lived together and got pregnant within a few months." Faye smiled faintly. "I wasn't exactly thrilled at first, but I fell in love with my little surprise. But Ryan, my boyfriend, was very unhappy about it. He began to treat me horribly. I loved him, and I expected that if I was patient enough, he'd grow into his role of fatherhood eventually.

"Partway through the pregnancy, I began attending church again. I wasn't totally on speaking terms with God, but I wanted my baby to grow up knowing him. So I figured that would be a good place to start. Ryan didn't attend church with me, but he was willing to try a few of the couples counseling sessions one of the pastors offered.

"Almost immediately, the pastor pressured us to get married because it would be the best thing for our child." Faye looked around the room. "I'm not here to say that's always bad advice in general. But in our case, it was advice—scratch that, it was *pressure*—given to an emotionally abusive relationship. The pastor didn't know that, because he never tried to figure out our background. He was only interested in what he thought we were supposed to do next.

"When I finally got up the nerve to tell the pastor what Ryan was like to me behind closed doors, I was advised to be more submissive. That submitting to Ryan would not only cause him to treat me better, but would be a witness to him and bring him to Christ. He used all kinds of Scriptures to try and prove his point, including the one we just read. By then, my spirit was so broken and confused, I believed him. But no matter how much I tried to show respect and deference to Ryan, things got worse. He never hurt me physically, but the things he yelled at me began to get directed toward our child. Even though he wasn't born yet, my eyes snapped open and I realized I couldn't raise him with a dad who treated him that way. So I left. I left Ryan, I left that church, I left Regina. I came home and started to see a Christian therapist my parents recommended, who helped me start to untangle some of the damage that had been done. This therapist also runs a support group for women who've been hurt by the church." Faye looked around at the group again, as if assessing their reactions. "I know it's an uncomfortable thought, but there are lots of us out there. Most of the ones I met in group therapy were told to stay in abusive relationships at one point or another. We've all had to untangle the way Scripture was used to manipulate us, on top of the effects of being abused. We've all had to learn our value and identity in Christ, because we were taught that our value and identity was in how we performed 'for Christ,'" Faye used air quotes as she spoke those last words, "in our relationships. A lot of people stayed in marriages that were toxic for far too long, because their commitments seemed to be badges of honour for the churches they attended…never mind that the underbelly of those marriages were dark and evil and full of sin."

"I'm sorry you were hurt," Theo said. "But are you suggesting that churches should be perfect? They're full of imperfect people. Even the leaders make mistakes."

Faye scoffed out a laugh and looked at Theo incredulously. "Of course not. But the problem of spiritually guilting women into staying with abusive men is worth examining, don't you think?"

Theo opened his mouth to speak again, but April put her hand on his leg. She removed it as soon as he looked down at it.

Please don't hate me, she begged. But she couldn't let him press the issue when it was clear that sharing her heart had been a brave, vulnerable move for Faye.

"Thank you for telling us your story, Faye," Patrick said. "I'm sorry this topic hits on some painful triggers. I would have tried to ease into it a different way if I'd known."

"No need," Faye replied. "I've worked through it enough to know how to handle the memories. It was the hardest part of my life, but also the place that God's power and love poured into the most." She smiled. "And contrary to what it may seem, I'm not here to hate on men or the church. I'm here, aren't I? And I'm raising a son with full respect for who God created him to be. But I'm not afraid to focus on this issue that is far too often swept under the rug."

The discussion continued from there in a calmer manner, but April was too uncomfortable to pay attention. She had silenced Theo. What had she been thinking? Despite her appreciation for her group member's brave vulnerability, she hated the situation that had forced her to intervene.

Thanks a lot, Faye, she thought with resentment.

Patrick closed the conversation by reminding everyone that there would be no gathering the following Thursday, as he and Robyn and Linus were going to be taking an extended weekend vacation at a rental cabin a few hours away. When he followed that up by asking for prayer requests, he wrote down the items that the group members brought up, then mentioned his own.

"Robyn and April are going to Edmonton this weekend." He looked affectionately at Robyn, who briefly met his eyes with a small smile before looking down. "We can pray for their travel safety, and for the kind of refreshing that a getaway like this can bring."

* * *

About an hour after small group disbanded, Robyn sent a text:
I'm going to Edmonton with a friend this weekend. Would you be free to do coffee?

Only a few seconds passed before the response came through.
For you, I'd cancel my own open-heart surgery. When and where?

She snuffed out a giggle behind her hand and typed: Our plans aren't nailed down yet, but I'll be in touch.

Do I get to meet the little guy?

No, he gets to stay home and have guy time with his dad.

Lucky them. And lucky me. I can't wait to see you in person again after all these years.

Robyn sighed, closed her eyes, and reached across from her perch on the bathtub edge to flush the toilet. Patrick was probably sound asleep, but it never hurt to prop up a believable story any time she snuck into the bathroom late at night.

On top of everything else, the thought of leaving Linus for an entire weekend gave her equal amounts of anguish and reprieve.

"Leaving him for a few days won't hurt him, and feeling relief at having a break from taking care of him doesn't make you a bad mother," she whispered to herself. In moments like these, when the fraught journey of motherhood made it hard to see clearly, she purposely spoke to herself as if she were her own best friend. The language was a lot kinder and more helpful than the first thoughts that came to her mind.

In truth, the prospect of leaving Linus was what had initially shot down the impulse to invite herself along on April's trip. But on their recent walk, when April had mentioned her plan with a contagious level of determination and enthusiasm, Robyn's interest had spiked through the roof immediately.

Devon lived *so* close to Edmonton. Although she would never have made a trip out that way on her own, she simply couldn't pass up this opportunity to tag along.

Yes, she would benefit from the time away from home. Yes, she was enjoying April and wanted to keep getting to know her better.

Yes, she needed to get away from Patrick and her confusing lack of affection that weighed her down like a heavy stone whenever he was near.

Most especially—yes, she needed to see Devon like she

needed to take her next breath.

* * *

The silence on the ride home was thicker than April had expected. She wanted to reach over and help Theo feel better, but she was worried that it would cause an accident. Was he mad at her, or Faye, or women in general? Maybe this small group hadn't been such a good idea after all.

When Theo pulled up to her curb, April turned to him and murmured nervously, "Well…I guess I'll see you after the weekend."

"Yeah," he said, looking at her with a troubled expression. "I didn't realize Robyn was going with you. I guess it'll be nice to share the driving."

"It will, yes," April replied. "And just so you know, it's not like I meant to not tell you. It kind of came up last-minute and I haven't seen you since then."

Theo shook his head.

"What a night," he muttered incredulously. "April, do you really see me as one of those boyfriends who has to know who you're hanging out with all the time? It just, for us, it feels like there's this theme of you not letting me in on things. This is a small example of a larger issue that keeps dividing us."

April looked down. She didn't know what to say or think.

"I'm sorry," he muttered. "I think I need to clear my head. Faye was just a little too much tonight, and I got frustrated by some of the things she said."

"I'm sorry I cut you off at small group," April blurted out quickly. "I just didn't—"

"It's okay."

Hand on the door handle, April wondered how to gracefully exit the conversation and the car.

Theo smiled at her, although the warmth didn't quite reach

his eyes. There was a poorly-masked hard edge to them.

"You'd better go get some sleep before your trip," he said. "I'm going to miss you."

"I'm going to miss you too," she said.

"Kiss for the road?"

April unbuckled and leaned across the console, planting as much energy into her kisses as she could manage. She had the power to make Theo feel better, and through her kisses, words and choices, she was going to exercise that power to the best of her abilities.

- Chapter Sixteen -

Robyn held on to Linus for dear life on Friday afternoon. April would be here to pick her up in a few minutes, and she didn't know if she would physically be able to let him go.

"He'll be fine, Robyn. You will, too," Patrick said gently, putting his arms around the two of them. "Just imagine how happy he'll be to see you on Sunday. Letting him miss you a bit will create such a great reunion."

"But what if he looks for me all over the house and doesn't find me?" The image almost made her cry.

"Then he'll learn that the world doesn't end just because Mom isn't always here. This is good for him, honey. Missing people is part of life. It's okay for him to experience that once in a while."

"It's not going to make him resent me?" Robyn couldn't believe the way she was gushing. She hadn't pressed into Patrick like this in ages.

She needed Devon so badly it hurt.

April's car turned into their short driveway. A bass beat had been pumping loudly enough to be felt in the house. They watched as April killed the engine, abruptly ending the musical onslaught.

Patrick and Robyn laughed.

"This is going to be fun," Robyn sighed, nuzzling her nose into the soft spot between Linus' neck and shoulder. "Sounds like April is ready to make me feel young again."

Patrick went to the front door and opened it as April stepped out of her car.

"Hello!" he greeted. "Ready to whisk my wife away?"

"Yes, if she's ready."

"You might have to pull on her while I pull on Linus. Make sure you pump her with a lot of distractions for the first little while."

Robyn swatted his arm, gave Linus one last squeeze, and was prepared to hand him over when his chubby little arm squeezed her neck.

"Mama," he said, breaking her heart completely in two.

"Oh, baby, Mama loves you so much," she said, pushing through her husky voice. "You and Daddy will have lots of fun, and Mama will see you in two sleeps. Okay?"

"Mama," Linus said again with a proud face.

"Hey, buddy, look what I have!" Patrick held Linus' favourite stuffy, a brown dog named Pup-Pup, in his hand. Linus dove out of his mother's arms and snatched Pup-Pup while Patrick pulled him into a bear hug.

I'm even going to miss Pup-Pup, Robyn realized with chagrin. She smiled bravely at her boy, then bent down for her purse and suitcase. She should leave right now, while Linus was happy.

She turned and looked at April with resolve. "Let's hit the road!"

"Just a sec," Patrick said from behind her.

She turned back and offered him a quick kiss, then leaned into his hug without setting her bags down.

"I'd better make this quick so Linus doesn't grab me," she said as she sensed Patrick's hold start to tighten. He hesitated for only a moment, then released her and stepped back. He and Linus looked at her while she walked backward toward the car, waving and smiling and blowing kisses to Linus the whole time. He giggled at the show and smacked his chubby little hand to his mouth then flung it out toward her, pursing his lips after the "kiss" had already been thrown. Robyn forced herself to keep walking.

Less than a minute later, they were blocks away and Linus was out of sight. He hadn't shed a tear, but that didn't mean he wouldn't cry later. Robyn batted the picture away.

April's heavy bass music was too quiet for Robyn's emotional needs. Robyn huffed and said, "Okay. Leaving him was hard." She turned up the volume and allowed the music to drown out how much she already missed Linus and how much she craved texting Devon about it.

April drove toward the edge of the city. Robyn set her purse on the floor and stuffed her hands under her thighs for a few minutes. Familiar buildings slipped past her window and reminded her of the fact that she hadn't left the city since before she'd become a mother. She determined to herself that she wasn't going to ruin her long-awaited prairie landscape views by drowning in her inner storm.

A glance at April revealed that there were big things on her friend's mind, too. Time to pull out of her own mess.

Robyn turned down the volume.

"That's better. I just needed the music to yell my feelings away for now. So…how was work today?"

April's face brightened considerably. "You know, it wasn't the best day, but some good things came out of it." She paused to safely complete a left-hand turn. "Seth and I had a walk at Meewasin Park, but the path is kind of hilly and that made it tricky for him. He had a slow fall, but I was holding his arm tightly so we both kind of slow-fell, and someone behind us asked if we were okay. I thought Seth would be upset about the whole thing, but he only screamed for a few minutes, and the guy behind us stayed close by and kept asking me if we needed help. I was explaining that we would be okay and stuff. Eventually Seth calmed down and allowed me to help him stand up. While we were walking away, this guy told us to enjoy the rest of our walk, and…I don't know, maybe it sounds silly, but when people are kind, it really makes my day."

"That's not silly at all. It makes perfect sense. The kindness of strangers is powerful."

"I know, right? When I think about Seth or anyone else who's typically on the margins of society, I think of how often other people ignore them out of discomfort. There's something about normal, simple kindness that goes a long way. I just want the world to be a safe place for all the vulnerable people. Guys like the one I saw today make it seem more possible."

By now, the buildings outside of the vehicle were becoming fewer and farther between. The rope between her heart and Linus' was stretching, but what lay ahead put butterflies in her stomach.

"How was the rest of your time with him?"

"Seth was so crabby after that," April replied with an affectionate laugh. "We finished the walk, and I took an extra-long drive home because he sometimes likes that, but when we got to the house and went inside, he really didn't tolerate much. He was making angry noises about pretty much everything I said and did, and I was feeling a bit frustrated because he's never been that grumpy around me before."

"Is he getting sick, or maybe he had a rough night?"

"I didn't figure it out. But I think what surprised me was… I don't know if this will make sense, but after I left, I was thinking about it and I realized that I didn't take it personally. Like, most of the time, when someone is upset around me, I automatically assume it's my fault and I'm busy trying to figure out what I did wrong, and how I can make it better."

"Hm."

"And I guess I realized that there must be something about Seth. Or something about our connection. But whatever it is, I could identify that I feel one hundred percent emotionally safe with him. Safe to be myself, safe to assume the best about his feelings toward me, safe to not overthink everything. It's just…yeah, it was just a neat realization. His bad mood might not have had anything to do with me. I've never assumed that about anyone's bad mood before."

"In a way, that sounds like the way we're meant to be free in our relationships with God," Robyn said. "Free to assume the best about his feelings for us, free from overthinking. That all sounds very much like what he wants for us."

April seemed to consider this for a moment. "Yeah," she finally agreed, putting on her sunglasses as the sun peeked out from a small break in the clouds. "I know that in my head. I'm starting to experience that, I guess. Still have some trust issues that he isn't bored with me or wanting to punish me for every little thing I've done wrong, or things like that. But I've had a couple of breakthrough moments where I sensed the truth of his love tangibly. In between those moments I'm still bouncing around like a nervous cat. I'm looking forward to my heart fully feeling it and resting in it all the time, if that can ever happen for an anxious person like me."

In the silence that followed, Robyn began to formulate a response. *Hypocrite, hypocrite, hypocrite* something screamed inside as she opened her mouth, but for April's sake she ignored it and pushed on.

"I used to be able to relate to that."

They passed a field of cows.

Linus would love those, she thought before continuing.

"I grew up with a lot of good things, including healthy family and church and friends. Oh, by the way, two of those friends are Devon and Carly, the people I'm planning to meet up with for coffee tomorrow." She inwardly winced at the lie, chided herself for babbling, and righted her train of thought. "That's beside the point. Anyway, I guess what I'm trying to say is, even though I grew up with all of that going for me, I didn't have a close relationship with God. I knew all the right stuff and I believed it was true, but my real growth with God seemed to start after I left home. I began to learn what it was like to walk *with* God, and not to walk *before* God, as if I was on a stage and he was in the audience. You know what I mean?"

April nodded. "Definitely. That's a good way to put it."

"Yeah, they talked about that at Bible School as being performance-oriented. You're trying to please God and sometimes it's also about being pleasing to others, so you're more focused on your outward actions than you are about what's going on in your heart. Or, to make it trickier, you're trying to straighten out your own heart, using your own strength, because you haven't learned how to rest in God's salvation, and in his love for you. You're trying to clean your inner world up before you surrender it to him."

April was silent, her lips pursed in thought.

"And it wasn't just Bible School that helped me grow. It was one of the biggest influences toward helping me realize just how vast God's grace is, but so was Patrick." At this, she squeezed her own lips tightly and paused. Could she go down this road? She considered April; how her anxiety covered her like a shroud when they had first met. She considered the way Theo's presence overshadowed her during small group meetings, increasingly more so as time went on. It was so subtle she was convinced neither party had even noticed what was happening.

But could she talk about the wonders of Patrick without hating herself and resenting his perfection for setting her up for such a catastrophic failure within their marriage?

What failure? Nothing has happened. Nothing is happening.

If nothing was happening, there was no problem; therefore, this wasn't a hard thing to discuss.

"How do you mean?" April prompted.

"Well, he showed me unconditional love in ways that opened my eyes even more to God. My parents were very loving as I was growing up, but at the time, I didn't recognize the power of that. But when Patrick and I started dating, it made me aware of deeper things. We've had our ups and downs, and I can get a little intense sometimes, but whenever I've been at my lowest lows, he's never stopped looking at me with love. If I look at myself through eyes of hate, his view of me never changes. If I want to run away from myself, or question everything, he gives me space to figure it out, but he never leaves. He gives me space without leaving…" Her voice trailed off. She gave her head a little jerk.

"Does Theo help you draw closer to God?" she finally said. She hadn't meant to lob the conversational hot potato into April's face like that, but her own hands were suddenly on fire.

April's tone simmered with masked defensiveness. "Yeah, he and I study the Bible together, and he really encourages me to keep loving God."

Robyn glanced over. "Well, that's…that's good. He seems to take Scripture very seriously."

"Oh, he does." April uncapped her water bottle and took a sip. "He does, and it's a good encouragement for me to do the same. I'm trying to, for sure. I'm trying to apply it as best I can."

"As best you can, while knowing that you're already fully loved by God just as you are, right?"

"I know he loves me just as I am, but he loves me too much to leave me this way," April replied. "There are *so* many—"

"Sorry to interrupt, but you should back up a few words and stop there."

April tilted her head.

"What you said, that phrase, it's true for all of us. Definitely. But I think you're too quick to rush past the part where God loves you just as you are. I think you need to camp out there for a while."

"I don't want to settle for less than what God has in store for me, though," April responded.

"You don't have to settle for less. Settle into his perfect love. Let that be your primary focus, and see what amazing things come as a by-product of simply resting in his grace. You *do* know you're fully loved by God just as you are, right?"

April gave her a little half-smile. "Getting there, I think."

"And fully loved by Theo just as you are?"

"That's what he says."

The clipped tone suggested a danger zone. Robyn wanted to help, but maybe they'd both had enough danger zones already. Time for a break.

"So. What are you thinking for supper?"

- Chapter Seventeen -

Ten-year-old April lay awake, listening to the sound of four-year-old Britney's even breathing from across the tiny gap that separated their beds with matching Tinkerbell coverlets. She thought again of how much she wanted a bunk bed—how much that would make sense, since they didn't even have room for their dresser in the room they had shared since Britney's first birthday. Until recently, April didn't question the system of choosing her clothes and changing in the playroom downstairs. Then a few months ago, she had seen a picture of a bunk bed in one of her books, and it started turning the wheels. A bunk bed would allow their dresser to fit against the wall where Britney's bed currently sat.

Mom and Dad weren't open to many of April's ideas about how things could be done differently around the house, but she had to admit that most of her ideas involved adding things to the house that they simply didn't have room for. This, on the other hand, would actually *save* space. If their dresser could be moved upstairs, that opened up a spot in the playroom downstairs for…what? What would Mom and Dad like to put there? Maybe she could suggest that it would free up a spot for another couch or a bigger TV? Or, since Dad had his favourite chair upstairs, could she recommend that they buy a favourite chair for Mom that would go downstairs?

Armed with a week's worth of preparation for her airtight argument, April brought it up over supper the following evening. Her parents had been very distracted as of late, but when she started off by saying, "I have a really great idea for saving space in our bedroom," they both looked at her and stopped eating. They glanced at each other while she pressed through the rest of her speech. Her little heart was racing by the time she'd finished. She hadn't wanted or anticipated something so much, not since giving up the dream of having her own puppy a couple of years ago.

"April," her dad said, setting down his fork.

"Max," her mom said quietly but firmly. Even Britney stopped eating as she recognized a tone of importance.

Her dad looked at her mom and gave a little shrug. "Now's as good a time as any," he said, then he turned his attention back to his eldest daughter. "April. What if, instead of getting a bunk bed, you were able to get your own room? All to yourself?"

Well, this was unexpected. April sat back with a frown, trying to peg this curveball into their current reality. She already knew she wouldn't want to have a bedroom in the basement. Besides, where would the office go? Or were they going to put a wall right down the middle of the bedroom she shared with Britney?

That won't even work, though. Who gets to have the door?

"I want my own room!" Britney piped up. "Yes, yes, yes!"

"But wait…how?" April asked with a tilt of her head.

Her parents both started to speak at once, and then her mother deferred.

"Well, we can't fit a new bedroom in this house," her dad continued. "And even though this house has been very good to us, it's time for us to get a new one. In fact, it's time for me to get a new job, too. So your mom and I," he paused and reached over to take their mother's hand in his, "have decided that we're going to move."

The silence hammered loudly.

Her dad continued, "I just found out yesterday that I got a job in Baylor, and we're going to move there this summer. Won't it be great to live so close to Grandma and Grandpa?"

The longer he talked, the more April felt like everything was turning into a bad dream. Things didn't seem as sharp as they did a minute ago. Thank goodness she was going to wake up soon and realize that they weren't *actually* moving.

But wait, this was more real than dreams usually felt. Except it was more dream-like than life usually felt. Which way was it?

Her dad was still talking, and Britney looked excited. April's mom was looking at her with a smile, but her eyes were a mix of sadness and worry. Words weren't making sense anymore.

April looked past her family's heads, taking in the skinny, white kitchen cupboards that reached all the way up to the ceiling. There were four beside each other, just like there had always been. She observed the arched doorway into the living room, where the lights were off, but the sunshine cast the room in an early-evening glow that conjured up all the quiet times spent reading and watching dust motes from her favourite spot on the couch. Her eyes landed back on the table, where all four of their plates were touching each other. They didn't have space for serving dishes on their little table in their little kitchen, so Mom and Dad always served them directly from the pots and pans on the stove. Movies that portrayed large dining-room tables full of steaming casserole dishes, and people helping themselves directly from those dishes without having to stand up, used to fill April with a certain type of longing. Now, remorse washed over her for every moment she had ever thought about how nice it would be to have that. Remorse over bringing up the bunk bed, and for wishing away the cramped space in her room, made her stomach tighten into a solid knot.

How badly had her longings betrayed this house that had loved her as best it could—and in three months they were going to abandon it like it meant nothing.

* * *

April knew she had lived a simple life compared to many people, but there was no denying the big slash in her timeline that corresponded with the big move. Throughout the grief of leaving the only home she had ever known, and the excitement of starting over and getting her own bedroom and living close to her grandparents, a shift occurred in her spirit.

It seemed like everyone else was thrilled. April recognized this and tried to sell herself on embracing the idea of being happy for everyone else's happiness, but some part of her wasn't giving up its right to feel pain. She did her best to shove it deep inside, knowing that it wasn't helpful to focus on it. Her parents gave April space to cry when she was too overwhelmed to hold it in, but the real attention came when she put on her brave face and convinced them, if not her own self, that she was happy too.

"See, it's great to be living here, isn't it?" her dad said one time when she burst into a giggle at Britney's antics on the swing set in their backyard—an apparatus they certainly hadn't had the space for back in Edmonton. He pulled her in for a hug. It felt so good to be held; it didn't happen as often as it did when she was younger.

It wasn't just the fact that she missed the house. She missed her family *within* that house. She was lonely whenever she couldn't see or hear anyone else at any given time, but it seemed she was the only one who craved sidling up to her family members. They all seemed to be enjoying the extra space in their new dwelling. There were several times she had thought, in a panic, that she was home alone, only to leave whichever room she had been in and find another family member doing their own thing somewhere else. Over time she developed a sense of appreciation for having that kind of solitary space. Yet when she got caught up in memory lane, picking away at and pressing into remembrances of what it was like to live constantly in each other's presences, a reassuring pressure would enter her spirit and make her feel safe. Thoughts of the way it used to be became a warm blanket she could pull over her mind whenever she was anxious.

As time wore on, the new house became another home. It even became good. But it was never the *real* home. Home was on a pedestal, untouchable yet ever-present.

The idea of re-visiting home had occurred to her constantly while growing up, but in the busy-ness of establishing her wings in the adult world, it hadn't taken form until last week.

And now, here she was, waking up in a motel bed just a few blocks away from her old neighbourhood on a sunny Saturday morning.

Eagerness ran through her veins, but it was only seven-thirty. Robyn was still sound asleep in her own bed just a few feet away. Assuming that the young mom hadn't slept in for ages, April stayed quietly in place and tried to savour the simple fact of being where she was: in her childhood city, away from Theo, and with a new friend who seemed to really care about her.

Why am I happy to be away from Theo? she prayed after recognizing the thought. *I miss him, kind of. I want to share this part of my life with him, kind of. I also feel like I need the comfort of my old home* because *of him…kind of. Is this a normal thing in a relationship?*

Was it odd that she felt more comfortable with Seth and with Robyn than she did with her own boyfriend? He lavished more love on her than anyone she knew. It was easy to soak up his affections because they rushed in like rain after a drought.

Why am I always in a love-drought?

With Theo, April had direction and a sense of purpose. She had always wanted to get married to a solid Christian man and have kids. Theo's dreams aligned nicely with hers, and his rock-solid love of God was inspirational. She knew he wouldn't be swayed away from his beliefs, no matter how the wind blew.

And yet—even as she thought these things, the stubborn

storm clouds of doubt continued to roil in the distance. She had been ignoring them and praying against them for weeks now. No doubt Satan was trying to get in the middle of a good, God-planned, God-honouring relationship. What great plans God must have in store for them since the enemy was working overtime to convince her that this might not be the right fit for her.

April spent some more time praying to that effect. When she heard Robyn shifting in her bed, she looked over.

Robyn groaned happily as she stretched her arms above her head, bending them when her fists connected with the wall. She opened her eyes and rolled over, first taking in April and then the digital clock on her nightstand.

"Whoa! If I was at home, I would have been up with Linus two hours ago!" she marvelled. "Thanks for letting me sleep in."

"I kind of figured you could use it," April yawned. "How did you sleep?"

Robyn winced. "Could have been better, but it was my own fault. I stayed up late texting after you fell asleep. Texting Patrick."

"Ha! Scandalous." April sat up and pushed off her blankets. "Is it okay if I use the bathroom first?"

"Go crazy," Robyn yawned and stretched again. "Then I'd be up for grabbing some breakfast."

* * *

Breakfast consisted of fast-food egg sandwiches and hash browns at the nearest greasy joint. They had decided to go cheap on most meals since they were planning to splurge on shopping and eating at the West Edmonton Mall after lunch. April didn't love the idea that Devon and Carly would be joining them for that chunk of the day, cutting into her vacation from being "on" and anxious, but she knew she couldn't begrudge her friend this connecting time. If she had comfortable childhood friends, she would probably love meeting up with them too.

In fact, wasn't that essentially what she was doing, but with a building instead of a person?

By mid-morning, the ladies were ready for the day.

April planned to drive up to her old house and just look at it from the outside, soak in its presence for a bit, and see what that might do to her. Next, she would deliver Robyn to Tim Hortons for her lunch date with Devon and Carly, and then she planned on returning to the motel room to do some journaling. If some clarity could be gained, or some reassurance that she was on the right track in life, or even just some comfort for her anxious thoughts, April was going to count the day as a win.

She was thankful Robyn had come on this trip with some of her own plans, allowing for that anticipated period of solitude.

"I feel creepy," she admitted to Robyn as her car turned onto the familiar street. Pangs of nostalgia were already kicking in. "But I'm trying not to care. It's not like I even live here. People won't recognize the weirdo who's stalking the neighbourhood."

Robyn chuckled. "I still think it's completely fine to knock on the door and ask for a look around, but I won't push it. Maybe." She gave April a teasing grin. "Okay, maybe I'll push for it if the moment seems right."

"No, seriously, don't! Or I'll drive away and leave you here." April laughed nervously, then blew out a deep breath. "Robyn, these trees. I swear they still know me." The foliage cover created a tall, dark tunnel down the street. A strong force hit her right in the lungs.

April glanced at the houses marching slowly past her car. Hers was a block away on the passenger side, but many of these homes had a similar look to the one she'd lived in. This was a neighborhood of wartime homes in various stages of modernization—an eclectic mix of overgrown lawns and well-kept yards; rusty, unhinged gates and storybook white picket fences; old metal door latches and keypad entries. Most of the colours were the same as she remembered. There was the dark gray house beside the white one (which still needed a good power wash) beside the pink one, where a small dog barked at their intrusion while its front paws rested against a low fence. How many former neighbours still lived here? Would any of them remember her if she told them her name? She couldn't recall knowing any of their names when she was little, and the passage of time had faded their faces into the background.

She stopped at the yield sign, her eyes trained on the lush oak tree half a block away on the right that called to her like an old friend. Reminding herself to check for traffic, she rolled forward and slowed the car down to a crawl, forgetting any concerns about what the local people might think.

Home was hiding behind the oak tree at first, but as her car practically tip-toed past, the large front window came into view.

As a child, it had felt like the tree and window had a vast amount of space in between them, enough for her to play quiet games in a secluded spot. Her adult eyes took in the five-foot space and wondered if the roots were causing damage to the foundation. If so, she mentally thanked the current owners for not having the tree removed before she had a chance to see it again.

The front entrance, accessed by four concrete steps and a thin metal banister, jutted out just beside the tree. The storm door looked different from what she remembered, but the wooden door behind it still had those three windows in a fan shape at the top. The door was white, and the house was pale yellow. Once, after reading *Little Women* and becoming enamoured with the idea of naming one's home, she had looked back in her memories and dubbed this place "Daffodil House." She could see now that she'd been wrong on the vibrancy of the yellow, but it was the way it made her feel that gave the name some weight.

Did I ever name our new house? she wondered, then pushed the thought aside in favour of looking ahead.

Her car was veering to the right. Correcting course, she glanced back over her right shoulder and was caught off guard by the comical sight of Robyn pressing herself as far back into her seat as possible, so as to avoid blocking the view. April laughed, looking past her to take in the image of the two side windows before they disappeared behind the next building. The two bedrooms! Those windows were insanely close together. How was it possible to have two full-sized bedrooms along that one wall?

"Well," she said, "I'm sure we have sufficiently creeped out the neighbourhood. I think I'm going to…yes, I'm going to park, and we can walk past it now."

"Sounds good to me," Robyn replied. "You seem to need more time with this house for sure."

After parking around the corner, April picked up her purse and stepped outside, inhaling the slight summer breeze. These were smells she was accustomed to, from living in a mature neighbourhood in Saskatoon, but somehow there was a difference. Maybe it was just the filter of her psyche that made the scents go directly into her stomach. Whatever it was, she was starving to soak it in.

Robyn walked silently beside her as they rounded the corner. The sidewalks were still cracked and raised up by underground roots in various places. It must have been a challenge for her mom to push the baby stroller around here.

Seth came to mind and April smiled. This would *not* be a good place to go for a walk with him.

With that thought, the past and present collided with a resounding force. It hit April that she really was an adult. She had been conscious of that reality since moving away from Baylor, but apparently her subconscious hadn't been caught up to speed until now, when it seemed to be feeling that truth for the first time ever. It was a bit shocking.

"What are you thinking about?" Robyn prompted.

They were walking past the house now, and the inside of April's mind was so full that the question completely stumped her. How to find an end to any of the tangled threads?

"I don't know," she finally replied. "Lots of things. Too many things. I'm going to be busy with my journal later. Maybe even for weeks."

They had stopped walking and a *now-or-never* boldness took hold of April in a way that hurt. She knew that she would regret not attempting to see the inside, yet it was Saturday morning, and she was a stranger, and she *hated* even the slightest risk of intruding on anyone's anything.

But how much would she ache when she returned to Saskatoon, knowing she hadn't even tried?

Robyn took a small step toward the house and smiled reassuringly. "You know you have to."

"I do. I do, and I hate it," she muttered back. But she fell into step beside her friend and borrowed her nonchalance as best she could, putting one foot in front of the other until she was standing at the door and shaking. Robyn pushed the doorbell for her.

It felt like an eternity passed. Relief began to swarm. If no one was home, then at least she would know she had tried and yet hadn't intruded. It was for the best, really.

But then there were footsteps coming from the kitchen. She could picture the path like she could picture her house in Saskatoon.

The door was opened just a few inches, and a woman's face peered around the edge. April would guess she was in her thirties, although the bags under her eyes suggested she was a tired 30-something.

It hadn't happened in years, but April found herself unable to speak. The noise in her head had drowned out the synaptic reflexes of ordering her thoughts and sending them to her mouth.

Thankfully, Robyn didn't wait very long.

"Hi! My name is Robyn Zhou, and this is my friend April Vale. We realize this is unusual, but April lived in this house when she was a kid, and she was wondering if she could have a look around?"

The woman registered the expected surprise at this

unexpected request, but a gentle look filled her eyes. "If you can just wait out there a sec, I'll go get my husband. We'll show you around."

"Thank you!" Robyn said as the door closed and locked into place. April took a deep breath and squeezed her hands together. She wondered if cliff-diving into the ocean would be easier than this.

What an odd concept that homes traded hands like this. Where once she could have run straight through that door with complete abandon, she now had to be locked outside and wait for permission from people who didn't even know she had existed until this moment. Did they even appreciate the house for all its goodness, the way it deserved?

"It's... it's just a building," she said in a shaky voice to Robyn. "I feel like I love it more than I should. It means more to me than it should. Like I've defined myself by it somehow, and I don't know if that's healthy or not."

"I think we all define ourselves by our homes to some extent," Robyn replied. From inside, two sets of footsteps began to draw nearer. "Or maybe by our feelings about our homes, whether-"

The door opened all the way. They were now face-to-face with a large barrel-chested man with a dark brown beard and serious eyes. Beside him, his tired-looking wife was wearing pajama shorts and a zippered hoodie over an extremely large, round belly.

"My name is Cynthia, and this is James," the woman said. "James, this is Robyn, and this is April, the one who used to live here."

"Hi," James said in a deep voice, while Cynthia continued, "can I get you some coffee while you look around?"

"If you have any already made, I'll take some," Robyn said.

"Sure thing. And how about you?"

April shook her head with a smile. "N-no thanks." On one side she was squeezed by her social discomfort, and on the other side she was squeezed by the impact of seeing the white shag carpet in the living room. It wasn't the brown Berber she had grown up with, but the cozy effect was the same.

And the room was *so* small!

Cynthia waddled toward the kitchen while James held the door open for them to step through.

"Where are you two from?" he asked, his voice matching the suspicious tone of his expression.

"We're from Saskatoon," Robyn repeated. "April and I decided we both needed a getaway. She wanted to come see her old home, and I wanted to see some friends, so now we're in Edmonton. This house meant a great deal to her."

"When did you live here?" James asked.

From the kitchen, Cynthia called out, "Cream or sugar?"

"Both," Robyn answered.

"I was… I was here until I was ten," April said, trying to ignore how much she hated that stutter. "We… we moved to a small town outside of Saskatoon eight years ago."

"We bought this house from an older couple a few years back," James said. "Harv and Sarah Cowan. Are they the ones your family sold to?"

The names rang a bell. Overheard parental conversations during that awful transition period, no doubt.

"I think so."

Cynthia returned with a steaming mug in one hand and a glass of water in the other. She offered them to her surprise guests, then rubbed her belly absent-mindedly while saying, "I'm sure you remember that it's not a very big place, so I'm guessing you don't need a tour. We'll just have to avoid the back bedroom where our son is napping. Although he should be up soon anyway."

"Oops, sorry about the doorbell then," Robyn said with a wince. "I have a nine-month-old son. I know how disruptive that can be."

Cynthia waved an arm. "Didn't wake him, it's all good. What's your son's name?"

April stepped out of her sandals and away from the safety of Robyn as the living room pulled her in. She stood in the center of it and spun a slow circle, forcing her awareness of James' watchful eyes to the side.

The sun still dappled the floor, although the texture was different. In contrast to the overstuffed couch-and-chair set that used to reside here, the current furniture was sleek and modern. The wall still had those built-in shelves. In place of the Barbies and comics she had grown up with were board books and a plastic cash register, a jack-in-the-box, and two fabric bins filled with smaller toys. There was a large flat-screen TV mounted on the wall, and on the wall opposite the window was a display of wedding photos mixed with an assortment of baby, family, and maternity photos. Everything looked tasteful yet lived in.

Without really thinking it out, her feet led her through the archway into the kitchen. She inhaled deeply at the sight of the tall table, its surface area just a few feet squared; raised, and surrounded by barstools instead of the regular-height table of her youth. How her mom managed to cook full meals and bake cookies and cakes while two kids ran underfoot, she couldn't comprehend. Her admiration for her mom, and for Cynthia, rose a few notches. It was a darling kitchen, inviting and warm, but the impracticality of its size couldn't be ignored without her childhood lens. Still, the call of belonging in here tugged at her heartstrings.

Just past the table was the sliding glass door to the back. April wandered over and looked outside, noting the two cars parked beside each other. A sandbox was tucked away behind a plastic picket fence that separated the parking pad from the small grass-and-gravel yard. She didn't have a lot of memories from back here. Most of their outdoor time was spent in the front yard, or at a playground down the street. Mom had been more worried about drivers being careless in the back alley than they were on the main road out front.

She turned around and took in the four tall, white cupboards, which had been given new handles but still carried the recollection of watching her mom make food while April did homework or crafts at the little table.

As she turned the corner to leave the kitchen, she noticed that James was still pretending not to be keeping an eye on her from the living room. Robyn and Cynthia continued their engaging mommy chat by the front door. April smiled at James, willing him to understand that she wasn't a kleptomaniac. The bathroom door to her right was closed.

"You can take a look in there if you want," James offered gruffly. "It's not the cleanest space though."

April turned the glass knob—that was something that had been kept to the original, and it felt like the last time she had put her hand on it was just yesterday instead of eight years ago.

The toilet, pedestal sink, and bathtub were all upgraded, but the layout struck her in a fraught way like everything else so far. There were towels on the rack and on the floor, and bath toys scattered all over inside the tub.

As she stepped back out and closed the bathroom door, the bedroom door kitty-corner to her cracked open to reveal a tousled blond head of hair about two feet above the floor.

"Hey, buddy!" James greeted, squatting down with his arms out toward the boy.

The toddler's eyes locked on April immediately. His face twisted in angst, and he slammed the door.

Compassion welled over. April completely understood. James glanced at her and shrugged. "He's pretty shy," he said. She nodded as he knocked on the door, then gently slipped inside.

"Yes, sorry about that," Cynthia said. She and Robyn made their way over to her. "He's always like that with new people. Actually, he's like that with pretty much everyone who isn't me or James." Her sentence ended with an affectionate yet nervous laugh. "Sometimes I worry about him, but I've learned there's nothing I can really do about it. I'm hoping he'll grow out of it someday."

"He may, or he may just find ways to cope," April surprised herself by saying. "I was…I was very much like that when I was a kid. Still am, sometimes. I think it's just part of me that will always be there, but I've learned ways to not let it always get in my way, if that makes sense."

Cynthia looked at her with unguarded appreciation. "Thank you, that is helpful to hear. A lot of people like to give us advice on how to help him stop being shy, but I don't even know if I'm comfortable with the idea of treating it like it's a problem. You know?"

"You're already on the right track." April looked to Robyn after she spoke, and felt emboldened by her friend's smile. "Your son will know that you're not holding it against him. And that's huge. In a world that will pressure him to 'come out of his shell,' that's going to hold him up. Total and complete acceptance is the best foundation for him. Maybe you'll think of methods that help him stretch out, but it starts with love for everything he is. Even the shy part." *You're rambling. Time to shut it down.*

With a start, April realized that Cynthia was staring at her in awe.

"Ah, these silly pregnancy hormones," the young mom laughed, shaking her head. "You seriously have no idea how much I needed to hear all of that."

Neither did I, April thought as she looked down at the floor her family used to walk all over in their former life.

- Chapter Eighteen -

The coffee shop Devon had chosen was only a twenty-minute drive away, but to Robyn it felt much farther. Her anticipation had stayed neatly hidden behind her focus on April's situation, yet now that they were moving in this direction her heart was thumping hard against her ribs.

Robyn was certain April had been holding back tears ever since they left the house. As much as she wondered if she should offer to keep her company, she couldn't bear the thought of changing her plans with Devon. It was easy to justify this train of thought, trusting that April truly did need alone time to process the morning. She was deep waters, that one.

By the time they had pulled up to the brown building with the red signage, Robyn knew for a fact that this lunch date had to happen. She would have mentally exploded if it hadn't. It was long overdue, by several years.

She glanced at her phone. Devon's latest text had said he was holding a table in the corner farthest away from the north doors. She quickly tapped in just pulled up, be there soon! She hit *send,* then mentally rebuked herself. Of course she'd be there soon; she just said she had arrived! Why did this giddiness have to mess with her brain so badly?

What are Patrick and Linus up to today?

She gave her head a slight shake at the intrusive thought, then looked over at April.

Yep. She's definitely repressing tears.

"You going to be okay?" she asked.

April nodded. "Yes, this is a good thing. It needed to happen."

Robyn nodded back, then gave April's arm a squeeze. "I'm glad I got to see your house with you," she said.

April glanced at her and tried to smile. "Don't be too nice to me. I can't cry till I'm done driving. But thanks for being there."

Taking her cue, Robyn gathered her purse and opened the door. Stepping out, she wondered if Devon could see her and recognize her from his seat.

"I'll text you when we're ready," she said. "But no rush. Take all the journaling time you need. We can easily kill a few hours around here."

April smiled at her and said, "Sounds good," then immediately backed out once Robyn had closed the car door.

With a little wave to her friend, Robyn then turned toward the restaurant and gave her heart over to its wings, ignoring the heavy unease that competed with her excitement.

* * *

April barely made it into the parking lot of the motel before the tears surged out, and then she may as well have been driving underwater. Easing into her parking spot, she tried for a minute to get her crying under control, but then quickly realized that she was far more likely to attract attention for bawling in her car than if she made a mad dash to her room.

Once safely behind the door, she fell back against it and slid to the floor and sobbed. It was the kind of crying that felt like fists pulling up clumps of sludge from the bottom of her soul.

Cleansing, she knew, was the word for it. Didn't mean the cleansing process felt tidy.

And what are these clumps of sludge? she wondered. *What exactly am I dealing with here?*

On one hand, she had expected an emotional reaction from herself. On the other hand, she hadn't expected it to resonate from a much deeper place than the grief over the house warranted.

Maybe, along with that grief, was the loss of the self-acceptance she'd had in early childhood. Likely the struggle would have begun even if they'd never left Edmonton, but would it have been easier to bear within the comfort of familiarity? She wondered who she would have been if they'd never moved to Baylor; if she'd never met Cosette and learned that most people seemed to like her better when she was acting like someone else. Even her own father had made that clear. Maybe it was the wondering if April out of her shell—forget whether or not it was all a farce—was better than April *inside* her shell any day.

Clarity struck like a bell. That was her takeaway from her growing-up years. That was the takeaway that still impacted her unconsciously every day.

She started to pray, then realized she should grab hold of her journal. The pressure of pent-up processing was about to burst the dams. April stood up and sat on the edge of her bed, pulling her journal and pen off the night stand.

The world went timeless. At some point, when things had ebbed enough for her to give her writing hand a break, she read over her words.

Something came to mind just now as I considered the pain that was conjured up after visiting my house and talking to Cynthia about her shy son. I already know I feel anxious most of the time, especially about what people think of me. Is that at least partly because I felt like my parents didn't know what to do with the part of me that didn't line up with their hopes and expectations? And partly because the only friend who was able to handle me back then wasn't interested in me, so much as she enjoyed that I never gave her any trouble by standing up for myself?

She felt guilty at the weight she'd been carrying over the pains of such an unremarkable life, yet she knew that talking herself out of feeling this way wasn't possible. If this counted as having a pity party, then so be it. Her writing continued.

It hurt that Cosette didn't see that she was molding me after herself and that she didn't try to leave space for who I really was. It hurt that Dad was happier with me like that. It hurt that Mom never said anything about this, never talked about my feelings or her feelings or anybody's feelings...until recently when she brought it up. Which felt kind of violating, but it was also helpful to have her acknowledge it. But still, I have so much catching up to do. I don't even know how I'm feeling half the time, only that it's usually strong and it pushes me inside myself. Especially when I'm with Theo.

I think I love him, but I don't know how to stay unguarded with him. Not like I can be with Robyn and Seth. Why is that? I haven't even known them as long as I've known Theo. What makes the difference? Is it me or him? Or both? Is it something we can overcome, or is it a sign of trouble? I can't imagine a future without him, and I would never be able to break his heart. I just couldn't. Sometimes I crave breathing space, but isn't that normal in relationships?

By now her pen was pressing so hard into the paper that she was forced to stop. She tossed the journal onto the bed and flopped back onto her pillows. An image of the tiny, cozy kitchen from her old house popped into her mind. Except this time, she could only see the tall modern table and chairs instead of her childhood furnishings.

Surprising herself, a fresh wave of crying overtook her. She balled the pillow against her mouth to absorb the sounds. As she pondered how deep this wound really was, a single impression floated to the surface of it all: she had to forgive her mom and dad.

My parents are good people, she thought defensively. *They were dealing with a massive transition when we moved. And neither of them had ever been shy. They simply didn't know how to handle me, and that's not their fault. They've always taken good care of me; they did the best they could.* It was enough to make her angry at herself.

Then a deeper, gentler voice rose within her with a message that was too deep for words, yet her mind translated it this way: ***Don't let your loyalty block your healing.***

She sat back, absorbing this idea and the source of it. An atmosphere of love enveloped the delivery of that message, just like that time in the car with Seth. She picked up her journal and continued:

I know it's possible to hold two ideas at the same time: that my parents did a fantastic job of loving and protecting and raising me, and that they also did things to accidentally hurt me. It's possible to hold those ideas because they're both true at the same time. It's also true that no one can expect anyone on this earth to know and love them perfectly. Because only you can do that, God.

"But how do I get there? To the point where I trust your perfect love all the time, and not just hope for it? For it to be real to me?"

Her voice sounded shaky to her own ears. She took a deep breath and let it out. At least hoping for God's love to feel real was a good place to be, better than where she'd been a few years back.

One of her favourite Bible verses was 1 John 4:18: "There is no fear in love. But perfect love drives out fear." She considered that verse now as her mind slowed down. She also remembered her conversation with Robyn on the drive up yesterday, and she chose to camp out on thoughts of God's love, ignoring her insecurities and confusion for the time being. Laying down, she took deep breaths and closed her eyes until emotional exhaustion pulled her into a glorious afternoon nap.

* * *

When April had backed out of her parking spot, Robyn had surreptitiously glanced at her dark reflection in the restaurant door. She knew it wouldn't do to linger. Devon was probably already watching for her, and she didn't want her nervousness to show.

Who's nervous anyway? There's no reason to be, so I'm not. With that, she pulled the door open and stepped inside to the welcoming aroma of coffee and donuts.

A brief scan caught sight of him rising from a table for two, and she felt herself go weak at the knees. She remembered that response—how it used to cause her to walk too quickly and talk too loudly in an effort to overcompensate—so she poured all of her focus into taking normal steps toward him. There was nothing to be done about the smile that made her eyes squint.

Like lights shining from across the room, there were those same mischievous blue eyes that had blazed their way into every daydream of her teenage years; the same sandy hair that she used to imagine running her fingers through. She remembered him shaking the water out of his locks after their swims in the lake, and how she would shriek and jump away.

His body was the only thing that had changed. It had filled out with muscles that were only beginning to thicken that final summer they were together. Now, well-developed biceps bulged against his t-shirt sleeves. Even the outlines of his pecs were visible under the dark gray material.

Devon opened his arms, his grin rivaling hers, and Robyn stepped into the hug. Her face pressed against the front of his shoulder, and she most definitely picked up on the racing heart that now beat against her own.

Sensations she hadn't felt in ages were coursing through her veins. Devon's hug was unrelenting, but a dash of self-consciousness caused her to slowly pull back and look around the restaurant at all the strangers who didn't even notice what was going on over there.

All the *strangers*. Oh good, someone she knew from Saskatoon hadn't randomly chosen to eat at this Edmonton Tim Hortons on this particular Saturday morning. Robyn shook her head at herself, then looked up at Devon from a few inches away.

"Hi," she said on a giggle that she hated herself for.

"Hi," he replied with an affectionate tone that implied he had enjoyed her giggle.

"I don't even know what to say," she finally admitted after staring into his eyes for a few silent beats. "It's been…"

"A few years," he finished for her. He stepped back, then hesitated, then stepped forward again. "Should we—"

"Let's get—" she said at the same time, then giggled again. *Good grief! What am I, fifteen?*

Devon pointed to the service counter and pulled out his wallet. He pointed to that, then to the table, then gave a thumbs-up with his eyebrows raised. That pulled a full-on laugh all the way up from Robyn's toes.

"Since talking is hard, I figured that was a better way to go," he said as they turned together and made their way forward.

"Definitely a good call," Robyn replied.

"Can we try the talking thing again?"

"Let's practice on the staff first."

"Good plan." Devon ordered his meal, then turned to Robyn. "And you'll have…?"

Robyn had her hand on her wallet, but she slid it back into her purse and placed her own order. After Devon paid for both meals, they waited over by the pickup counter.

"You did well there," Robyn told him.

"You too. Let's try it again with us."

Robyn laughed. "You know, you're almost as funny as I remember you being. Almost."

"You mean I've lost some of my teenage charm?"

"Just a little bit, but I suppose you've traded it out for some adult charm." The second the phrase was out, Robyn wanted to disappear.

Devon threw back his head and laughed at her embarrassment. "Wow, you really know how to plow ahead, don't you?"

The heat that flooded her face was scorching. "Maybe the talking thing still isn't working for me. I didn't mean it that way."

Devon laughed again, but with an underlying tone of kindness. "I know, I know." And the joke went flat as instantly as it had popped up. An awkward silence passed, then was mercifully broken by the arrival of their food and drinks. After thanking the woman who had placed it on the counter, they made their way back to the table and tucked into their lunch.

Robyn wondered if Devon would have said grace under other circumstances, or if he—like she—knew on some level that it would have been weird in this context. Not that there was anything weird about two old friends meeting up for lunch, but still.

"So, Birdie—how has your girls' trip been so far?" Devon asked, his leg fidgeting slightly under the table.

"Good," Robyn answered, blushing yet again. "We got in late last night, and this morning we did the childhood home tour for April. It was a huge deal for her. Things seemed to hit her even harder than expected."

"What part about it was hard, do you think?"

His gravelly voice did something deep inside of her that she tried to ignore. She took a sip of her iced tea, which gave her a moment to refocus.

"She's a really quiet type of person," she began. "Very underconfident but deep. I don't want to share any details from our private talks, but my take is that she's quite sensitive and has a lot of things to work through. I don't think she ever fully dealt with the pain of moving when she was a kid, and on top of that I suspect she's never fully dealt with anything that's ever bothered her. And...her boyfriend is kind of controlling."

At this Devon tilted his head in concern.

Robyn continued, "It's subtle, and I don't think she sees it yet, but the dynamic just seems off. Like, I don't think he's a bad guy, I just think he's taking advantage of her nature without even realizing it. And I think she lets him because she doesn't recognize it, so she doesn't know she can do anything about it." Feeling guilty for saying so much about her friend, Robyn dipped her sandwich into her soup and took a big bite.

"Have you told her what you see?"

Robyn shook her head and finished chewing. "You're the first person I've sounded off to about it. But as the words are coming out now, I'm wondering if I should say something to her." She looked up at Devon and met his gaze, which happened to be full of tender fire. She hid her responsive smile behind her sandwich. "Anyway, how's Carly?"

Devon ducked his head slightly and shrugged. "She's doing alright. Enjoying her new place and her job. She's already talking about getting out there and dating again, and I'm trying not to be the overprotective big brother who tells her she should wait a while longer."

"Do you think she'll be able to join us for the mall this afternoon?"

"I texted her, but she had to pick up a shift for a sick co-worker. She said to say hi, though."

A flit of discomfort crossed Robyn's mind. How would it look to April if it was just the three of them spending the afternoon together? *It would look like your friend Carly got a last-minute shift, and that it ended up just being you and her brother, and there is nothing wrong with that.*

"That's too bad." Besides balancing out the group, Robyn had looked forward to seeing the younger woman again. "And yeah, I hope she isn't jumping back in too soon. But maybe she'll be quicker to notice red flags the second time around."

"I hope so."

They discussed Carly's situation a bit more. Robyn watched Devon's features carefully, moved by the depth of struggle he was willing to re-count with her now that they were sitting across from each other. The topic eventually shifted to their careers, hobbies, and mutual acquaintances. Their meals were eaten, and second coffees ordered while tables around them filled and emptied and filled again. The conversation was interspersed with memories of their times at the lake, the lighthearted youthfulness of those days being conjured up in their laughter and lingering looks.

Then the question was asked that they both knew needed asking, yet neither of them had especially wanted it asked: "How is Patrick?"

Robyn shuffled around in her purse for some lip chap and smeared it on. Her hand trembled slightly. "Oh, you know, he rocks at being a dad. Enjoys his job at the garage. He really is great with Linus. He's texted me a few cute little stories already. Sounds like they're having a great guys' weekend."

"And how is married life?" This was asked after a quick glance down at his steaming coffee.

"It's great," she said against a sudden brick wall in her brain.

Devon chuckled. "I'm asking as a bachelor who likes the idea, but after getting dumped by my girlfriend of two years, I'm a little gun shy about the whole prospect. Dreaming of permanent attachment is tough when you've been burned."

"You never mentioned that before," Robyn said, automatically reaching across the table to put her hand over his. It sent a jolt of electricity up her arm, but his hand felt so different from Patrick's. She pulled away, ears burning.

"Her name was Madison. Well, is, I guess, it's not like she stopped existing." He gave a humourless laugh. "We met on a construction site when we were both apprenticing. We started dating pretty much right away, and it was going well for a while. But then she told me she was considering a move to B.C. to be closer to her family. I had no interest in moving, but I thought I could convince her to stay." He looked up at Robyn. "Short story is, I couldn't convince her to stay. She'd always been really close with her family, and it was too hard for her to be so far away. I guess I wasn't enough of a pull to keep her here."

"And…you didn't think she was enough of a pull to move

with her?"

Devon winced. "Touché." He wrapped his hands around his paper cup and sighed. "To be honest, by the time we were having those discussions, things had already cooled off between us a bit. I think we both knew the end was coming, but neither of us had addressed it. Sometimes I wonder if things cooled off because she had started detaching herself from me in preparation for the move. And I wonder if I had tried harder, maybe we would have found our spark again."

Robyn hurt at the thought of Devon experiencing the pain of rejection. He was such a kind, generous, fun-loving person. Really, how could Madison have let him go? Didn't she realize that she had given up what any girl in her right mind would have held onto with all her might, if given the chance?

Like you would have? And then not ended up with Patrick or Linus?

It wasn't the first time the thought had cropped up, but now it flew at her from a slightly different angle and struck deeper. She couldn't help but acknowledge it before swiping it away. This was neither here nor there, especially since things hadn't turned out that way.

But you wouldn't mind a small taste of what could have been, would you?

"Are you okay?" Devon asked. Robyn realized that she hadn't only imagined the jolt that passed through her body.

She smiled, his concern for her etched deeply in those warm blue eyes. Her heart melted. "Yes. Just got a chill from the air conditioning, I think."

"Would you like to take a walk, or—"

Robyn gasped. "What time is it?" She pulled out her phone and noted the lack of texts before seeing the time: two-twenty-five.

"Wow, time flies!" she remarked. "I'll just…are you okay if I text April? I didn't realize it was getting so late. I don't want her to worry that we forgot her or something."

The disappointment that flashed across Devon's face was replaced by an acquiescent smile. "Sure thing."

After reluctantly sending the text to ask if April was ready to pick them up, she set her phone on the table.

"I feel awful cutting in like that just as you were sharing something so painful," she said. "I really want to keep talking, but I just don't want to leave April hanging."

"I get it. I wish we could do this again before you leave, though. Is there any chance of coffee tomorrow morning?"

Robyn gave a sad smile. "I'd love to, but I can't imagine how it would look to…" she fluttered her hand in the air uncertainly.

With a nod, Devon rescued her. "I know."

Their eyes met and held for the hundredth time that day, but this time a shared understanding passed between them. Desire and alarm bells rang out with equal fervour.

Devon placed his palms down on the table and took a deep breath. "Robyn, I know we might not see each other again for some time."

She nodded, growing breathless. "Right."

"And I hope we can keep in touch like we have been. It's been…amazing...to have you as a friend again."

"I've enjoyed re-connecting with you too."

The phone buzzed. They both glanced down at it and mutually chose to ignore it, looking back into each other's eyes with undeniable attraction.

"After all this time of getting to know each other again, and after knowing how it feels to be in a relationship that didn't work out…I just want to say this so that you know it. I was an idiot for not asking you out when we were younger."

Robyn took in a sharp breath and held it as Devon quickly added, "I actually had a pretty heavy crush on you that last summer, but with college coming up and knowing that I'd be going away, meeting so many new people and all, I didn't think it made sense. But it's one of my biggest regrets that I didn't reach out for you when I had the chance.

"I wasn't surprised to hear that you'd gotten married, but

when my parents told me, I couldn't believe how jealous I felt. How hard the regret hit me." He exhaled heavily. "Patrick is the luckiest guy in the world. And I hope he knows that."

He reached across the table, taking her hand in both of his. They were calloused like Patrick's, and while there was a spark, there was no familiarity.

He held her gaze with a steady look that held both declaration and question.

As a teenager, Robyn would have given anything to hear those words and feel these hands over hers. As a young woman, the *what-ifs* had never been too far from her mind. And after the last several months of holding onto that tantalizing dream behind a shield of denial, hearing these words now reminded of her of the time she stood in a boat beside the roar of Niagara Falls. Everything else was drowned out as she basked in the glow of his profession.

Then came the still, silent voice that she knew so well.

He's not for you.

It was quieter than Niagara Falls but held an undeniable authority that left very little room for questioning.

Another buzz erupted from her phone.

Devon's words lingered between them, but ***he's not for you*** had shot an arrow through her resolve to ignore her convictions, no matter how natural it felt to follow her heart.

With an apologetic grimace, Robyn used her free hand to turn the phone over and read April's texts.

Just woke up from a surprise nap. I'll be there in 20.

The other text was from Patrick:

I put Linus down for his nap a few mins ago. I told him not to tell you that we had chocolate chip pancakes for lunch. We miss you, by the way. Love you.

"She'll be here in twenty minutes," Robyn said, looking up at Devon's conflicted face. She so desperately wanted to address what he'd said, but felt near-panic at the need to transition the tone between them so that April wouldn't sense anything unusual. She closed her eyes and took a deep breath, then blurted out, "So, what mall ride are you most excited about? The roller coaster or the Drop of Doom?"

Devon smirked and looked out the window, but kept his hands around hers. After a moment he feigned a cheerful tone. "Can I convince you to try either one of them with me?"

"Not a chance, mister." She gently pulled her hand back to her side of the table.

They both stood up and brought their trays to the garbage. Devon put his hands in his pockets. Robyn wanted to link her arm through his and enjoy what she knew would be their last time alone together. Ever. It would have to be. But at least they could continue calling or texting. After all, they were only friends. The distance would preserve that.

Devon turned to her and put his arms around her and held tight. She leaned into the embrace, moisture lining her bottom eyelashes. As before, her heart was racing directly across from his.

His hand moved up to cradle the back of her head, weakening her at the knees for the second time that day. All she had to do was lift her face slightly, just one time, knowing that this was good-bye. No one else would ever know, and it wouldn't have to mean anything other than a farewell gift to this precious man who had shown her his heart just a few minutes ago, the most long-awaited gift she had ever wished for—

He's not for you.

She turned her face down and stepped out of his arms.

"I'm so sorry," she whispered, tasting the promise of a peace that she'd been denying herself for months. "We can't do this."

His hands slid down to her arms. She felt the battle raging within him as he slowly released his grasp. Devon and Robyn inhaled and exhaled for a few minutes, an out-of-sync duet that held them together in a static moment.

"I'm sorry too," he finally murmured, shaking his head. "I don't know what I was thinking."

She forced herself to look at him, but took another step back.

"What you said back there is what I wanted to hear for so long. For *so* long. And I didn't let you go when I should have," she stated softly. "I led you on. I apologize for that. But we've already crossed a line. We can't cross any more. We can't be friends anymore."

"Robyn, that was my fault," Devon said with a frantic edge to his voice. "I'm so sorry. I won't ever try to kiss you again. I don't want to lose you as a friend, so I'll keep my distance, but I don't want to stop being in touch. You have no idea how much you matter to me."

Robyn tilted her head and bit her lip. "I don't think we can do that, Devon. Being here with you…I want you too much. But I want my marriage more." A new resolve inflated her lungs while she closed her eyes. "I want Patrick more. This has to be the end of everything for us."

Devon looked at his feet. "I don't want to lose you," he said again.

"You won't be better off holding on to me," Robyn replied. "It's not fair to yourself. You'll be stuck." She waited a beat and said, just above a whisper, "I'm going to delete your number from my phone. This has to be completely over. For both of our sakes."

And for Patrick's. Remorse charged in with all the weight of the world behind it.

Devon looked like he'd been physically struck.

Robyn glanced behind her shoulder to scan the vehicles in the parking lot. No April yet.

The silence was difficult to bear, but what more could words do?

She forced herself to turn around and walk out the door, looking back to note that he was watching her from where she had left him. His hands were in his pockets, his countenance shrouded in dejection. Catching her eye for a second, he nodded his head once in some kind of acknowledgment, and then looked at the floor.

Robyn nodded at his downturned head, said a “good-bye” that he probably couldn’t hear, and stepped out into the sunlight, shattered.

- Chapter Nineteen -

April held Seth's hand, the soft pads of his fingers slick with sweat as they navigated a broken piece of sidewalk. It was one of the hottest days of summer, so April had planned to stay inside with Seth and bask in the air-conditioned living room—but for the first time in their entire relationship, he initiated going out. It was an unusual start to a Monday after an unusual weekend. Regardless of the heat, there was no way April was going to stifle his sudden initiative.

When she had arrived at his house that morning, Vanessa had asked her how her weekend was.

"It was…" April didn't know how to sum it up. She never knew how to succinctly answer questions like this. Saying "fine" or "good" wasn't natural, yet she had come to realize that most of the time, most people were content with that simple reply. But first she had to categorize the person, the context, and her own mood to decipher just how much to say. Settling on a happy medium for this moment, she said, "I had fun with my friend, and I got emotional about my old house. It felt like a lot to process, but it was overall good." *Ramble alert, full-stop now.*

Vanessa had come to be a comfortable touch-base person

framing each of her days with Seth. Over the course of the past few weeks, April had happily recognized the shedding of her stutter with her.

"Things from childhood have that effect on a person," Vanessa replied, settling her sunglasses onto her head and grabbing her keys from a bowl on the entryway table. "Just wait until you have kids and watch them grow up. Then things from *their* childhoods hit you in a way you can't really explain."

They had said their good-byes and April had turned the corner into the living room, where Seth stood up abruptly and made a happy sound at the sight of her. Then he had gone to the bathroom, come back out, and walked straight toward the door without hesitation.

"Happy Monday to you too, Seth!" April laughed, following his lead. "I guess we're going for a walk today."

Making their way to her car, she racked her brain for the most sheltered walking path she knew of. The best one that came to mind was Victoria Park in Riversdale. They hadn't been back since the falling incident, but maybe she had to borrow some of Seth's determination and try it again. Time to build a good memory there on top of the bad one.

As they walked along, the heat slowly gaining on them, April reflected on how refreshing it was to have this lighthearted time with Seth. The weekend had been heavy, with not much fun to offset the weight. Robyn hadn't been her usual self ever since her visit with her old friends at Tim Hortons, so April had spent a good portion of Saturday and Sunday wondering if she should pry or just leave it alone. There must have been a serious falling-out, or maybe some bad news was revealed during that lunch date. Devon and Carly hadn't joined them at West Edmonton Mall, and Robyn had given no explanation other than to say that they were busy.

After picking Robyn up from the coffee shop, April had planned to share some of her thoughts from her journaling time at the motel. Robyn was such a great listener, and her insights often gave April the words she needed to hear. Yet Robyn seemed to be barely holding herself together, so they both tried for the fun, lighthearted shopping experience they'd had planned. Going on a few rides in Galaxyland helped a bit, but not by much. Robyn had closed into herself by the time they got back to the motel, and when April asked (not for the first time) if she was okay, Robyn had said, "I will be. I just have some things to talk to Patrick about before I talk to anyone else." They had watched a movie in silence before turning in that night.

April's mind went a little haywire trying to think about what it could be, but with no leads, and out of respect for her friend's reticence, she tried her best to shove her inner brainstorming sessions down. It was difficult, with a long and silent drive home the next day, to not fall into the realm of overthinking. Loud music accompanied them for the 5-hour trip. The drop-off at Robyn's home had been a little intense, with Robyn holding back tears when she stepped out of the car and into Patrick's welcome-home hug. They'd stayed like that for a long time, so April had gotten out to pull Robyn's luggage from the trunk.

"Thanks for driving," Robyn had called in a quavering voice, and Patrick wished her a good night.

April shook off her curiosity about Robyn as she and Seth meandered past the pool. She could hear the mix of lifeguards' voices leading different swimming lessons while the scent of chlorinated water filled the air.

For herself, upon arriving home she had texted Theo that she was back. He'd replied that he would be back quite late, so he would see her the next day.

Tonight, they were going to hang out. April's feelings vacillated. She couldn't wait to drink in the sight of him and snuggle up to him, but she didn't know if she would feel safe discussing the reality of what her house visit did to her. Sometimes getting real about herself went well, and other times he took over and figured herself out for her. Or thought he did, anyway. Often, her own explanations offended him. She didn't know how to say things in a way that wouldn't hurt his feelings. She still hadn't decided if and how to combat that tendency of his, or if it was something she could learn to live with. Making him uncomfortable wasn't a very loving thing to do, especially since he was just trying to show how much he cared.

April's attention landed on the spot, just up ahead now, where Seth had tripped and fallen before. Pretending she didn't feel nervous, she tried to gauge Seth's body language. His pace hadn't slowed, his grip on her hand hadn't changed, and he still emanated happiness. Once they were a few feet away, April wondered if she should remind him to lift his feet higher over the upcoming bump, but something made her hold it back. Seth's toe caught momentarily, but April stepped in front of him and he grabbed onto both of her arms, steadying himself without too much effort, and then he kept moving forward without a moment's hesitation. April was still holding both of his arms, walking backward and smiling at his determination to keep moving. Where was this energy coming from?

"I guess we're dancing now," she joked. She kept up the ruse for a few more feet, quietly singing a song they had heard on the drive over, then she let go of one hand and walked beside him again.

They were almost to the car. But Seth kept moving, ignoring April's reminders that they were beside the parking lot.

Are we doing another loop?

If it hadn't been such a sweltering day, she would have been happier. Yet it was hard to deny the excitement of Seth taking charge.

"This is a good idea, Seth," she told him. "Probably just one more loop, though, so we can grab our water bottles from the car.

"You must have a lot of energy to burn, hey? Sometimes I feel like that too. Not just from my body, but from my mind. Our minds need the exercise just like our bodies do."

Seth was still moving at a good clip, and she could see that he was breathing harder than he did on the first loop. She had never seen him like this—looking like any other young man pushing himself through a workout.

"We can slow down if you need to, Seth."

He kept up the pace. April saw a proud gleam in his eyes that wasn't usually there.

It was what he wanted to do, and he was doing it because the hot air was like a heavy blanket against his body, face, and even inside of him, which made all other loudness and brightness become less so, and April—who he always missed on Saturdays and Sundays—was here, and she was not stopping him from being in charge of their walk. She was beside him and holding his hand. They were friends, and she didn't tell him what to do, like most other people did, and so he was sure that it would work for him to make his own decision, so that's what he did, and April didn't stop him, and Seth was so pleased with how he could make his own choice. Even though Dad and Mom sometimes let him make choices, they weren't the same as friends, so with April it was different. They were side-by-side and he knew he was safe to show her what he wanted to do.

It was getting slippery between their hands and his throat was getting dry and he was thirsty, but this pressed-in hot feeling from the air was too good to ignore. April was singing that song again, and he didn't always like that because it didn't sound as good as the radio, but it was okay enough not to complain.

Now he heard April tell him to look at the birds in the tree, so he looked up to where she was pointing. He didn't see the birds, but he could hear them, and then someone was walking past them, and the person's voice got louder and then quieter once he was all the way past, but something had flashed just as he was near them. Seth turned around to look back because now the man was past them, and he thought he saw something. The man had his hand to his ear, and there was a shiny spot coming off of a small line of black between his hand and his ear, but when Seth thought about following him, April told him that the birds were flying toward a different tree now, but he didn't care about the birds anymore. The man pulled his cell phone away from his ear and there was a glint off of the screen as the man touched the screen, and the force that moved up inside of Seth made him forget all about the hot pressure of the air and April's okay singing, and Seth started to walk after the man because he had to go see that screen. He was tired and suddenly a little angry and he needed to touch that screen and see the lines on the screen and make them move and move and move and move…

"Sir, can I ask you to put your phone in your pocket?" April called after the man. She was trying to calmly pull Seth's hand toward her, but his momentum was gaining strength by the second; she knew there was likely going to be an interaction.

The man glanced back. April registered the surprise and impatience in his eyes as he said, "What? No, I have to make another call."

Seth's hand was about to slip out of her grip. Of all the days to forget her book! She had forgotten to return it to her purse after the weekend.

She implored Seth firmly, enthusiastically, and she even tried for silly, but she'd seen that tunnel-vision look take over his eyes. He was in compulsive mode now.

The man was talking on his phone again, walking with the same leisurely pace as before, but glancing behind himself a few times.

Seth's sweaty hand suddenly slipped free, and as he loped toward the stranger, April ran past him and accessed her fake-calm and called out, "Sir, he will try to grab your phone, please hide it and walk away quickly. He can't run very fast."

Arriving in front of Seth on the path, she put up her hands

and bounced from side-to-side in the ready position, shadowing his movements to try and keep him from getting past. He started to press into her, so she steadied her feet and used her body to press back, her hands open and nesting against his flailing arms. From a few feet behind her, she heard the man say loudly into his phone, "Sorry, gotta run. Some retard wants to grab my phone and his mom can barely control him." April didn't bother looking back, but the direction of the man's voice changed as he said, "You need to teach him how to respect other people and their property."

The man's footsteps faded. Although Seth's pushing had moved April back a few steps, he soon stopped trying. His pressure went limp, so April relaxed her own body and moved her hands away from his arms.

She looked into Seth's face, her heart pounding like it always did after a moment like that, but she managed to force a smile. "I guess I'm your mom now."

Seth was deflated. Whether from the loss of opportunity to scratch the screen itch, from shame, or from hurt feelings over the man's words, she didn't know. Maybe it was from all three.

"That guy was worried, but he shouldn't have said those words," April told Seth. She took his hand and led him back to facing their original direction, then started walking slowly. He fell into step beside her.

What she wouldn't *give* for her water bottle. The sweat between their hands was way more slippery now, but they eventually completed the loop and got back into the car, where April turned it on and blasted the cold air, then handed Seth his water bottle while she guzzled hers.

Okay, so it wasn't a perfect outing, she prayed. *But Seth took charge of both loops, and he didn't fall. How do I get him to focus on those things, instead of focusing on his weak moment and that man's rude words?*

Somehow, even before Seth's parents had explained to her that discipline didn't work for addressing Seth's screen obsession, April had instinctively known that it wouldn't. He might not ever stop having this struggle with screens his whole life, but if he wasn't fully accepted at that level, shame could trap him against that weakness even harder. The cycle of shame to struggle and back to shame was far too easy to enter, and incredibly hard to get out of. April wanted to be a force in Seth's life that pointed away from it.

* * *

It was the third time Linus pulled open the plastic container drawer and pulled everything out one-by-one, while Robyn tried not to reach out every time it looked like he might lose his balance. As much as she didn't want him to bang his face on the drawer or floor, she told herself it wouldn't be the worst thing. It was all a part of learning his own physical boundaries in the world.

Playing with Linus was a welcome distraction. There was nothing she could do right now; she knew that very clearly, even as her mind raced in a million directions. She was somehow above all that, aware of it but not being pulled along with any of it. Robyn was grateful, but she knew she didn't deserve this gift of peace. Still, for the sake of following God's lead in this, she had to accept it and press in. No point burying herself in an ocean of guilt when it would take her eyes off of God whose help she needed more than ever.

She had wanted to talk to Patrick last night. Everything in her was begging to spill out, but Linus was frantic to be with her every possible second, and it had taken until almost midnight for him to fall asleep. The raging thunderstorm outside probably didn't help, but Robyn sensed it was more than that. Patrick tried to take over a few times, yet Linus made it abundantly clear that only Mommy was good enough for now.

Robyn felt terrible at the confusion and concern that Patrick wore as he watched his wife cry off-and-on during the entire evening of their reunion. He asked several questions. Did she and

April have a fight? Was there a problem with the old friends that she'd met up with? Was she in pain? Was she pregnant? She shook her head to every query and kept insisting she wanted to tell him sometime when Linus was asleep.

By the time Linus finally crashed and burned, Robyn slipped into bed beside her now-snoring husband. Deciding that he deserved a normal night of sleep before she broke his heart, she endured a restless few hours interspersed with lots of prayer and planning. How on earth to broach the subject when the time came?

What made her feel even worse was the recognition that her anguish wasn't just for her betrayal and her husband's imminent pain; it was for Devon. Half of her tears were for him, for the loss of him and for the pain she'd caused him when she walked away and cut him off completely. How cold could she be? But how could she not be, given the circumstances?

This morning, Robyn was surprised to find that she had apparently dozed off at some point. She only woke up when Patrick pressed a tender kiss to her cheek.

"I'm off to work," he whispered. "Linus is still sleeping. I guess you both partied too hard last night."

A forced smile lifted her lips. "I guess so."

"I love you, Robyn. Let's talk tonight. Even if it's midnight."

She simply nodded and said, "I love you too." He looked into her eyes for an extra beat or two, then said good-bye and walked out of the room. She heard him open and close the front door, locking it behind himself, and a few seconds later his car started up and backed out of the driveway.

The sound of his engine trailing off down the road gave her relief. In some ways, things would be better once the first conversation was over with. At least, it would start the horrible journey toward getting better. Yet part of her wished she could stretch out the day indefinitely.

Robyn usually prayed from whatever position she was in, whether it was sitting or standing or lying down. But this morning called for her to hit the floor on her knees beside the bed, and she talked to God fervently until Linus called out for her fifteen minutes later.

The day moved along at an alarmingly normal rate. As on any given Monday, it came to pass that Patrick returned from work at suppertime and they ate together as a family. It was an awkward meal, with Robyn laughing too hard at Patrick's little jokes and Patrick's face registering that her over-the-top efforts had been recognized as such, but the unspoken agreement was settled between them. They would keep at this until they were alone together.

Finally, and to Robyn's dismay, Linus was getting sleepy. She tucked him in at his normal bedtime in his normal way, then ducked into the bathroom and splashed cold water on her face. Her mouth felt like cotton; swishing it with water didn't help, and swallowing the water made her stomach clench even tighter.

Her husband's waiting presence seemed to scream at her from the living room, even though he was just sitting there quietly. Robyn didn't know how she could do this, but she managed to turn the doorknob, walk out of the bathroom, and sit down on the easy chair across from Patrick.

It was time to make the confession that would create a before-and-after moment to mark the rest of their marriage. It was too much power for one person to bear. How had she let it get to this point? The allowances, the indecisions, the giving-in, had all built up into something that was going to shatter the heart of the one she had promised to protect.

Patrick leaned forward, his countenance bearing the severity of her tone with a readiness to support her in any way he could. The love in his eyes was deep, his attention sharp. His hands were on his knees like he was prepared to spring up and take action.

Robyn looked into his open face and held steady.

This was her husband—the man who had never stopped reaching for her and believing the best about her. He was ready for her to tell him about a mental health struggle or a secret medical issue, a friendship fallout, or a major life decision that required his help. He wasn't prepared for what she was about to say. In this moment, she loved him as she had never loved him before, and she wanted desperately to shield him from the truth. How could she ever push the words out?

God, help me.

She licked her dry lips. Her mind flooded with infinite possibilities of how to begin, and nothing came out. Closing her mouth, she leaned forward across the small space, took Patrick's hand in hers, and tried again.

"I love you," she heard herself say, and then part of her listened in shock while the rest of the words tumbled out. "And after I say what I have to say, I hope you remember that, because it's the reason I'm telling you about this now."

Patrick's gaze intensified, his call to action being eclipsed by fear. Robyn squeezed his hand. He squeezed back without releasing.

"You know Devon, the old friend I've told you about? That I used to have at the lake growing up?"

She waited until Patrick gave a short nod.

"He and I started texting each other back in the spring," Robyn continued as her mouth ran even drier. "At first we were just getting re-acquainted, and he was telling me about the hard times Carly was going through—his sister—and it just started to snowball a bit."

Patrick's squeeze took on the tiniest hint of a tremor. Robyn forced herself to keep looking in his eyes. She needed to be his reassurance; she deserved the penance of observing his pain.

"I didn't want to admit it to myself, but we began to flirt over text. And talk about some deeper, more personal things. It got to the point where I felt guilty about it, and I was hiding it from you because I knew it was going too far, even though I didn't want to believe it was."

Patrick pulled his hand away and rubbed his jaw. Shock had replaced the look of readiness in his eyes. He had been prepared to take action, not to absorb a blow of this magnitude.

"And on the weekend, while April was busy, he and I met up for lunch."

"You went on a date," Patrick muttered in disbelief, blinking rapidly as he looked away.

"Well, we didn't call it that, but…anyway, that was the end of it," Robyn said quickly, reaching for his hand again. After a beat, Patrick seemed to realize she was holding it and he shook her off.

"What do you mean, that was the end of it?" Patrick asked, standing up and pacing. His voice began to rise. "Did you officially call off your relationship? Did he come to his senses and remember that you're a married woman? Did *you*?"

"It wasn't an actual relationship, Patrick. It wasn't anything, really."

"But it was enough of something that you went out of your way to hide it from me, to drive five hours for a date, to feel guilty about the whole thing? That doesn't sound like nothing. Don't give me that it wasn't anything. It was *something*."

"Okay, yes, it was something, but I mean…it never became an *official* something. I never went so far as to consider leaving you for him, or…or…*sleeping* with him, or even…"

Patrick stopped pacing and stared hard at her. "Did you kiss him?"

"No!" Robyn felt a tear drip off her chin. She hadn't realized she was crying. "No, we didn't kiss, we didn't…we didn't…all we did was hug twice, and in the spirit of honesty, yes, the hugs lingered longer than they should have, and there was one tiny moment where I thought we might kiss, but I pulled away from him because that's when I first fully recognized what I was doing to you behind your back. What I was doing to God and myself, but most of all to you."

Patrick waved an arm. "I don't want to hear about this. I don't want to picture it. I don't want to know any more. Not right now." He looked at his wife, his pain so striking that Robyn knew she would never recover from the image of it. "Robyn, you're my wife." The last word ended on a hoarse whisper. Twin tracks rolled down his cheeks as he bent toward her, shoulders slumped with a weight he didn't deserve to bear. "You let yourself fall for another man. You went behind my back. You didn't kiss him or sleep with him, I know, but in your *heart* you betrayed me."

A whimper escaped from Robyn's throat. "I know I did, Patrick, but I can promise you it's over, and I promise I'm choosing you, and I promise it won't happen again. I've deleted his number, I told him we couldn't talk ever again-"

"I need some space." Patrick started toward the door.

"I understand," Robyn whispered to his back. For the first time, she was coldly aware of the possibility that this could end their marriage. That Patrick could choose to leave her, and that she'd have no right to try forcing him to stay.

Let him go. Trust him to me.

He needs to see me fighting for him, God, she prayed frantically. *I'm losing control here. He needs to see me trying. I need to say something, go hug him, anything! I can't just sit here and let him leave!*

Let him go. Trust him to me.

Robyn planted herself where she was and bit her tongue, her mind railing against the quiet order. She wanted to make everything better, starting right now.

Patrick yanked the door open. He hesitated for a moment and turned back to Robyn. "I don't know what to say," he said. "I just don't know what to do right now." And then he was gone into the night.

I will never leave you nor forsake you.

Robyn was in the fetal position, vacillating between blinding numbness and intense pain.

God, how can you say that? How can that be true? Look at what I did to Patrick. I don't even know where he is right now. I don't even know if he's safe. Look at what I did to our marriage. He's the best husband there is, and look what I did to him.

When you pass through the waters I will be with you.

Robyn shook her head. *I made this mess, God. It's my fault I'm going through these waters. Why should you have to be with me through it? It's my sin that caused it.*

Nothing can separate you from my love. I am with you and I am for you. You have not fallen out of my hand.

Robyn continued to shake her head, God's grace stinging like lotion on raw skin. She deserved to hurt. She had earned the pain from her own unfaithfulness, and she would rub her mind over the memory of Patrick's stricken face every day for the rest of her life so she could never forget what she'd done. Yet God's love was pressing down on her with an insistence she needed and resisted, both adding to her inner storm yet promising hope and peace if she would surrender to the truth that his view of her hadn't changed. She was not separated from him or from his love.

Allowing herself to believe that felt like yet another betrayal against her husband.

God, Patrick deserves for me to suffer. How can I face him if I don't pay the full price for what I did to him?

God's response was instant. ***Because I already paid the full price.***

She squeezed the pillow harder. *I know that technically you did, I know that, but I need to do something too. I can't just act like I'm not deserving of punishment. We all know that I am. I have to pay some kind of price.*

Through blurry eyes, Robyn looked at her digital clock. It was past midnight. Where was her husband? Was he being rushed to the hospital after an adrenaline-fueled car accident? Had he taken off down some dark highway to escape the city without a plan? Was he at a bar somewhere, drinking his way through the mess she'd put on him? That wouldn't be like him, but then again, he'd never been hurt like this before. He wouldn't drive drunk, would he?

Or, she thought with a shudder, *is he getting back at me by going to a strip club, or charming someone with a low-cut dress somewhere who'd be only too eager to see how far she could get with an attractive guy on the most vulnerable night of his life?*

I guess I am *paying a price,* she realized. It was inevitable. The worries, the heartache, the hard work of sorting through what fueled her choices while also working toward the healing of their marriage—those were all realities that she would now be living with. It might never seem like enough—yet the truth was, she was already forgiven by God. She didn't owe him anything in payment for her wrongdoings.

And, oh, was that good, because she would need the air clear between them so she could lean on him for guidance as she sought to love Patrick and repair their marriage. She knew she couldn't do it on her own.

Lord, keep him safe, she implored. *I'll do whatever it takes to fix this, but you'll have to tell me because I want to smother him with love and make it all better, but I have no control over what he needs to go through now. Please guide me and help me and heal our marriage. Please.*

- Chapter Twenty -

Low rumbles of thunder accompanied the view of April's car pulling up to his house. Theo was watching, ready to get the door. Rob was in one of his snits this evening, and despite the progress they had made in tolerating/sometimes enjoying each other in small doses, Theo knew that their tenuous roommate friendship wouldn't spare April a snarky comment or two. He didn't know if he had the energy to deal with the oversensitive fallout tonight. His two nights in the tent had proved restless, and all he wanted to do right now was to have April in his arms and relax with a movie.

He thought again about what his dad had said last weekend while casting into the lake. Over the faint whirring of the line, he had asked Theo, out of the blue, what he thought about his future with April.

Theo had looked over from where he was putting a new lure onto his hook. It was Saturday morning. They had been out on the water for three hours already, and Theo had only caught one trout. While Theo had been considering which new tackle to try, his dad had apparently been considering how to broach a big subject, his question heavily weighted with his own unspoken thoughts on the matter.

"I don't know," Theo mumbled, busying himself with the task at hand. He reprimanded himself for sounding like a sullen teenager, then sat up straight and looked out over the water. "I mean, I don't know when to start planning to get engaged. But I know she's the one for me."

He waited for the follow-up questions that hung invisibly in the air between them.

They never came. In the distance, the roar of another motorboat mingled with a dog's excited barking, their echoes skipping across the water like a flat rock.

Theo loved being out here on the lake—had grown up fishing here with his dad ever since he was a young boy—but the awkwardness between them was almost as bad as the time his dad tried to have "the talk" with him in seventh grade. Why did serious things have to come out when they were trapped in the boat together?

Theo cast his line, taking great interest in the sharp *plop* of his tackle while his dad reeled in an empty hook and prepared for another cast.

While it whirred through the air, another question came out. "Have the two of you discussed your plans for after she's done school next year?"

Stifling a sigh, Theo replied, "Yes, of course we have. She wants to look for work in Saskatoon while I finish my degree. She'll try to find a job in her field, but if she can't find one, she's willing to take anything so we can stay together."

"Is that what *she* wants?"

Theo glanced at his dad, who was looking intently at his slack line while he slowly reeled it in. Why didn't the old man ever buy a new hat? That wide-brim number was new about twenty years ago.

"Yes, Dad, she's the one who brought it up." He didn't like the edge in his own voice, but he couldn't help it. Feigning nonchalance had never been his strong suit, especially when he was being challenged.

Another few minutes of silence passed. When his dad prepared for another cast, Theo inwardly flinched. Sure enough, as the line whizzed out, another question sliced through the air.

"How do the two of you handle disagreements?"

"Geez, what is this, Dad, a test I didn't sign up for? We talk them through and work it out, just like all couples do."

"Okay, then, son, let me ask you this." He turned his full attention toward Theo and asked, looking him straight in the eye, "What does God have to say about your relationship with April?"

Theo returned the stare. "I think God is pleased that we chose each other. We both love him, we both want to help each other grow in our faith, we study the Bible together…I mean, do you and Mom have a problem with April? Where is this coming from?"

His dad shook his head. "No, Theo, we think April is wonderful. We don't have a problem with her at all. Your mom and I think she is a fantastic person. We just wonder…do you realize that you've become angrier and angrier the longer you've been with her?"

Theo bit his lip and cast his line so forcefully he wondered if his rod was going to go flying away with it. He didn't say anything for a long time. Let his dad stew in the uncomfortable silence of what he'd just suggested. Served him right.

"I'm just trying to help you see what we see. Whoa, hold on a sec," his dad suddenly interjected on his own thoughts, pulling back while his rod curved into a taut *C*. "This is a big one!"

It was hard to ignore the flip of excitement upon seeing the fight this fish was giving. Theo set his own line down and grabbed the net, eyes trained on the disturbance in the water. There was a quick silvery splash at the surface before it submerged again.

"Whoa! We got a scrapper!" His dad gave just a little slack, then pulled hard again, the boat tipping ever-so-slightly. Theo leaned back and watched as the entire side of the fish broke through, revealing part of the length that they were dealing with.

"Looks like the baby of one of the ones I caught last year," Theo teased.

"Yeah, he sure outgrew his mother!" His dad laughed. "Nearly doubled her in size. Okay, ready with the net."

The trout was now within arm's reach of the boat. Theo scooped the net into the water while his dad pulled up on the line, and in a few fluid motions the fish was deposited on the floor of the boat, flopping around with admirable ferocity.

Theo grabbed the scale while his dad worked his fingers into the mouth, removing the hook as quickly as the flailing fish would allow. As soon as the fish was dangling from the scale, Theo snapped the requisite photo. His dad's proud smile beamed beside the silvery-gray scales that flashed in the sunlight—one moment captured amongst years' worth of moments like this—and then, without preamble, his dad released the fish from the scale and set it gently back in the water. Theo said nothing while he watched the creature stir groggily in his dad's immersed hands before it thrashed its tailfin toward the boat and dived away.

Theo grabbed two Cokes from the cooler and tossed one to his dad.

"Not bad," he admitted. "That would've looked nice mounted on the wall above the fireplace."

"You know how much your mom would love that," his dad laughed, taking a big drink.

Theo pictured his family home, the fireplace with a photo-studded mantelpiece—much like the one in April's home in Baylor. He had already envisioned a future where their wedding photos were on display in a similar fashion in their own dream house. Yet he had to admit the conflicting feelings that arose with that image lately. Would admitting that to his dad make it more real?

They enjoyed a companionable silence, the earlier tension broken.

"Dad…" Theo finished his drink and set the can on the floor where the thrashing fish had left a sizeable murky puddle. "You and Mom don't always understand each other, right?"

"That's a good question." His dad was already re-baiting his hook. "We certainly don't always get each other, no, but we take time to figure it out. Or do our best to, at least. There are some things we disagree on, but we respect each other's positions."

Nodding, Theo looked into the water. "That's the way it is with me and April," he said with resolution. "We don't always get each other. But I love her, and I'll never stop trying to figure her out."

His dad's line flew out. "What don't you get about her, exactly?"

Trying to organize his thoughts, Theo selected yet a new lure and began to work the old one off.

"She's really shy, of course," he began. "Really underconfident in some ways. I don't see why she still struggles with that. She grew up in a good family and she has friends. She has goals, she works hard, she makes a difference in the world. I mean, just look at the way she talks about her days with Seth. She's pretty, and smart, and she can be really funny when she's not on edge…and I just don't understand how she can hold herself back so much. It doesn't make sense to me. And…and she gets really upset about little things. She's oversensitive, and sometimes that gets directed at me. I usually don't even know what I've done to bother her, but suddenly I'm getting pushed outside of her walls again, after working so hard to get inside of them. I can't understand how not to upset her, but I also think she needs to get thicker skin, you know? I'm always on her side, but she doesn't seem to trust that, and then suddenly I'm the bad guy and I don't know why. She makes my head spin."

Theo cast his line and waited, allowing his dad time to ponder. One thing he knew from years of doing these weekends with his dad—nothing, especially conversation, ever had to be rushed. The essence of time seemed almost nonexistent on a fishing boat.

"Does she talk about her insecurities?"

"Yes, sometimes."

"Do you listen well?"

"I think so, yes."

"Would she be comfortable telling you if she didn't think you were listening well?"

"Of course she would." He paused, catching himself. "Well, at least she *should*. I think she would."

His dad nodded his head at that but said nothing more. Theo wondered if he had passed the test, or if he was supposed to be considering the questions further. Option *A* was more palatable.

There was a sharp tug on his line. He had gratefully let his thoughts disappear as he focused on his second catch of the day.

Now, watching as April walked from her car to the front door, the questions tried to surface again. Just like that huge fish. But instead of pulling them into the boat, he willed them to let go of the hook and disappear back under the water.

She caught sight of him in the window and flashed a smile, waving happily. It warmed his heart and made him ache to hold her. It looked like it was going to be a good night.

"Oh, another evening in paradise," Rob sighed from the couch. "Excuse me while I go nurse my lonely heart in privacy." He stood up and left the room while Theo opened the front door, pulling April into a hug before she even had a chance to say hi.

"You look beautiful," he said into the top of her head. Her giggle reverberated against his chest.

"So do you," she replied. "Fishing with your dad seems to agree with you."

"None of my catches were as good as you."

April pushed away and rolled her eyes. "Lame," she said on a laugh. "But for real, how was the trip?"

Making their way into the living room, Theo filled her in on the logistics of their trip—the number of fish caught, the weather, the food. They sat on the couch and held hands, chatting and laughing for an indeterminate amount of time. Occasional flashes of lightning added a dramatic flair to the otherwise relaxed atmosphere. After yet another oppressively hot day, it was no surprise nature was getting this tension out of its system.

Rob stepped out of his room, shielding his eyes. "Are you decent out here? I need to get some supper."

April blushed and Theo laughed. "All good, Rob. Are you decent?"

He walked through, shirtless and rubbing his eyes. "As decent as I care to be in my own home. April, how's it hanging?"

Theo felt her hand tighten ever so slightly. "G-good, how are you?"

"G-good too." He carried on past them into the kitchen.

Theo looked at April and raised his eyebrows, but she shook her head quickly. *It's okay,* she mouthed.

"Speaking of supper, have you eaten yet?" Theo asked. He was already rising. "I can whip something up. I think I have soup."

"Soup sounds good," she replied, following him into the kitchen. She tried to avert her gaze from the shirtless Rob standing in front of the open fridge.

"You haven't said much about your girls' weekend," Theo said while he rummaged through the cluttered pantry.

"Girls' weekend? Nice!" Rob said, kicking the fridge door closed. He grabbed a fork off the counter and dug into a box of Chinese takeout. "See any good male strippers?"

"She's practically looking at one now," Theo said drily. A few pots clanged while he pulled one out of the bottom drawer, wishing he'd waited until Rob was back in his own room.

Rob laughed. "Jealous, Theo? Your girlfriend can't keep her eyes off of me."

Theo shook his head and glanced over at April, who stood in the kitchen doorway with a red face, staring hard at the floor. He thought of his sisters, whom he'd seen dish it back easily against guys like Rob. He thought of other girls who could crack a joke to diffuse the situation. Heck, he knew some girls might even slap the guy. But April did none of that, and he knew it was all going underground to come back on him later. The familiar tension began to build between his shoulder blades. Maybe he should say something to Rob, regardless of how much April begged him not to intervene.

This was not going to keep on being the fun, easygoing night he had longed for.

"You know what, April? Let's eat out." Theo turned on his heel, abandoning the pot and the unopened tin of soup, and walked briskly out of the kitchen. April fell into step beside him and grabbed her purse from the coffee table on their way out.

* * *

It was all going so well, April thought as she raced to match her steps with Theo's. *I know he's mad at Rob, but now he'll be mad at me too for some reason.*

They slipped wordlessly into Theo's car while April tried to think of a way to keep him from remaining upset. She reached over and placed her hand on his thigh, giving a sultry squeeze. Theo glanced at her with a hint of surprise.

"You have nice quads," she offered shyly.

"And you have a nice hand." He placed his hand on hers while he drove. "Grrr, I'm sorry about that guy. Sometimes he's okay, but it just seems like he has this big thing against you. Or against girls in general. That Cosette of yours must have broken his heart pretty bad."

"That's okay," April said. "But just so you know, I wasn't staring at him. I was trying not to."

"I know." Theo was driving toward Eighth Street, where restaurants abounded. "How about Moxies?"

"Sounds great," April answered.

"I'm not jealous. I know you weren't staring at him," Theo continued. "It's just…it gets under my skin that he makes these digs at you, and it bugs me that…"

April waited for him to continue, but the silence stretched on.

Moxies came into view and she realized that her stomach was growling. Theo parked as close as he could and they ran inside, unable to avoid getting a little damp. Once they were settled in their booth, April once again marvelling at the luxury of ease with which Theo's financial status allowed them to eat out without considering a budget, they both seemed more relaxed. Theo smiled across the table from her and released a heavy sigh, then asked her again about her weekend.

He listened while April described the emotional experience of visiting her old home, the surprisingly meaningful conversation with the new homeowner, and the tension that had completely changed Robyn after her lunch date. The server interspersed their conversation a few times. Theo ordered an appetizer and entrées for the both of them. It wasn't until their server walked away that April realized she still hadn't told Theo that she didn't like salmon.

"Why do you always order for me?" she asked, interrupting her own story about the awkward ride home from Edmonton. She felt her face burn up, regretting the spewed question.

Theo raised his eyebrows in surprise. "I thought you liked that. You've never complained about me doing it before."

"No. I don't, like, hate it or anything, and I'm sure you're just trying to be nice, but I keep forgetting to…I keep not telling you, but I actually don't like fish."

"Well, let me catch our server and I'll let her know you want something else. Sorry, April, I—"

"No, don't bother her. It's a busy night. I don't mind it tonight, but just…going forward, I'd like to order my own food, if that…if that's okay with you?"

Theo laughed humourlessly. "If that's okay with me? Am I that much of a control freak for just trying to take care of you?"

His attempt at flippancy fell flat, but April tried to go along with it.

"Yeah, you know, just trying to be so considerate and ordering me the most expensive meal on the menu and, you know, trying to take a decision off of my mind," she said in a lightheartedly sarcastic voice. "You know, *so* controlling and *so* considerate." Her cold hands repeatedly crumpled her napkin under the table.

His eyes pierced hers from across the table. "That's exactly what I was going for. Considerate. I'm glad you told me you don't like when I do that. Now I know, after half a year of dating, that you don't like it."

April felt herself shrink a little. She wondered what had come over herself. Putting his needs above her own, considering him more important than herself, submitting herself to him, all those Biblical principles of love she kept trying to live out with him, and she just smashed right through them tonight without considering his feelings.

"So, umm…oh yeah, back to my story." She continued her retelling of her curiosity about Robyn's scenario, and she watched in appreciation as Theo's body language relaxed. Soon they were back on track with each other, brainstorming about what could be going on with Robyn.

It seemed neither of them wanted a fight tonight.

"Maybe she's having an affair," Theo stated bluntly as their food arrived.

"Okay, whoa, that's going too far," April stated firmly. The smell of the salmon wafted up her nose, about as appealing as Theo's theory.

"I'm just making a joke," he said. "Lighten up, Vale."

"I'm plenty light, McTeague," she muttered, digging into the wild rice.

They ate in silence for a few minutes. April ran through their conversation several times, trying to think of a line she could pull on to explain herself more clearly. There were a few places where things had started to fall apart. Should she try to explain herself in a better way and apologize for something?

"I see you're wearing the earrings I gave you," Theo mentioned in a softer voice. "They still look beautiful on you."

April smiled and reached up with her right hand, feeling the familiar pattern of the stone's cut against her fingertips. "I still love them just as much as I did that first night."

Theo put his fork down. "And I still love you just as much as I did back then," he said.

Unbidden, April's mind superimposed his first-ever "I love you" on top of this one and her stomach knotted up. The first one had been tender and sincere. This one was forced, almost desperate, like he needed something from her. What did he need? Why was she so bad at this?

"April, do you love me too?"

Of course that's what he needs. Why can't you say it back again? You've already said it once before.

But I don't know for sure. I don't feel safe anymore.

"I…I love you, too," she heard herself whisper urgently, cutting off her inner realization before it was fully formed. It didn't matter how she felt anyway. Her insecurities weren't to be trusted. Love put his feelings first, and if Theo still loved her after dealing with all her issues and imperfections, then she could most certainly continue to choose to love him back.

Are you pleased, God?

Theo's beaming smile from across the table was her reward. "Then stay with me, April. Not just in our relationship—I hope that's a given. I mean, keep your heart open. Don't pull away. You have this tendency to shut me out. I don't know what causes that, but I hope you know that you can trust me. You don't have to hide from me. I'll never hurt you, and I'll never steer you wrong."

She knew these words should be settling over her like a balm. Why couldn't she receive them like any normal girl would?

Glancing up at her handsome boyfriend with the pleading eyes, she wanted to make everything better for him. If he needed more from her, then that's what she was going to give.

"I know that," she finally responded. "You're very good to me, and you take good care of me. The next time something bothers me, I'll try not to shut you out."

"And I don't mean you can't show that you're upset," he said earnestly. "I mean, tell me about it and let me try to help. When you go all quiet, I don't know what to do, and it hurts that you don't trust me to help you."

Taking a deep breath, April tried to harness her thoughts.

"Okay, so this is me trying to keep my heart open with you," she said. Their server came by to ask how the food was, and they both glanced down at their barely-touched plates.

"Very good," Theo told her with a curt nod. She smiled and walked away.

April twirled her fork over and over against the table. "So, you know how I get overwhelmed in group settings and just crave some time alone afterwards? Like after the first few times of doing small group, or being with your family?"

Theo nodded.

"Well, it's not like I don't enjoy bits and pieces of those times, and it's not like I don't want to have you around. It's not like—it's kind of like, my battery is drained, and it can only recharge when I'm alone. Not because people are bad or you're not needed, but because that's just the way I'm wired. I'm an introvert."

"I understand that," Theo said, and then he seemed to remember his food. He started eating. "I know how introversion works. I just thought that, maybe after being together for so long, I could become part of that battery." He chuckled nervously. "Because to say that I'm not, it's kind of like saying that I drain you. And, I don't know, that sits wrong when almost everything I do is for you. Haven't I earned a spot closer than that?"

"Theo, even my parents and sister drain me, if you want to see it like that," April said quickly. "It has nothing to do with how much I love people or how much they love me. It's just, it's just the way I work. I don't know how else to explain it."

"Tell you what. Oh, your food is getting cold." Theo waited until April started in on her rice again. "How about we try something. The next time you feel like you have to re-charge, let me stay with you. I won't say anything. We can just watch a movie, or I can give you a back rub or foot massage, or you can take a hot bath while I just hang out in the living room watching TV. Are you willing to try that?"

Taking a long drink of her water, April felt a vise grip tighten somewhere deep in her gut. At least now she knew something concrete that Theo wanted from her. It was time to dig in and put strong legs on the principle of considering him more important than herself. She put down her glass and said, "Sure. Sounds like a plan."

- Chapter Twenty-One -

Never had Robyn clung so tightly to Scripture. Two days had passed since her confession to Patrick, and while the weight of untruth was lifted, the heaviness of guilt and grief nearly crushed her as she tried to go about her normal routines.

Patrick had come home that first night at about two in the morning. Robyn had been aroused from a fitful sleep to the sounds of his quiet footsteps in the kitchen and hallway. Gratitude for his safe return caused her to fling off the blankets, but she stopped herself just before running out to him.

Slow and steady, give him space, she reminded herself based on the guidance God kept pressing onto her heart.

Creeping gently toward the open doorway, she caught sight of his shadowy form slipping into the bathroom down the hall.

She leaned there and waited. Listening to the familiar sound of him brushing his teeth, a new thought struck her. His everyday noises hadn't only been something she took for granted, but she had come to despise them over the past few months. Part of the reason for that resentment was that he'd kept on doing his normal life, even though she knew he had sensed the distance growing between them. Why hadn't he fought harder to unearth the issue and bring her back?

Knowing that the thought was ridiculous and unfair didn't matter. Robyn knew it had to hit the surface so she could properly unpack it—just maybe not right now.

The bathroom door opened a few minutes later. She ducked back into the bedroom so as not to startle him.

Patrick walked right back down the hall without a glance. Robyn watched as he took a few weary steps into the living room and lowered himself onto the longest couch, curled up his legs so he'd fit, and draped the throw blanket around his waist. Moonlight cast muted echoes of light onto his shirtless torso, the familiar muscle ridges taunting her with the loss of her right to run her hands over them. She yearned to have their connection back to what it was before.

On the day they'd said, "I do," it never crossed her mind that she'd be wondering if their marriage could survive down the road. The ball was in Patrick's court now, but it was an unfair play he hadn't asked for.

Ultimately, if things didn't work out, she knew she would only blame herself.

She watched for a long time as his chest heaved up and down far too fast for a sleeping person. He tossed and turned several times, at one point sitting up to disentangle his legs from the blanket before flopping back with a heavy, shaky sigh.

She had to do a touch-base. He deserved the space he'd asked for, but she had to let him know she was here. That she saw him.

"I'm glad you're safe," she found herself whispering. His breathing stilled for a second, then continued as he kept his face turned toward the couch.

"No need to talk," she continued. "I'm just glad you're home." She forced herself to turn around and go back to bed, leaving the door ajar.

* * *

The next morning, by unspoken mutual agreement, their bodies carried them through the automatic motions of the family morning routines, both of them avoiding looking at each other. Patrick's chatter with Linus lacked any shine, but he was trying. Robyn's over-the-top cheerfulness seemed to be making up for it, evoking a lot of giggles from their innocent little boy.

When the time drew near for Patrick to leave for work, Robyn busied herself with the dishes. Normally the good-bye included a kiss for Linus and for her, but she didn't know what she would do if Patrick tried for that. Would she flinch because of her own guilt, thereby putting him off even further, or would she respond too hard and scare him off? Or would she be unresponsive, making him wonder if she was still thinking about Devon? It would be a lie to say she wasn't, but her lens had changed completely. She still pined for him and wondered if he was okay, but her stonewall resolve to cut him off hadn't budged—especially now that she was re-acquainted with walking in full honesty before God.

And in light of being witness to her husband's agony.

"Good-bye little buddy." Patrick kissed the top of Linus' wispy-haired head, and Linus threw his jam-grubbed hands around his dad's face. A little too eagerly, Robyn knew, she grabbed the sink cloth and handed it over to him when he pulled back from the sticky baby love.

Here, take this, I love you, please know that I love you.

Patrick wiped his cheeks and handed the cloth back across the table to Robyn's outstretched palm, a quick brushing of their fingertips sending a cold jolt up her arm. Their eyes met for a split-second, an ocean of pain barely concealed behind the guardedness in his own.

"Good-bye," he said flatly, then turned and walked away.

* * *

They repeated the routine later. The night was spent apart

again, Patrick insistent that he was fine on the couch when Robyn offered to trade places with him. The next morning they coped with each other's presence, and in the evening they focused separately on Linus. As soon as Robyn tucked Linus into bed, Patrick went outside to putter in the yard. He didn't come in until well past dark.

During Linus' daily naps, Robyn pulled out her journal and jotted down thoughts that peeked through the haze—like her misdirected anger toward Patrick for not protecting her from herself, or was it anger due to his leaving her open to wanting the kind of attention Devon gave? And if so, what was it she'd been looking for?—and she wrote in detail about missing Devon.

These pages would be destroyed one day, she knew, but in her Intro to Psychology course at university, her instructor had taught the students that it was necessary to feel the full pain of something before you could properly let it go. The last thing she wanted to do was suppress her grief over Devon, only for it to crop up destructively down the road. It seemed obvious to her, now, that she'd never fully let go of the dream of him when she married Patrick. The distraction of new love, marriage, and her teaching career had kept the suppressed dream so convincingly buried she would never have imagined the power it held—until the subject of that power came back into her life, needing her as she once ached that he'd need her.

The vulnerability of new motherhood had been the perfect timing, really.

God, why did he have to contact me at all? Why did this have to happen? she prayed now, having just put her journal away at the sound of Linus waking from his nap.

I provided the way out of temptation, beloved, just like I promised I would.

"But I was a little slow to listen," she acknowledged out loud.

Yes, but you did listen. And I never left you then, and I won't leave you now. Cling to me.

Robyn walked into Linus' room, which was filled with an eclectic mix of handmade décor from all angles of his life. The canvas painting of Noah's Ark that took up residence over his change table had been made by Patrick's sister. The rocking chair in the corner had a large quilt made by her own mom, green-and-yellow patterns reflecting the 9-month period in which nobody knew whether this baby would be a boy or a girl. The small quilt that now lay in a heap on the floor beside the crib—tossed there by a standing little boy who made certain to draw a clear boundary on the end of his nap time—had been made by Myla.

Myla! She hadn't touched base with her at all since small group last week. How was her pregnancy going? And how was Robyn going to tell her about what she'd done? She loved Myla like a sister, but she knew that she couldn't trust her to keep a secret. Come to think of it—how were they going to tell anyone they knew? Did they have to? If their marriage fell apart they would certainly have to, but what about right now?

Thank goodness small group was already cancelled for tonight.

Linus had his arms outstretched. His huge smile showed that he trusted his mom's love for him without question. Robyn felt humbled by how little she deserved that trust as she picked up her son and held him close.

Ironic that last week's study of Ephesians 5 had included discussions on men and women submitting to each other in marriage. How could she have sat there amongst those other believers, knowing the secret she held in the back of her mind? Knowing that she was mere days away from going out for lunch with her secret crush?

Kissing the sweet-smelling crook of her son's neck, Robyn determined to herself that she'd re-read Ephesians 5 later tonight and review the study questions. On this side of the previous days' events, she wondered how differently she'd perceive things now. What might God tell her that could help her stay in the ready position to support Patrick and save their marriage, if given the chance?

* * *

It felt odd to be staying home on a Thursday evening. April was surprised to realize that she missed going to small group, although with only two sessions remaining, the disbanding was rather imminent anyway. Maybe another group would start up in the fall. Even without Theo's encouragement, she was open to the idea of joining another one.

Theo was off playing pool with some friends, and April sat in the living room at home wondering who to call. While being alone with her thoughts wasn't usually a problem, she found that re-reading her journal entries from Saturday was exhausting and fruitless. Robyn, the first friend she'd allowed herself to really open up to, had introduced her to the power of a nonjudgmental listening ear. April craved that connecting time right now. But she hadn't worked up the nerve to text Robyn all week, being uncertain about whether that would be welcome or intrusive. Wouldn't she get ahold of April once she was ready for…once she was ready for anything outside of dealing with whatever she was dealing with?

Not for the first time, April shot up a quick prayer for her burdened friend. Then she called her parents' number, only to be greeted by the answering machine.

So. She really was destined to have a lonely evening. Even her roommates were gone, either at work or out having fun.

"Well, God, I guess it's just you and me." She winced. "I mean, not that I don't want to spend time with you. It's just that I wish I could be with someone in the flesh right now. I feel lonely and out of sorts. What should I do?"

Without waiting for an answer, her feet carried her to the door. A walk would feel nice right now, just to take the edge off. Like she'd said to Seth on Monday, exercise was for the mind as much as for the body. While she walked, inhaling the neighbourhood's earth-rich fragrance of preparation for the weighted air's promise, her thoughts rolled over her mind like the distant thunder. She offered them to God without trying to alter them in any way.

I'm confused about everything. I'm trying my best to act in loving submission with Theo, but I have to admit—I don't think he gets me. Sometimes he says things that really bug me. But if I tell him it bugs me, he gets all upset. I just don't know what to do about that anymore. But anyway, is it even my job to be looking for him to treat me the way I want to be treated? Isn't it my job only to be concerned about my own performance instead of judging how another believer is living out their faith? Besides, he treats me well in lots of other ways.

And then there's the whole business of my old house, and the resurrection of hurts from my past with Cosette and my family. Why is all this stuff coming up this summer? I was doing fine until I kept on being reminded of how people have hurt me before. I thought those things were all buried and gone, in the past. It's been whack-a-mole all summer. I hit down one thing, and then another pops up. Why can't I just rest from the game?

A favourite Bible passage came to mind, hitting differently than it used to: "Come to me, all you who are weary and burdened, and I will give you rest. Take my yoke upon you and learn from me, for I am gentle and humble in heart, and you will find rest for your souls. For my yoke is easy and my burden is light."

Jesus' soothing words from Matthew 11:28-30 washed over her, teasing her with the promise of calm. She wanted to press into that more than ever, but she shook her head at the idea.

"God, I can't do that. I have so much to sort out first. I'm still trying to figure out-" she stopped her spoken prayer when she noticed a young couple walking toward her up ahead. No sense being seen as a crazy lady. *I'm still trying to figure out how to keep on putting others first even when it's uncomfortable. I can't rest until I do. There must be a plateau or something coming up, right? So I can take a break while I'm climbing the mountain of trying to become a better person?*

Come to me.

Jesus, I am talking to you.

You're talking to me from afar. Come closer.

I can't. Tears pricked her eyes. She passed the couple, keeping her face down so they wouldn't see. Her feet had carried her to the first corner of her usual route, and she turned right without thinking.

Lightning flashed. The thunder's response was delayed, but she picked up her pace. These frequent storms of late seemed to be appropriately accompanying the amping-up of whatever it was she couldn't put a finger on.

Why can't I come closer? she asked herself now, pushing Jesus aside. She was such a mess. For being one of the ninety-nine in the flock that he didn't have to go seeking, she sure wasn't making his job as Shepherd any easier.

Nor was she making Theo's life any better. She always seemed to be one misstep away from bothering him. He deserved better than that. He deserved more than what she could give, and yet he'd chosen her. Shouldn't she continue to try to live up to that honor? But at what cost? Should she even count the cost, though? Wasn't putting someone else first supposed to hurt a little?

Suddenly Seth's face came to mind, and she smiled. Good old Seth. There was no way she could let him fade out of her life after this summer gig was up. How ironic, it seemed, that his challenges sometimes placed her in the most socially awkward situations she'd ever faced, yet he was one of her safest people.

By the time she arrived back at her house, darkness was settling in and her feet were ready to be put up. She plopped down on the couch with a glass of water, then got up again to fetch her Bible and study materials from her bedroom. Maybe it wouldn't hurt to study ahead for next week.

As she flipped through Ephesians, tracking quickly for the big number 6, her attention snagged on chapter 5 verses 13 and 14: "But everything exposed by the light becomes visible—and everything that is illuminated becomes a light. This is why it is said, 'Wake up, sleeper, rise from the dead, and Christ will shine on you.'"

Obviously she would have read these verses at least a couple of times last week, but today they jumped out as if they were highlighted. In her rush to get to the submission verses, had she not noticed them before? Or was she just not ready to notice them until now? Either way, they were here now—front and center and clicking into place with a clarity she'd been craving.

Things were being exposed. Old hurts, hidden wounds; this seemed to be the summer of exposure. Had she been sleeping all along, at least as far as these painful infections were concerned?

Perhaps that wasn't what the original context of the verses was getting at, but she couldn't deny how God seemed to be illuminating her own situation with them. Was this what was meant by God's Word being living and active?

But my life has been so good and relatively easy, God. Why should I hurt? I don't have the right to hurt.

You* do *hurt. Let's deal with it.

April read on to verses 15-17: "Be very careful, then, how you live—not as unwise but as wise, making the most of every opportunity, because the days are evil. Therefore do not be foolish, but understand what the Lord's will is."

"That's what I'm trying to do, God. To walk as wise, to understand what your will is. I'm trying to do that, especially with Theo. But…do my old hurts play into all of this somehow? Is that why everything is tangled in my head all at once? What are you trying to teach me?"

Come to me.

There it was again.

I don't know how. But I want to. Show me how, please!

The sweet communion went quiet.

- Chapter Twenty-Two -

Robyn hadn't brought it up, assuming that Patrick wasn't ready to consider spending so many days in the same space as her. Yet indecision had kept her from making the call to cancel their reservation, and she was glad for that when Patrick came home from work on Thursday and asked if she was ready to go to the cabin.

"N-no," she stammered, unable to decide if this was a good or bad idea. "I mean—I didn't think…um, I can be ready, I just have to pack and…"

"I don't want Linus to miss out just because of what you did."

She would have liked to mask how much that stung, but she hadn't been given time to prepare.

Patrick closed his eyes. "I'm sorry. I'm a mess, but I really do want to make this vacation work. For Linus."

Robyn nodded, willing to do anything he wanted. It wasn't even worth considering whether it was a good idea.

"You bet," she said softly. "For Linus."

* * *

Packing took a few hours, and by the time they were on their way it was already growing dark. Robyn rode the current of Patrick's determination to have this family vacation, beat-up though their family was now.

The night drive would have been soothing under different circumstances. For the first time all week, the crystalline stars weren't hiding beyond storm clouds. Linus had fallen asleep within minutes of the drive, and although Robyn was partly worried that it would throw off his night's sleep once they arrived at the cabin, she knew it didn't really matter. It would have mattered before the Before she had created, but here in the After she still couldn't find her bearings. She couldn't imagine how Patrick was holding up.

Patrick turned off the Baby Einstein music. The default soft rock station took over. Robyn leaned against her window, head in the crook of her arm, trying her best to look relaxed. She allowed the familiar songs to bring back echoes of her teen years, skipping past all the memories of her summers at the lake. Right now, it felt like nothing good came from them and she wished they'd never happened at all.

Patrick seemed very focused on his role as driver. At least, from what Robyn could discern through her peripheral reconnaissance. So long as he didn't look like he was about to fall asleep, she decided she would keep her presence as inobtrusive as possible.

They were about half an hour along when a horrifying assortment of familiar swaying notes filled the car's interior. Robyn glanced at Patrick; Patrick glanced at Robyn; the cruel mockery of the song, *their* song, the music of the first dance at their wedding, raised the atmosphere of tension so drastically Robyn had to fight the bizarre urge to laugh. Her hands were frozen, but Patrick's weren't. She watched in awe as Patrick turned the volume knob up ever so slightly, and she met his eyes. Moonlight reflected off the bare pain and love they conveyed to her. She couldn't look away.

Naturally his focus had to return to the road, but Robyn

continued to stare at him. As the music played, she watched the mystery of her husband and wondered what in the world was going on inside. She had tried to imagine, many times over the past week, what it might be like to have the tables turned—yet she knew it was only speculation. And then having this unexpected trigger thrown in between them…she didn't even understand how *she* felt about it, let alone how he must be feeling.

Two things were clear to her: the affection and heartache at the replay of their shared memories with this song. She pondered the promises she'd made in that white dress, across from him in that handsome black suit, just a few hours before they swayed around the great big reception hall in their first dance as man and wife. Was Patrick trying to hurt her now, with the reminder of the trust she'd broken? Was he trying to remind himself of the goodness they'd shared, and the goodness they might share going forward? What on *earth?* That tiny little twist of the knob spoke volumes, but in what way?

Finally, the song was done and Robyn dared to breathe a little easier.

But when the car slowed down and she saw Patrick's shoulders shaking, her heart sank.

The gravel on the shoulder crunched under the wheels for a moment, then Patrick's deep intake of breath and his release of a shuddering sob was all she could hear. It penetrated to the very core of her. Her husband's arms went up on the steering wheel and he buried his head in them, crying in a way she had never known she would ever see him cry. He seemed like a completely different person, yet intimately familiar all at once. She reached across the console to him, then pulled her hand back. Then she forced herself to reach again and complete the connection, her hand landing in the middle of his back. Pressing it there, she held still and waited for the rebuff. It never came.

Several minutes passed. From the backseat, she could hear Linus making a few mewling noises, but she shoved her maternal instincts aside.

Patrick's breathing began to level out. Through his back, Robyn could feel his heart racing. Linus began to amp up his own fussing at having his sleep so rudely interrupted, but Patrick seemed not to hear. Keeping his head in his arms, he spoke.

"I don't know what to do."

Robyn nodded, realized he couldn't see her, then just rubbed his back gently in response. Tears welled in her eyes; she didn't bother wiping them away.

The silence stretched on long enough that she began to wonder if he wanted something more from her.

"Me-" she had to stop and clear her throat. "Me neither."

Another beat of stillness fell between them. Linus' crying in the backseat dropped off to a low, drowsy keen.

"You haven't texted him this week?" It sounded like a question, a challenge, and a statement all at once.

"No, I haven't. I blocked his number as soon as I could."

"Do you…" he paused. A vehicle passed them, spitting a few grains of sand against the windshield. "Do you want to be with me?"

It was all she could do not to throw herself against him, but she channeled that energy into her voice.

"Oh, Patrick, yes." The conviction that thundered through her took her breath away. "Yes, yes, all the way yes."

He took a deep breath and released it slowly; Robyn hoped it wasn't just in her imagination that a touch of his tension faded.

"I have so many questions," he muttered. "So many things I need to say. But I don't know where to start. I don't want to say terrible things, but I'm so messed up inside. I don't know if I can trust myself not to lose it if I try to talk about it."

"I understand."

Patrick sat up straight and leaned back against the headrest, closing his eyes. Robyn quickly removed her hand from his back and set it on his armrest instead. She wasn't ready to retreat into her own space just yet.

"I would…I mean, I've been thinking that it might be a good idea to see a marriage counselor," Robyn said softly. "If you're up for that."

This time when Patrick looked her way, she saw the tiniest hint of hope flickering there.

"Yes," he answered in a hoarse voice. "Let's do it."

- Chapter Twenty-Three -

On Saturday afternoon, Theo and April made the short trek out to his parents' place for his mom's birthday supper. She had turned sixty the day before, so tonight promised to be a major event. Not only would the entire family be showing up, but dozens of their friends and relatives as well.

Having just the immediate family all together was overwhelming enough. Tonight promised to be a doozy.

"So, what are everyone's names again?" April asked as Theo directed the car off the poorly-maintained highway and onto a gravel road.

Theo laughed. "Do you want physical descriptions too? So you can match them up?"

April smacked his arm with the back of her hand. "No, just the names, McTeague. So I can memorize them in my head and possibly even regurgitate them back if my stutter doesn't ruin every attempt at conversation."

Theo looked at her and raised his eyebrows. "I keep telling you, if you focus on your stutter, it's more likely to happen. Like hitting a deer that's standing in the middle of the road."

"I don't think it's an inappropriate focus. It's the dependability of a set pattern. Crowds full of unfamiliar people plus social anxiety equals stutter. Tale as old as time."

"Look, all I'm saying is, try not to think about it too much. Think about the things people are saying, instead of thinking about what you're going to say back. Imagine everyone naked if that helps. Just don't keep your mind only on your nerves. And remember…" he gave her hand a squeeze, "after the party we can re-charge you together."

She forced a smile even though he wasn't looking at her.

They pulled into the large circular driveway, where half a dozen vehicles had already found places to park.

This colossal house never ceased to amaze April. The very first time Theo brought her out here, a few weeks into dating, she had actually gasped. It was wintertime, and the late-afternoon winter darkness had cast the cloudy sky in a navy hue. When they turned left through a wide break in the neatly-trimmed hedges running parallel to the gravel road, thousands of diamond-white Christmas lights surrounded all of the house's features, putting on a brilliant display.

"I know it's the end of February, but my mom insists on keeping the lights on all winter long. She wants to drag out the Christmas season for as long as possible," Theo explained.

April had thought *this is where we'll celebrate Christmas every other year*, already formulating in her head that they would alternate years between families, much like her family had done when she was younger.

The two-storey sprawl could have fit ten of her old Edmonton houses inside of it. Having an attached three-car garage on its right side did nothing to diminish the ultimate size of the living quarters.

Six uniform windows took up the second storey. Underneath, two impossibly large bay windows occupied either side of the portico, which encased wide wooden double doors and four glittering potted evergreen trees along both sides. Light spilled out of all the ground-floor windows, inviting travelers to come in and find respite from the darkness.

"This is where you *grew up?*" April had breathed, excited to explore the beautiful house yet mortified at how much she didn't measure up to the lifestyle it proclaimed.

"Home sweet home," Theo had replied happily, as giddy as she'd ever seen him.

That first visit had been with only his parents. April had found it uncomfortable, but her enamoured state of the house had thinned out her reserves a little more than usual. By the time they left, April told herself it went okay, trying her best to combat the self-reproach that followed almost all of her social interactions.

Later, she learned that his whole family had wanted to be there for the first "meet the family" meal, but Theo had insisted on keeping it small. April's heart had swelled when he admitted it later.

He saw her; he cared about her struggles, and he would support her. That was the moment she felt truly known, and she believed she was falling in love.

Now, six months later, they were parking on the far edge of the loop and April still loved the grandeur of the house, but she didn't feel the tug of future memories like she once did. *Probably just because I've never been here with such a huge crowd before,* she told herself.

When she got out of the car and looked over the roof at Theo, she recognized that sparkle in his eyes. He was going to be in his element, and she was going to be left behind. Her stomach sank.

He deserves someone who's as outgoing as he is, she thought, feeling her inadequacy down to her toes.

She wanted Theo. Yes, he deserved better, but she would have to learn how to be that better person. Even if she had to fake it somehow, at least for tonight.

One major social event at a time.

* * *

It had been a strange but alright day. With the uneasy truce resting precariously between them, Patrick and Robyn had woken up (she in the cabin's one bedroom with Linus in a playpen against the end of the bed, Patrick on the living room couch) after sleeping past the rising of the sun. It had taken Linus a good few hours to settle upon arrival, as expected, and now this morning he continued to slumber on while Robyn slipped out of the room to find Patrick sitting up and rubbing his eyes with the heels of his hands.

"Morning," she greeted softly. He nodded in reply. Robyn scooped some grounds into the cabin's miniature coffee maker and pressed the button, then quickly stopped it to add water. It was going to be one of those days.

There was a small dining table pressed under a side window that framed a view of the nearby mix of poplar and evergreen trees. When the coffee was finished, Robyn brought one steaming mug over to Patrick on the couch, then she took her mug to the table and stared outside.

Awkwardness had become like a third person in their marriage. Robyn was growing used to dancing around it. She felt she could relate to the main character in an action movie facing a deadly bomb: should she cut the red wire or the white one? The right choice would save everyone, and the wrong one would make her marriage explode. Thankfully, awkwardness didn't have a clock ticking down the seconds.

When Linus began babbling from behind the closed door, both parents jumped up eagerly.

At least we have something in common. We both want to avoid being alone together for too long, Robyn thought to herself as Patrick glanced over and deferred to her with a nod of the head. She nodded back and went to their son, eager not just for his presence to shrink the tension, but to start sharing a fun-filled nature day with him.

* * *

Later that evening, Robyn tucked him in after wiping as many grains of sand as possible away from his diaper area. The bathroom had a stand-up shower, so she had bathed Linus in a basin that she brought along, but that early afternoon at the beach was still clinging to him.

Once Linus was settled in the playpen, Robyn gently closed the door and sank down on one side of the couch with a weary yawn. All the rough nights of sleep were catching up to her. She closed her eyes and leaned her head back, the warmth of the day's sun soaked into her skin even in the shelter of the cabin. She knew Linus wouldn't remember this trip, but discovering so many new things had surely etched something meaningful upon him. If nothing else, he had been entertained and delighted to no end. A nature boy—a boy after her own heart.

The bathroom door opened and Robyn, still with closed eyes, heard the unmistakeable sound of a sudden stop of footsteps.

"Oh," she murmured in embarrassment. "Sorry, I'll give you your space back."

"No, no, you stay. That couch is as much yours as it is mine."

"Well, I guess it doesn't actually belong to either of us. Seeing as it's a rental cabin and all." She tried a little smile, and he tried for one as well.

Patrick resumed walking through the small kitchen and sat down on the far side of the couch with a sigh equal in exhaustion to the yawn she'd emitted earlier.

Awkwardness was already elbowing its way in, but Robyn wanted to elbow it back.

"I loved watching Linus in the water today," she said. "Going back and forth and back and forth with such a huge smile on his face."

"That was pretty cute," Patrick replied. "I was surprised he didn't mind getting splashed by those older kids. The water wasn't as warm as I hoped it would be."

"Maybe all the exposure to splash parks this summer helped," said Robyn.

"Or maybe he's just like his mom." Patrick looked over at her. "Remember when you asked me to drive through that huge puddle in the road so you could stand on the side and get soaked?"

"Oh, yeah!" Robyn wanted to laugh, but she'd noticed the amount of effort Patrick was using just to have this conversation. It was a sobering reality.

That puddle moment had happened shortly after they'd gotten married. It was an impulse borne of the exultant happiness and freedom she felt as a new wife, with a man whose love surrounded every aspect he knew about her at the time. There was nothing he hadn't accepted about her, nothing he'd tried to change. She felt the same about him and wondered how they had gotten so lucky to end up together—two imperfect people who embraced each other entirely and celebrated each other fully.

How well she remembered the sensations: it was a warm summer evening. The puddle in question was on a lesser-traveled secondary highway, spanning almost the entire right lane after days' worth of summer storms. She stood on the shoulder, anticipation rising like a quick tide as she watched the car racing toward the water. Suddenly, her reality became a roar of exceptionally chaotic water, the warm and asphalt-scented wall of it descending and ascending upon her all at once, completely immersing her in a world that would last only a moment but leave her pondering its richness for years to come.

When Patrick pulled over up ahead and walked back to her, he was laughing. Robyn was laughing, too, and cheering and jumping up and down. Celebrating happiness for its own sake was fun on her own, but when Patrick grabbed her and got his own clothes soaked and kissed her with a fierce passion that branded the occasion against her brain, she recognized what power her happiness had over him.

That thought struck her anew in this moment, sitting here with a big space between them.

She blurted out, "None of this is your fault, you know."

"Robyn…" Patrick sighed again.

"I mean, I don't know what thoughts you've been having, but just in case you've wondered that, I just want to say that. It's completely my fault."

"Okay, Robyn, I'm tired and I don't know if this is a good idea to try, but here goes." He leaned forward and stared at the coffee table. "I know it's your fault. Sometimes I'm so angry at you I can't think straight. This is the worst betrayal I've ever had, and I honestly don't know how I can ever trust you again."

"I promise you can. I'll work on that-"

"But one of the other hard things is that, yes, I've wrestled with wondering what I was missing. Maybe it's a fault with us men, but one of our greatest accomplishments is knowing that we make our wives happy. So to have you look to another man for happiness, it digs at my manhood and self-worth in a way I can't fully explain."

"I'm so sorry…"

"I'm also angry at myself, because obviously I must have missed some signs. I thought it was all the adjustments you were going through as a new mom, missing your job, all that stuff." He rubbed his face with both hands. "Robyn, I was trying so hard to be supportive and available. I knew you were growing distant, but I figured if I waited patiently enough, you'd feel free to tell me if there was something going on inside of you that I didn't understand, or anything…I just didn't expect this. And I hate that I didn't see it coming. I hate that I wasn't paying enough attention. I hate that you let it happen, that you didn't value me enough to protect our marriage when an old flame came sniffing around in secret. I hate that…" his voice was rising in volume and Robyn forced herself not to flinch, but Patrick suddenly rested his fist against his lips and stood up, pacing around the small room.

"I'm going for a walk," he said. "This is me leaving before I say anything I'll regret."

He was out the door before Robyn could react. She sat there massaging her chest as if that would release the tightness inside, wondering if his words were a sign of progress or a setback.

Either way, she stayed on the couch and prayed for him, for her, and for their future.

She moved to the window and watched him return about half an hour later, then started toward the bedroom before he entered the cabin.

"Good night. I love you," she whispered with her hand on the knob.

Patrick's eyes were wet and red-rimmed, his jaw tense. "I love you too," he muttered angrily.

* * *

A few hours away, Theo's jaw was also clenched. He and April drove through Saskatoon on their way to her house, coming to an abrupt stop at her sidewalk.

"Umm," April said quietly. "Maybe…maybe it's not a good idea for you to come in tonight."

"April." Theo turned to face her, holding the steering wheel with both hands. "It's up to you. I'm not going to force it. But I have to tell you, after the way things went tonight, if you send me away right now, I'm going to seriously question the value of this relationship."

April bit her lip and looked down, her mind racing. The threat of rejection struck hard. She wanted to ask God for strength to do the right thing, the loving thing, and she hoped that just feeling that way was enough of a prayer for now. She couldn't lose Theo over her own stupid insecurities and issues. She *couldn't.*

"Those are my friends and family, April," Theo continued. "I know you don't like people, but have you no capacity to consider my feelings in this?"

What? All I do is try to consider how to make you happy! she wanted to say, but she didn't want to upset him more. She ignored the thought and tried to think of an honest response more suited to his needs.

"I do like people," she said on barely a whisper. "I just get intimidated sometimes. You know this about me. I think your family is great."

"You had a funny way of showing it tonight," he muttered. "There's nothing wrong with getting through the night and accepting that you're going to be stuttering half the time. There's nothing wrong with pushing yourself out of your comfort zone a bit, April. Especially for my sake, if I mean anything to you at all. But for you to go missing halfway through the party, and then for me to find you hiding away in my bedroom after half a dozen people start asking where you went…do you realize how embarrassing that was for me?"

"Telling them I felt sick was fine, Theo! No one would have reason to believe otherwise!" she pleaded.

"Yeah, but after that lie slipped out it wasn't possible to stay at the party without looking like a complete jerk. We hadn't even done the birthday cake for Mom yet. And this, April, this is what really gets to me." His hand sliced the air and bounced off the steering wheel, making April wince. "I bend over backwards to try and help get you out of your shell, to make you feel safe, to expand your world, and I don't see you making any effort to meet me halfway."

"I'm sorry, Theo, I really am. You're always welcome to go back to the party without me. No one would expect you to stay with me just because I'm sick. Tell them I sent you back with my blessing, that I went to bed right away…"

"No." Theo firmly turned off the ignition. "If we're ever going to get anywhere past this point, we're sticking to our plan. I'm coming in, and we're going to watch a movie or something. You're not getting rid of me so easily."

He exited the car and marched around to her door, wrenching

it open. So much for making it her choice.

April saw the bulging muscles in his arm and became instinctively aware of her vulnerability.

I'm scared, she wanted to say, but instead she said, "Okay."

She wanted nothing more than to get in a hot bath or go to bed, but even with Theo's reiterated promise to just hang out quietly in the living room with the TV or a magazine, she didn't want any decreased guardedness of any sort tonight. Instead, she let him pick a movie and they sat on the couch together, where she laid her head against the armrest opposite from him. Her empty reserves were bombarded with a hyper-awareness of every move and noise he made.

She still loved him. Convincing herself of this, she decided to table any major decisions about their relationship for now. Maybe in a few days, when they were both calmer, she'd have a renewed sense of how to love him better, and he'd have a renewed sense of why he fell in love with her in the first place.

- Chapter Twenty-Four -

Robyn and April met up at a coffee shop on Broadway Avenue. After purchasing their drinks, they sauntered out into the warm Monday evening, jostling their way through the crowded sidewalk. The Fringe Festival was in full swing—street performers and artists of various media were strewn along the entire road, which was blocked off to vehicle traffic for the duration of the night. They stopped to watch a man on impossibly high stilts as he called forth a brave young volunteer to play catch with him. The hot summer air was fully loaded with the smells of deep-fried wares, handmade soaps, cigarettes, and the occasional whiff of marijuana. People-noise and music created a pleasant clamor that echoed against itself as far as the ear could hear.

Making their way toward the Broadway Bridge, the ladies stopped at a few of the artisans' booths. April splurged on a hand-knit shawl for Britney. Robyn picked up a wooden train for Linus and some knitted baby booties for Myla.

"I guess I didn't plan ahead," Robyn laughed as she tried unsuccessfully to stuff her wares in her little purse. "I was so happy to not need the diaper bag that I went a little overboard."

"Or maybe underboard," April replied. "Here, you can put

them in my bag for now."

The crowds were thinning out as they neared the bridge, but foot traffic was very steadily moving in the opposite direction, so they found it necessary to walk in a line. As they descended the slope of the pedestrian sidewalk toward the lower riverbank of the North Saskatchewan River, they both couldn't help but look toward the wide vista of water and sandbars spread out to their right. There was a small group of people sitting around a campfire on one of the sandbars nearest the shore. A duo of kayaks cut gentle swaths in the middle of the river. The sun, hovering between horizon and mid-height in the clear sky, sprinkled the water's surface with a smattering of brilliant little flashes. From underneath the span of the downriver University Bridge, the iconic Prairie Lily passenger steamboat was midway through its evening tour.

In a few minutes they had completed their crossing. Turning right into a graffiti-strewn concrete staircase down off the side of the bridge, they ended up on a gravelly patch of grass with bits of broken glass scattered amongst the rocks. The city was vibrating with the festival essence of summertime, even though they had left the official festival behind. The riverside park they were now jaywalking toward was filled with picnickers and bikers and walkers; people and dogs; groups and couples; people on their own; and Canada geese mixed in with them as naturally as you please.

"Have you and Seth walked here yet?" Robyn asked, now able to stroll side-by-side with her friend again.

"Yes, it's not usually quite this busy during the day," April answered. "But finding nearby parking can be a problem. We've had to abandon a couple of times."

April was full of so many conversation topics at once, she didn't know where to begin. When Robyn had texted the invitation to hang out tonight, she had responded casually enough, but in reality she had just about burst out of her skin.

For her part, Robyn looked a bit nervous. April sensed an

invisible force of unspoken words, as well as the counterforce that Robyn was trying to overcome.

Maybe it would ease Robyn into opening up if April did it first.

"So, Robyn," she began, "I wanted to ask you something."

"Go ahead." Robyn's eyes were unreadable through her sunglasses, but her voice sounded like she was preparing to face a firing squad.

"It's about God."

Robyn glanced at her, nodding encouragement. "Shoot."

April filled her in on the things she'd been struggling with since the beginning of summer; her thoughts about God, and her confusion that old wounds were re-surfacing even though she was also feeling God's love and presence more often. Especially when she was with Seth.

By now they were walking past the towering hulk of Saskatoon's famous old red-brick hotel, the Delta Bessborough. The foot path grew narrower, with an ivy-covered chain-link fence to their left and the river view to their right. People were weaving slowly in and out along the way in the casual dance of strangers making their way past each other with no particular place to go.

"I think God often uses our relationships to help us see him more clearly," Robyn said. "Maybe he's trying to teach you something through the freedom you experience with Seth."

"That could be. I'm kind of hoping for a breakthrough with God. It seems close, but I can't grasp it yet."

"Hm. I know that feeling. If it's any encouragement, I've had that inner sense happen to me a few times in my life, and God has never failed to follow through."

April felt her spirits lift. "Can you tell me about one of those times?"

"Well," Robyn said after a thoughtful silence, "there was a big one that happened at Bible School. It was when God taught me that he doesn't turn away from me even when I mess up."

April frowned. "I thought that sin causes a barrier to go up.

That's why we need to ask for forgiveness each time. So we're not separated from him by our mistakes."

"That's what I used to think, too," Robyn replied, "but back then, one of the teachers taught a class on grace. It was eye-opening, but it didn't really sink in right away. I wouldn't be able to do it justice, but the sum-up is that, yes, original sin separated us from God. That's what we are all born into. It's like a disease that we didn't ask for, but it's the unfortunate reality of coming into existence in a broken system. So, when we first realize we need a Saviour and we ask him to forgive us, or ask him into our hearts or however we word it, we instantly fall under his perfection. That's one of the things Jesus' sacrifice gained for us. When he died to save us from sin, it was once and for all." Robyn stopped and looked up at the treetops as if searching for words. "We don't have to live in constant fear of asking for his forgiveness after each screw-up. It's not like sunscreen that you have to re-apply every few hours. It doesn't wash away, no matter how much we think our worst thoughts or behaviours are capable of doing that. God's not looking for reasons to walk away from us."

April pondered this. Something inside of her rejected this dangerously careless notion while something else pressed the "come to me and I will give you rest" verse against it.

"But I always feel especially distant from God after doing something wrong," she admitted.

"And you think that distance is a result of God-imposed guilt?"

"Well, yes."

Robyn touched her arm, causing her to look at her own reflection off of Robyn's sunglasses. "April, that's not from God. It's shame imposed by yourself or the devil."

April's feet steered her back toward walking, a nervous energy buzzing through her body. "I don't know, isn't that splitting hairs? I mess up, therefore I'm guilty, therefore I feel shame. Shame, or I guess sometimes we say conviction, isn't a bad thing when it reminds us to repent."

"Shame and conviction are two different things, though. Conviction is when God calls our attention to something that needs addressing, and it's wrapped in his love. Shame is when we know we've messed up—or sometimes just *think* we've messed up— and we hate ourselves. Usually because we think he's mad at us."

"Isn't he, though?" April asked uncertainly.

"But what if—okay, let's look at it this way. Remember that first time I met Seth, and he went for my phone?"

It all came rushing back to April—the power of that moment, of seeing the shame come down over Seth and how hard she and Robyn tried to speak words of love through his fog.

"Was he guilty of doing something wrong?" Robyn asked. April nodded with a noncommittal shrug as Robyn continued.

"Technically, yes. Did you put the guilt on him and disengage from him because of that? No. But there was a new distance created. And it wasn't by you."

"But I'm not God," April pushed back, resistant. "God still loves us, but he can't abide sin. So when we sin, he can't abide us."

"But if he's already forgiven us, if we're living in salvation, he doesn't see the sin on us. He only sees the perfection Jesus gave us. Once and for all."

"So, what you're saying is, even when we're messing up, he still sees us as perfect."

Robyn was getting excited now. "Yes!"

"Even when we're right *in* the act of committing a sin…he doesn't see it?"

"Well, this is where we have to be willing to suspend our own limited understanding of what God is and isn't capable of." Robyn lifted her drink to her lips, sipping loudly through the ice cubes at the bottom. "The Bible does talk about how God sees everything and knows everything. However, it also talks about how nothing can separate us from his love, and the entire book of Romans is a major in-depth study on how our standing with God is reliant on Jesus, not on ourselves. We've moved under his salvation; our entire status is changed. It has nothing to do with our performance or whatever screw-ups we make along the way. His view of us, as perfect children because of Jesus, never changes."

"And yet, he sees how we hurt him and other people." As an afterthought, April added, "And ourselves."

Robyn winced. "Yes, he does."

"But he doesn't turn his back on us."

"No."

"He doesn't see us any differently."

"No."

"Hmm." April took a long sip from her icy drink too, trying to process all of this. Her desperation for rest, and for a closer relationship with God, cried out for this to be true. Yet it didn't fit with her understandings. It was an uncomfortable mental space to be in. She wondered whether she should be encouraging the spark of hope that flickered in her heart.

A large circular water fountain infused this section of the park with the sound of millions of delicate water droplets spraying up into the air, then hitting the coin-filled pool. The noise grew louder as they walked past, filling in the space after Robyn's excited ramble.

"It sounds kind of like believing that what we do doesn't matter, though," April finally said with confusion. "Like we can get away with murder, figuratively and literally."

Robyn tilted her head back and forth a couple of times. "Well, yes and no. I think it depends on how you're looking at the entire issue. If a person is using God's grace as a get-out-of-jail-free card, then it begs the question of whether or not that person has actually grasped their need of him. Like, yeah, we all mess up, but a willful pattern of going against God should raise some red flags for that person to examine. The book of James really makes you think about the relationship between faith and works, and how they go together. And the thing is," Robyn paused and lifted her foot, shaking a pebble out of her sandal, "I guess, in my case, I think God has taught me the difference between trying to do works to get grace, versus having good works come as a *result* of trusting in his grace. And, it's a *relationship* with God…not a formula to solve in front of God. Does…does any of that make sense?"

"I think so," April replied. "You're giving me a lot to think about."

Silence settled between them. Birdsong began to trickle into the background noise the farther they got from the crowded areas.

"So, did we ever get to your actual question about God?" Robyn asked.

"Hm?" April looked up from the sidewalk just in front of her feet. "Oh yeah, that first question…yeah, I guess, kind of. I was basically going to ask you how you yourself get closer to him. Because I've been trying for years, and now that I can feel his presence more often, I guess I just want to keep it going. I don't want it to pause, you know? Or to stop happening altogether. And you seem to have your ducks in a row-"

The guffaw that burst out of Robyn made April jump, and she couldn't help but giggle nervously in return. "Oh…okay, not so much with the ducks, then?"

"April, that makes me want to laugh and cry at the same time," Robyn said, quieting her voice a degree. There were even fewer people out walking this way, but she was looking around nervously. She waited for a group of teens to pass before she spoke again.

"I need to tell you something. Something hard."

April noticed that Robyn's voice was shaking.

"Are you okay?"

"Yes," Robyn sniffed. "Let's sit down over there."

They had just gone up a short stone staircase beside a dark wood gazebo, and past that was a bench surrounded by flowers. Making their way over to it, April looked carefully at her agitated friend.

Robyn twisted her hands in her lap and looked down.

"I owe you an explanation for my weird mood last weekend," Robyn started. "And first of all, I'm sorry for turning the second half of the trip into such a bummer."

"It wasn't so bad," April lied.

Robyn smirked. "You're nice. Anyway. Just so you know, Patrick and I have talked this week, and we've decided to go to marriage counseling."

April nodded her head and forced her bubbling questions down.

"So, I was having an emotional affair this year." Robyn grunted in disbelief. "Wow, saying that out loud makes it really real. What I did. That really sucks."

The bubbling questions vanished, replaced by nothing but dead air.

"I know. It's shocking," Robyn said quietly. "The gist of it is…you know Devon, the old friend I told you about that weekend? He got in touch with me in the spring. I had a major crush on him when we were teens—like, major crush. The kind of crush that lasts for years and you desperately hope that one day you'll get married and have a family together. Anyway, Patrick is an amazing husband…but when Devon started texting me, I let it snowball. I knew what I was doing, and yet I didn't because I was very good at denying it to myself. And then…when I found out you were going up to Edmonton, and I knew he lived close by, I…"

April looked at Robyn and waited patiently as an ache rose in her heart for Patrick. Good, solid, loving Patrick.

"I just want to be clear that I *did* want to spend that weekend with you. It lined up nicely with my wish to get to know you better, and to get away from home for a break. But unfortunately, it also lined up nicely with giving me a chance to see Devon in person."

"So…" April interjected, "that lunch at Tims…there was no sister, was there?"

"Technically, there is a sister. She was going to join us for the mall after lunch. But the lunch date was always planned to be just me and Devon."

"So, you lied to me." April said it with more surprise than anger.

"I did, yes. April, I'm so sorry. I can't tell you how sorry I am."

"I mean, it sucks to be lied to," April said slowly, noticing how the sun was edging closer to the horizon. "But I care more about how you're doing. This must be…really tough times for you right now."

Robyn's downturned face studied the tops of her sandals with great care.

As delicately as possible, Robyn shared how the lunch date had ended, and how Patrick had received the news. She told about the fraught weekend at the cabin, and about how she had researched a few local marriage counselors to start determining who might be a good fit. They had narrowed it down to two; tomorrow she and Patrick would choose which one to contact.

"April, I wanted to let you know all of this because I wanted to be up front about my dishonesty toward you. I also wanted to tell someone I trust. I haven't figured out who else to tell, or even if I'm going to. For now, anyway. But I would love and appreciate it so much if you could pray for me and Patrick."

"Of *course* I will," April reassured, wondering if she should offer a hug. If Robyn sensed how unnatural it felt for April, would it help or make her uncomfortable? In the end, she decided to sit on her hands and just be near.

"And I won't tell anyone."

"Not even Theo?"

"No, not even him."

In the silence that passed, April debated whether to bring up her own pressing troubles with Theo. But the shock of Robyn's confession, and the desire not to drown out her moment of truth, surpassed her need for a fresh perspective. Besides, she still didn't know what questions to ask about her situation anyway.

Lord, if Robyn and Patrick are going through a major relationship crisis, what hope is there for any of us?

- Chapter Twenty-Five -

Two summer storms rolled through the city over the course of the following week, rivaling the turmoil in April's mind. Thankfully only one of them had happened during the day, so her hang-out times with Seth hadn't been affected too much. Being with him continued to provide a respite from the rest of her days, which were filled with thinking about Theo, or being with Theo, or trying to decide what to do about Theo.

"It's not like you're married," her mom said to her on the phone one evening, when she had finally gotten up the nerve to ask for her advice. "If you were, I'd recommend that both of you look into getting help to make it work. But what I'm hearing is very similar to what went on with Cosette, and I think you need to take some time for yourself. You're making this relationship all about him and burying yourself as you go. You've already experienced how unhealthy that is."

April had found a feasible excuse to finish the call shortly after those comments. Theo was *nothing* like Cosette. For starters, he cared about April. Secondly, April was in complete control this time—she was controlling her own choice to put Theo first out of obedience to God. Thirdly, he loved God, and this was a God-honoring relationship, not a friendship borne out of desperation. If she didn't practice making it all about Theo, what kind of Christian love was that?

So much for going to her mom for advice on this stuff.

Maybe Robyn would be willing to share some of the wisdom she'd soon be learning in marriage counselling.

* * *

By the time Thursday rolled around, Robyn and Patrick were anticipating their first appointment with Rick for the following Wednesday evening. He was a Christian marriage counsellor who worked out of a church office in the south of the city, who had come highly recommended by several online reviewers.

In some ways, it was nice to see that people were willing to openly talk about and make recommendations for this sort of thing. Maybe it wasn't shameful to seek marriage counseling after all.

Yeah, but it's a huge blow to the pride when you never even considered it in the realm of possibilities before, Robyn thought as she collected cups to bring to the living room.

Linus was sleeping and Patrick was downstairs grabbing the bags of chips they had bought for tonight.

It felt like an eternity had passed since their last small group gathering. Robyn looked forward to the healthy distraction of having these familiar faces back in their home all together, eager to catch up and dig back into their Ephesians study. Tonight, they were going over the sixth and final chapter, and the following week would be their windup barbecue. It was hard to believe the students would be starting classes again so soon and the small group would be disbanding. Robyn knew she would miss the discussions and the group dynamics.

Yet because of the stilted state of their marriage, Robyn had asked Patrick if it would be wise to cancel small group for one more week, just to avoid the possibility of their tension being noticed.

"No," Patrick had replied matter-of-factly. "We'll be just fine for that. It'll be better to stick to the schedule."

Robyn was all too aware that if tonight's chapter had been the previous one, which included a significant portion on marriage, his answer might have been different.

Robyn's journal was filled with pages about all the big and small ways she felt and saw God's mercy at work. She saw their entire weekend at the cabin as an act of mercy. The fact that new family memories had been formed, and that they'd been unified enough to have fun together for Linus' sake, was a big deal.

Their unified decision to seek counseling gave her immense hope that they could get back on track, and that Patrick was willing to put in the work to forgive her.

And God had mercifully listened to her crying in pain as she wrote down all the things she would miss about Devon, all the feelings she had toward him and the agony with which she grappled over walking away from him after he took that chance to open up his heart to her. She knew he was wrong to do that, but she wasn't capable of not caring that she'd hurt him badly. Yet whenever her prayers turned into supplications for his wellbeing and healing, the Holy Spirit told her that he wasn't hers to pray for.

But who will pray for him, God? Who else knows about what he's going through right now?

Trust me. He is not alone, and he's not yours to pray for. I can provide what he needs. Let him go. In every way, let him go.

Letting go of him was important, but it was difficult. Some moments were harder than others. She looked forward to the day she could think about him and not feel like her heart was twisting right up to the breaking point.

Patrick returned from the basement and loudly opened the crinkly bags, pouring their contents into a few large mixing bowls with reckless abandon. Robyn grimaced, despite the past few weeks demonstrating that Linus could sleep through his dad's noise pollution. The familiar resentment from before went coursing down their well-worn grooves in her brain, but she caught the thoughts that sought to throw her husband under the bus. *Lord, I'm taking more thoughts captive in obedience to you,* she prayed silently. *Here's another one.*

Patrick caught her looking at him. She averted her eyes and carried the cups out to the living room, then came back to pull the pitcher of fruit punch out of the fridge.

"I wonder how big Myla will look," Patrick said as he walked past her with two bowls in his hands.

Robyn waited a moment, then replied, "I guess it could go either way. Either she's showing already, or she'll be one of those moms whose baby belly doesn't stand out until they're, like, halfway along."

Patrick stood up after setting the bowls down, then gave Robyn a lopsided grin. "I hope she's over her morning sickness by now."

The food and drinks were all on the coffee table. They had each placed their Bibles and study notes on separate chairs. Robyn and Patrick stood in the living room and looked at each other, heavy with the awareness of what they usually did next.

Robyn lifted her hand timidly in invitation.

Patrick's eyes shifted down to it. Robyn saw the struggle there, but she didn't lower her hand.

He took a deep breath, reached forward, and took it in his own. The sudden warmth of his large palm against her smaller one brought a lump to her throat. She closed her eyes while Patrick prayed somberly for their evening to be filled with God's wisdom and revelation. Robyn finished the request by asking for encouraging fellowship for everyone. When she said "amen," she opened her eyes and saw that Patrick was gazing at her. His expression was unreadable, but his hold on her hand didn't change.

Outside, tires crunched slowly over gravel as somebody pulled into their driveway. They released each other's hands first and gazes second, then Patrick went to open the door while Robyn sat down and tried to decipher what had just passed between them.

"Helloooo!" Myla's voice entered the room before she did. Robyn turned around in time to see her step inside and give Patrick a side-hug. "You look like your puppy just died, Patrick!" she announced with a playful squeeze. "Maybe this will cheer you up—we brought donuts! Oh, hi, Robyn! How was your trip with April?"

Maybe we should have cancelled tonight after all…

* * *

Half an hour later, with the entire group together and in the throes of discussing what it meant to raise children in the discipline and instruction of the Lord, Robyn noted that April looked smaller than she'd ever seen her. Although she'd been happy to visit with her and Myla upon first arriving, then to join the conversation with Yvette and Faye when they sat down nearby, she visibly shrank when Theo squeezed in next to her after catching up with Patrick and Asher. For his part, Theo's leg was jiggling up and down at regular intervals. Robyn felt nervous just looking at them.

Samuel had been the last to arrive, and he entered the room with exuberant words of greeting that soaked the atmosphere with uncontainable optimism. It set the tone for a great discussion, both for catching up informally and then for moving into the formal study.

Discussing parental wisdom took up a large chunk of time, with Faye and the Zhous sharing their experiences thus far, as well as Myla and Asher's confident beliefs about all the things they were going to do well for their child.

Robyn noted that none of the child-free members of their group had contributed anything for a while, so she interjected with the suggestion of moving on to the next topic.

Patrick read the next study question aloud: "Marriage,

parent/child, and master/bondservant relationships have all been explored in chapters five and six. What are some common themes explained about each of these?"

"All three of them give instructions for both sides of the relationships," Yvette answered quietly, reading from the notes she had written. "And while in each relationship one entity is recognized as the spiritual authority, within that role the person is commanded to treat the other party with love, dignity, and respect. This went against the common understanding of the culture at the time, as wives and children and servants were often treated as lesser beings to be controlled and dominated."

"I think it's still that way, unfortunately," Faye piped up. "Not in every circumstance, but the instructions are still relevant. There's, like, this common force to control and subdue that never fully goes away. Humanity seems to be stuck with it, like a curse."

"I guess that's the gravity of sin working against us," Myla said with a hand on her belly, an obviously familiar gesture despite the current lack of baby bump. "I feel lucky that I never experienced being controlled myself, as a child or as a wife, but I know it's out there. And I want to raise this little one not to fall into either side of that trap."

"Exactly! And how do we, as a church, help protect people from that? How do we teach people how to respond when submission is abused?" Faye asked.

Theo spoke up. "I think it goes back to the parenting we just talked about. If we teach our kids young how to treat others respectfully, then hopefully that sticks when they grow up."

"True, but how do we teach our kids to respect themselves, too?" Faye pressed. "I think it's important to teach respect for others, but—again, I think the church has overall focused on that a lot. I have yet to hear a formal church teaching, *anywhere,* on how to protect yourself from getting caught up in a cycle of abuse and manipulation. There are lots of resources for that out in the world, but within the church…what are *we* teaching about it? How are *we* equipping people?"

"That is a great question," Samuel murmured, looking down at his clasped hands.

"Isn't the point of our faith to be focused on others?" Theo asked, his legs twitching even faster than before. "As soon as we start focusing on ourselves, we lose sight of what's important. We're supposed to look to God first, then others, then ourselves." He began to leaf through his Bible while Patrick spoke up.

"Bringing our attention back to these verses in Ephesians, it does look like some self-awareness would be necessary to know that we're on the right track," he posited. "I mean, how would you know if you were loving your wife and child if you were only thinking about them, and not examining your own self from time to time? So maybe focusing on yourself isn't inherently unhealthy. We're just not meant to make ourselves the center of the universe."

"Or what if you were operating from an unhealthy mindset, and your way of 'showing love' was actually your way of trying to earn something, like favour?" Faye asked quickly. "For example, say-"

"Here it is," Theo interrupted, lifting his open Bible. "Philippians 2:3 says, 'Do nothing out of selfish ambition or vain conceit. Rather, in humility value others above yourselves.'" Also…" he paused and flipped back a few pages. "In Matthew 22:39 Jesus says, 'And the second is like it: "Love your neighbor as yourself."'"

"Yeah, but what if you don't love yourself?" Robyn asked, stopping herself just as she was about to glance at April.

No one responded, so she continued. "If the benchmark for loving others is our self-love, how can we possibly be doing things from a healthy place if we haven't accepted our own value and worth? In that case is the love for others a healthy thing, or is it based on our need for them to validate our worth?"

"That's what I was trying to get at," Faye said. "I don't disagree with the Biblical notion of submitting the way we're instructed to. I just think it's dangerous for the church to be preaching this all the time as if assuming that every person is already prepared to do that in a healthy way. As if there's no one listening to those messages who is already being abused or repressed, or who's in danger of getting into that type of situation because they don't know the warning signs of being manipulated. They might just easily slide into it because 'it's what the Bible says,' but really that's not what the Bible is getting at."

"And what is the Bible getting at, exactly?" Theo asked.

"Godly relationships," Faye responded eagerly. "Most of all, our submission to Christ and our relationship with him, yes. But in these specific passages that we're discussing, the Bible is teaching about how godly relationships not only build each other up, but they actually bring glory to God himself. And how can we do that if we're not equipping people to avoid abusers? Submitting to manipulators and abusers doesn't bring God glory, no matter how much we try to dress it up as 'submission.'"

"Jesus himself submitted to the ultimate abuse," Theo stated with firm conviction. "I'm not saying we should strive for that, exactly, but are you saying we should see ourselves as better than that?"

"Really, Theo?" Faye threw up her hands in exasperation.

"I think," Patrick quickly intervened, "when it comes to the example of Jesus, let's remember that he submitted to the crucifixion with the specific goal of our salvation, and with full knowledge and acceptance of what he was going to go through. That's quite different than people who get manipulated and beaten down against their will."

"But aren't we supposed to have the mind of Christ?" Theo asked, flipping through his Bible again. "Where does it say that?"

"The Bible says we are to be imitators of Christ," Samuel said in his deliberate enunciation. "As a man, that relates back to what we are learning about in Ephesians regarding how to treat others, namely my future wife and future children and anyone in my employment. If I, as a man, am not loving them the way Christ loves the church, then I must repent. There is no room for manipulating them or causing harm in any way. That's all there is to it. Now as to me being submissive, I can ensure that I am not allowing someone to remain in my circle of influence if they are consistently harming me. I'm not to hate them or wish them ill, but I see no Biblical reason to remain in that situation."

"What about turning the other cheek, and giving them your other cloak, and all of that?" Theo asked. "Sounds to me like we're supposed to accept it when things like that happen to us."

"I studied this exact topic a few years back," Asher said. "What it boils down to is this: turning the other cheek isn't referring to staying in a situation where you're being abused. What that passage points to is that we're not supposed to retaliate or seek revenge. But to stay in a relationship or a job where you're being mistreated constantly, that's not necessarily what it means. In fact, if you look at Jesus himself, and his ministry on earth, he was constantly pulling full-stops or sidestepping manipulative people. He barely gave them the time of day. Until it was time for him to submit to being abused, for a specific time and for *our sakes,* knowing full well what he had to go through in order to save us—until then, he didn't put himself under anyone who demanded or twisted his words or tried to sabotage him. He kept his eyes on God and his feet on his mission and surrounded himself with imperfect but supportive, loyal friends."

"Yeah, except for that Judas guy," Myla interrupted with a little laugh.

"Well, even he was fully known and had a role to play that Jesus anticipated," Asher said, looking at her with pure adoration. She wrinkled her nose at him.

Robyn looked around the room at everyone, trying to read their faces. She'd never heard this perspective on Jesus and abuse before; she was curious about how the others in the group would react. There was silence after Asher's words wrapped up, but a few heads were nodding, and she could see the wheels were turning.

"Any other thoughts on these verses before we turn to the rest of the chapter?" Patrick asked.

The discussion moved to the Armour of God, but April heard almost none of it. She couldn't get her mind off what had been said, nor the way her inner self had responded.

Come to me, you who are weary and burdened, and I will give you rest…

- Chapter Twenty-Six -

April pulled up to the sidewalk in front of Seth's house the next day. Theo had insisted on staying at her place for an hour after small group. This morning she was particularly exhausted.

Clarity about their relationship was just a breath away. She could sense it the way a swimmer underwater senses the easing of pressure as they get closer to the surface.

"I love you, April," Theo had said when he finally stood up to leave last night. He had pulled her hands to lift her off the couch and wrapped his arms around her. "Thanks for letting me stay again."

If I said no, you would have been angry at me, she thought sadly against his chest. This chest had once spoken to her of being safe and loved, of being wrapped in his masculine protectiveness. Now she felt trapped there. How much longer could she put his needs first? She was running on empty.

But maybe her mom was right. Maybe everyone at small group was right. This relationship wasn't abusive, but it was growing manipulative. At least, that's what seemed to click briefly after that heavy discussion at the Zhous'. Or did it just seem that way, since she was trying so hard to surrender her own needs and wants to him? Was this just part of the growing pains of following God's will?

Theo was *not* a manipulator. She refused to think so poorly of him.

But what did you call it when someone emotionally strong-armed you into doing everything his way?

Yet she was *choosing* to do things his way. So, it wasn't his fault. Not completely, anyway. And was it really that bad after all?

God, are you happy with me? she asked with little feeling while waiting for Theo's hug to end.

Theo placed his finger under her chin and tilted her face up. She allowed him to kiss her, recognized her own cold-fish performance, and put a little effort back, begging it to be over soon. But Theo seemed determined to show her how strongly he felt about her, and she pretended to reciprocate until *finally* he pulled away and smiled down at her.

When he left in a happy mood, April knew she should be pleased with herself for a successful night, yet there was an underlying emptiness that gnawed at her until she fell into a fitful sleep.

The hot, sunny morning that had greeted her when she left her house spoke of things to come. On the way to Seth's, the weather forecast predicted strong thunderstorms this afternoon. Surprise, surprise.

She and Seth enjoyed a hot but successful morning walk under the tree-lined canopy of Spadina Crescent along the north side of the river. The loud rush of water from the weir provided a welcome distraction, as did the intense focus on helping Seth navigate the many rifts and cracks along the sidewalk. Thankfully, he managed them extremely well, and they made it all the way down to Queen Street and back without a single cell phone in sight.

Thank goodness. I don't know if I would've had the energy to deal with a screen-inspired episode today, April thought as she helped him back into her car afterward.

By now the sky had begun to cloud over. The temperature dropped low enough to cool their sweaty skin. When they pulled up at Seth's house to the sound of rolling thunder, a few fat drops plopped against the windshield.

"Just on time, Seth!" April said. "Let's get inside quickly." She helped him out of the car and, since he held her book in one hand with a particularly strong focus on the page he was lining, she decided not to bother asking him to leave it in the backseat for Monday. The sky could unleash at any second.

With his slow gait they couldn't quite get to the steps at a speed that matched her liking, but they managed to get inside the house and settled into the living room before the sound of millions of heavy rain pebbles unleashed upon the roof and windows.

"We made it!" she sighed, plopping down next to him on the couch. He was still lining, but had slowed down to take in the sounds of the sudden storm. His contented face relaxed even more. It was easy to imagine how this constant thrum of noise quieted his mind, much like it did hers. April closed her eyes and leaned her head back, soaking it all in—the rain, Seth's company, and her own deep breaths.

The flash of light that registered through her closed lids was followed immediately by a clap of thunder that shook the house and jolted her heart. Seth startled beside her and looked over at the window with alarm, dropping his book.

"Wow, that was loud!" April said with a short laugh as she bent down to pick up the book. "Here, you keep lining and I'll make lunch in case the power goes out soon. Don't want to keep opening and closing the fridge once that happens," she continued as she made her way down the hall.

"How about a ham sandwich and some applesauce?" she called out. Her familiarity with this kitchen had turned it into a place that felt a little bit like home. As she pulled the required foods out of the fridge and set them on the black granite countertop, the crescendo of the wind drew her attention to the window.

Just then another sound, quiet and musical, caught her attention from a corner of the house.

Her cell phone rang from her purse in the front doorway. She frowned at the intrusion. Theo, Robyn, and her family knew perfectly well that she was not to be called during her hours with Seth, and Seth's parents certainly would know better. Running to grab it, she stabbed the "end call" button before looking at the caller display. It was Seth's dad, Leonard.

"I'll be right back, Seth, just running downstairs for a minute!" she called cheerfully while fighting back concern. Shoving her phone back in her purse, she took the whole thing down to the basement. Even if Seth overheard the noises of a phone conversation, she knew he wouldn't be able to follow her down there.

She was halfway down the steps when another thunderous explosion jarred the house, accompanied by a seemingly unnatural flash of brightness. Seth's cry of alarm sent her running back up to him, abandoning her purse on one of the basement steps. She'd never heard him sound so afraid.

"Seth, it's okay," she said, dropping to her knees in front of him so she could hold both of his hands. "It's just noise and light, buddy. I know it's startling, but we're safe." His hands were trembling. A wave of compassion and protectiveness suddenly consumed her, but she knew she had to leave him to try calling Leonard back.

The cloudy sky had rendered it necessary to turn on the living room lights when they had arrived home. Now, with a flicker, they went off. Seth looked up and around with wide eyes.

"You can still see the book," April said, pointing to the novel that had dropped to the floor again. She picked it up and opened it in the middle, then began to follow the lines herself until Seth joined her. At first, his finger trembled along its dimly-lit path, but as she watched his progress the page grew darker and darker. She looked over at the window.

The sky had gone from gray to black.

When the first gust of the wind's new velocity hit the side of the house, April's mouth turned into sawdust. She could feel the pressure change with every fibre of her being. The hairs on her neck bristled.

"Seth, we need to get downstairs," she heard herself saying as she rose on mechanical legs. Her hands took his in a futile attempt to pull him up.

Something heavy thudded against the living room window. April and Seth jumped.

"We need to go *now!*" she commanded loudly, just above the ever-increasing howling outside. A mental image of Seth surrounded by broken glass and being pummelled by the wind gave her an extra burst of strength. She brought him to his feet, tossing aside any concern that she might be bruising his wrists. They moved toward the kitchen while Seth resisted weakly, making scared noises along the way. Then April turned toward the basement stairs and began pulling him down toward the top step as she made her way in reverse. His force of panic rivalled her will to save. He yanked back so quickly she had to grab the banister to keep herself from falling backward down the long staircase. Regaining her balance, she looked up to see that Seth was turning back toward the living room.

"No, Seth, it's not safe in there!" she cried out.

Terror was nipping at her heels, but concern for Seth propelled her down the stairs toward her hastily abandoned purse. April pulled out her cell phone, ran upstairs and into the living room, and saw that Seth was once again sitting on the couch with his hands over his ears, rocking back and forth with a keening wail that matched the wind.

"Seth, look!" April called, holding the object of his obsession straight out in front of her. "You want to see this? I'll let you hold it, but you have to come and get it."

The cell phone was right there, and all the noise outside and in his head funnelled into that one little direction, because all he had to do was reach out and take it. It was moving now and April was moving with it, so he got up as fast as he could to take it before it would get hidden away, but it kept moving and moving until now it was moving down. Seth felt his foot touch nothing when he stepped forward, so he reached out and grabbed something to hold onto, and he yelled because he had almost fallen down the basement stairs and because the phone was out of reach.

April was scaring him and the house was so loud, like he'd never heard it before. All the hairs on his arms were standing up, which usually meant it was cold, but now it was a different reason and he didn't like that feeling, and now there was also the NEED to grab the cell phone. His world was breaking apart until he could grab that phone and make everything stop because his arms, his legs, everything in him was moving in that direction but not actually going anywhere, and being stuck between moving and not-moving was the worst agony, and he couldn't shake it off, and he couldn't stop the NEED until he got to that cell phone, but it was down the stairs and he was stuck and he screamed, screamed, SCREAMED. Then it got worse because hands were grabbing his arm and pulling him down, and April's voice was saying things that he couldn't understand over the noise in his head. Why was April trying to make him fall?

She was pulling on him, but he didn't want her to do that, so he shook his arm but she kept holding on and then he started to lose his balance, but suddenly his foot touched down on the top step, but his toes were off the edge and it wasn't safe—didn't she know he couldn't do stairs? She released his arm and his hand shot out to press against the wall, and that kept him upright. Now was his chance, so he turned and tripped and fell, and he hated falling, but he had to get away, so he crawled back to the living room, even though it was noisier there, but maybe April would let him stay this time instead of trying to make him fall. Why did she want to make him fall down the stairs? Why was it so loud everywhere?

With her chest too constricted to breathe properly, April ran up into the kitchen. Watching Seth almost tumble headlong down the stairs on top of her was too much. This wouldn't work, and she might be running out of time to try this way. What if the wind died down soon, and she broke both of their bodies for nothing?

Another idea popped into her head as her eye caught sight of the window-less bathroom at the other end of the hall.

He was sitting on the couch again and the noise was unbearable, but then the cell phone was in his face and the NEED rose so quickly he shot his hand out toward it, but now the phone was moving away again. This time it was not going toward the kitchen, so Seth followed and felt the disconnect between moving and not-moving growing larger and more uncomfortable again, so he walked even faster until he had the phone in his hands as easily as if nobody wanted to hide it from him. He was lining, lining, lining on the lighted screen, and the disconnect morphed into a connected energy that burned like lava through his veins, and the pressure inside him was bulging through his entire body and then it reached the top and it BROKE OUT, so he threw the phone and heard the cracking sound when it hit something. That's when he noticed there was complete darkness all around him, and April's voice was saying things that he still couldn't understand. The noise in the house was loud, it was screaming, it was full of thousands of loud pops and then an exploding, crashing noise from somewhere. The screaming loud noise was even louder than before, and what was that new rattling noise, and that wind at his feet? And then the rattling stopped, and April was still talking but her voice was higher than usual and Seth had no control over anything, he couldn't see anything, but he could hear and feel it all, and he flung his arms around and kicked and scratched and hit because he didn't know what else to do with the TOO MUCH TOO MUCH TOO

MUCH.

April braced herself against the door and begged God to keep her strong while the wind from the broken living room window rammed itself relentlessly against the thin layer of wood at her back. She could feel the gust from the thin crack under the door blowing against her feet like a messenger announcing the advance of a merciless enemy. Seth was screaming in the dark near the bathtub. She knew there was nothing else she could do for him, and ached for his fear that she had no control over.

The first blow came as a surprise—just a grazing hand across her arm. But it was followed by another and another, all coming faster and harder and accompanied by Seth's screams. April held back cries of alarm while Seth's fingernails scratched her flesh and his hands struck her face and chest. He kicked her legs and the door beside them, almost knocking her down, but she couldn't lose her post between him and the storm.

"God, please!" The plea tore out of April's throat, detached from her ability to think while the wind shrieked in an unearthly multi-toned harmony, breaking down her sense of reality. She was aware of every detail of how the pressurized door felt at her back, yet disconnected as if experiencing it by proxy from within someone else's body. Death's possibility settled into her nightmarish haze, but just as convincing was the notion that she'd wake up soon in her own bed. She had no control over either outcome. All she could do was hold her post and wait to see what would happen. Images of her parents, Britney, and grandparents flew across her soul with a muted pang of regret that she might have to say good-bye; then Theo, with a sense of sadness and release.

A smack to the side of her head threw her off-balance. Her feet began to slip and she thought, *this is it.*

Other things started crashing around in the bathroom as Seth turned to flail in other directions. The lack of assault against her body allowed April to notice that the breeze against her slipping feet had stilled, and the noise of the wind had died down. The pressurized atmosphere was slinking away. The realization made her feel boneless.

She slid all the way to the floor and leaned her forehead against her raised knees, breathing erratically.

It was over. They were both going to live.

A minute might have passed, or it could have been ten. The crashing noises from across the dark room ceased.

April gathered her wits into order. Seth had needed her to protect him in the storm. Now he needed her to show him the way forward, at least until help arrived.

"Hey Seth," she said, faking confidence. "I'm going to open the door and see if it's safe out there."

He fell so silent she wondered if he had passed out in the panic, yet she hadn't heard him hit the floor.

When she raised herself up and cracked open the door, sunlight shot into the darkness as if the storm they'd experienced was simply some kind of lighthearted cosmic joke.

April looked back to see into the now-illuminated bathroom. Seth was standing perfectly still near the toilet, looking for all the world like the life had gone out of him. She took advantage of his numb state and stepped in the hallway.

Sparkles of shattered glass littered the floor about ten feet down the hall, right across from the living room. Making her way carefully along the corridor, she took note of where on the floor it would be safe to step.

When she turned into the living room, she gasped. A large, mangled tree branch lay across the area rug and angled up against Seth's favourite spot on the couch. Scattered leaves, glass shards, and ripped magazines cast a surreal texture over every square inch of the room. April had the sensation of watching herself from behind as she moved her gaze around to survey the damage, fixating back to the spot on the couch where Seth had been sitting in terror less than a minute before the branch was hurled through the window.

She watched herself with curiosity as trembling set in, but the logical part of her mind took over her actions.

Seth needed to rest. April rotated so that her back was to the living room, and she was now looking at Seth's closed bedroom door.

"Thank you, God," she muttered breathlessly when she opened his door to see that nothing was damaged. His bed and dresser were completely undisturbed. All the books, childhood toys, and decorations sat neatly on their shelves. Most importantly, his window was intact.

The impact of such a normal scene was jarring.

Seth was easily guided toward his bedroom. April helped him lie down on top of his dark-green duvet, when she noticed that he'd had an accident. With no resistance from him at all, she pulled off his soiled shorts and underwear and dug through his drawers for fresh ones. It was a bit awkward, but she managed to pull them back up his legs and over his hips while he lay on his back, staring upward with half-mast eyes. Then she sat on the edge of the bed beside him and dared a kiss on his forehead.

"You're safe now, Seth," she whispered in a husky voice. "You're safe."

- Chapter Twenty-Seven -

Sirens wailed in the distance. April let out a slow breath at the realization that someone else would be taking charge soon. The world outside was mobilizing to respond to whatever disasters had fallen. She trusted that Seth's parents would also be racing home as quickly as possible.

How were Robyn and Linus? Theo? Had anyone in the city gotten hurt…or worse? She wished she could go to her cell and try reaching out, but the way Seth threw it, she was positive it was broken.

Seth had fallen asleep on his bed, his even breathing becoming a pattern that she forced her own respiration to follow. April refused to leave his side, despite the growing aches that had begun to announce themselves from various places around her body. Wiping at a slow trickle of blood from just beneath her lip, she registered the slow pulsation of deep bruises forming on her arms and legs. There was a sharp throbbing in her lower ribs and several painful tingling sensations growing sharper along her upper arms and neck where Seth's nails had made terrified tracks.

"God, please help him to be okay," she whispered fervently. What had this experience painted on Seth's gentle spirit?

How would he see her from now on, after being confined in the dark against his will by someone he trusted? She didn't know if she could have done anything differently to keep him safe, but could she have at least made it easier on him somehow?

Traffic was starting to pick up, its noise amplified by the lack of sound barrier that the tree branch had created in the living room.

Someone pounded on the door.

"Are you okay in there?"

It was a man's voice, unfamiliar. April rose off the bed, stepped into a pair of Seth's rubber-soled slippers, and tip-toed through the shattered glass until she was safely in the front entryway.

"We're…we're okay," she announced after she pulled open the door. There was an elderly gentleman that she'd never seen before, hair disheveled and mouth agape.

"I'm Harold," he said breathlessly. "I live across the street and I just looked out and saw the broken window. How is the boy?" he asked, eyebrows angled up in deep concern.

"He's safe, he's sleeping now," April said.

"Oh my lord, look at you! You need an ambulance!" Harold gasped.

April's hand shot up to her face, but squealing tires caused both her and the man to look toward the street, where Leonard's car was careening up onto the driveway. It screeched to a halt and he was out in record time, running toward the door.

"April, Harold! Are you alright?" he asked, breathing heavily. His face showed surprise when he looked closely at April, but then he asked, "Where's Seth?"

"He's safe, he's sleeping in his bedroom," she said quickly.

"Oh, thank God," Leonard breathed, then took her by the arm and started into the house. He turned back around to ask Harold if he and Ruth were okay.

"Yes, yes, we're okay, just a bit shaken up. I saw the broken window and just wanted to check. Looks like your girl here might need a doctor," he replied. "I'll go check on the rest of the neighbourhood."

While the older man sauntered down the front steps, April and Leonard crunched their way to Seth's room. Father sat down beside son and felt his pulse. Seth stirred slightly, then rolled over onto his side.

"Leonard!" Vanessa's yell preceded her hurried footsteps.

"In here," Leonard replied with a deep voice.

She came flying around the corner and practically dove onto her knees beside Seth's bed.

April stood apart from them and answered their barrage of questions. Hearing herself talk made everything sink in, cementing the reality of what just happened. Vanessa rose and came to her, pulling her into a tender hug. The move was so unexpected, both in the simple fact of it occurring and in the welcome April gave it. She leaned into Vanessa and held on desperately.

"Thank you for protecting our boy," Vanessa said in a tone that implied the words were not enough.

* * *

Vanessa drove April to the nearest hospital, despite the young woman's insistence that she was fine. Leonard would stay home and keep observing Seth.

The waiting room in emergency wasn't as busy as April had expected. From some of the conversations they overheard, the storm had caused some structural damage in the far east of the city, but most of Saskatoon had only felt the effects of a stronger-than-usual wind. It was indeed a small tornado that had touched down on the outskirts of their suburb with unusual suddenness. With no media on in the house, April and Seth had had no warning other than what Leonard had attempted to provide by phoning her cell.

While they waited, Vanessa asked April who she would like to call.

"My mom." April's voice cracked on that. "If she sees the news, she'll be worried." *And I need her.*

Vanessa handed her the phone and said, "Take your time."

When April heard her mom's greeting, she nearly broke down.

After filling her in, she fielded about a dozen rapid-fire questions that eventually ended with, "We're coming down tonight. I'll bring supper and take care of you."

"Sounds good. Mom? Can you call Theo for me? The nurse is calling me in now."

She handed the phone back to Vanessa and stood up from the plastic chairs.

* * *

An hour later, April was being driven to her own house with a butterfly bandage on her chin and an ice pack against her lower ribs. She'd been prescribed antibiotic ointment for the scratches that had broken skin.

"Looks like you have company," Vanessa said, drawing April's attention away from the console and out toward her front yard, where Theo paced anxiously in his shirt-and-tie work attire while rubbing his hand through his hair. When he saw the vehicle pull over, his eyes met April's through the passenger window. He jogged over.

"Are you Theo?" Vanessa asked, stepping out while Theo yanked open April's door, unbuckled her, and pulled her out of the car before she had a chance to react.

"Ouch!" April yelped when he pulled her into a tight squeeze.

"Careful! Her ribs are bruised," Vanessa said sharply. "April, are you alright?"

"Yes," she gasped, leaning away from Theo. "Thanks, Vanessa. Please call me when you know how Seth's doing. I feel so awful about what he went through." Her words slurred slightly from the freezing in her chin.

"You went through just as much," Vanessa said in a kind but

firm voice. "Let your parents and Theo take care of you this weekend. We'll be in touch."

She drove away. Theo kept his arms around April, but he didn't squeeze this time.

"I'm so sorry, April. I didn't mean to hurt you, I just got overwhelmed with how good it is to see you. I'll be more careful. Can I get you anything?" They walked together toward the house.

"My parents will be bringing supper tonight," April said, wondering if she'd have an appetite by then. "I think I just need some water. And to lie down for a bit."

The keys were not cooperating with her fumbling fingers, so Theo took over and let them into the house. April sat down at the kitchen table and laid her head down against her arms while Theo filled a glass from the sink and brought it to her. After a few tentative sips, April drained the cup and asked for more. When was the last time she'd had anything to drink?

Thirst satiated, she made her way to her room and gingerly laid down on her bed, not even bothering to make a suggestion about how Theo might make himself comfortable. He pulled out the chair from her computer desk and sat down beside her, grimacing with concern as he surveyed her face and arms.

"When I heard about the tornado being right near Seth's neighbourhood, I almost lost it," he admitted. "Then I couldn't get you on your phone, and they wouldn't let us leave the building until the wind was over." He rubbed his hand over his face. "Seeing you here, safe, is the best feeling in the world. You have no idea."

"I'm glad you're okay too," she said tiredly. "Have you heard from anyone else?"

"My family's all good. Everyone on the small group chat checked in to say they're fine. I let them know about you. Everyone's praying for a quick recovery."

"That's good. That's nice of them. It's really not that bad."

"I know it could have been worse," Theo said, "but I hate that you got hurt at all."

April shrugged slightly. "I hate that Seth was so scared. I'll heal up fine. I'm just worried about what he'll be like after this. Like, I wonder if he thinks I was trying to hurt him, or-"

"Does it matter what he thinks?" Theo blurted out, then leaned back in the chair and shook his head. "Sorry."

"No kidding," she bit back. "I shouldn't have said anything about him. This conversation is over."

"I'm sorry," he restated while he stood up and paced away from her. "It's just that I feel so protective of you. And it wasn't the tornado that hurt you. It was Seth. If any other guy laid a hand on you like that, for any reason at all, I'd be kicking down his door right now. I know that's not appropriate for this situation, but I can't help it."

"Well, then, *learn* to help it," she said angrily. "I refuse to listen to anything else you have to say about it. He did *nothing* wrong to me. It wasn't his fault. End of story."

"Maybe not, but…you could have locked him in the bathroom and gone downstairs yourself. He would have been just as safe. Or you could have-"

"Stop."

Theo shut his mouth and looked down at her in surprise.

The silence grew heavy while Theo fidgeted, uncertain of how to proceed.

Suddenly, a look of alarm passed over his face and he said, "Whoa, April, be gentle to yourself. Take a slow breath." Caring and concern took over his voice again. April realized she was standing up, unaware of how she had gotten there. But she was breathing hard, punctuating the pain in her ribs fiercely, and she felt fire in her eyes.

"I *am* taking a breath, and you know what? I'm done trying to stuff everything inside all the time. I feel like I have a lot to say right now, so you'd better be ready."

Theo looked scared as he sat back down.

"Seth is important to me, Theo. Not only is he one of the best and purest and kindest people I know, but he's given me more in friendship than almost *anyone* else ever has. I chose to protect him and be with him at all costs, because there was no other thought. I love him, and I had to do it. That's all there is to it. I know you don't like it, but I'm done trying to bend over backward to fit into whatever it is you seem to like.

"And you know what? Theo, I'm sick and tired of this," she said, motioning her hand between the two of them. "I'm done trying to make you happy all the time at my own expense. Do you know what I realized today?" She shot out her open hand in his direction when she saw him opening his mouth. "No, no, don't interrupt me, don't you *dare* interrupt me."

Theo's eyes clouded over, but he closed his mouth.

April continued. "Today, I thought I might die. Like, I actually thought this could be it. And do you know what hit me like a ton of bricks a little while later, when I realized what a gift it was that I could keep on *living*?" She slowed down her rate of speech and forced a few long, slow breaths. Her pain was frustratingly opposed to the speed with which her thoughts wanted to tumble out.

"I realized…that I put Seth's safety first because I love him. Simple as that. And then…and then I thought about you, and how I've been trying to put you first in our relationship, but not for the same reason. It's because I haven't loved myself. With Seth, I never struggled with thoughts of my worth; I was only focused on his. With you, and with most people, I struggle with my worth all the time. And you…whether you mean to or not…*you* make me question my worth because you take over and squeeze me out for your own agenda. I've been trying to put you first because I thought that's what a good Christian and girlfriend does. But I've just been barely surviving, trying to gain approval from you and from God. I can't do it anymore."

Theo reached forward and clasped one of her hands with intensity. "April, listen to me. I don't know where that wrong motivation comes from, but I never asked you to try and be *approved* by me. In my eyes, you have more value than you seem to realize. And God, well, you know he loves you just as you are. You have nothing to prove, and you never did."

April held his eyes, confusion threatening the clarity that had flooded her system until a moment ago. Carefully, she sat back down on the edge of her bed.

"Maybe not," she offered. "Maybe you do value me, but… you seem to expect things of me that I can't give. We started off strong, but over time it seems like you've become harder and harder to please. Even when I try to do what you want, and even though I try to stuff my own thoughts and ideas down if I think they'll contradict yours, it seems like it's never enough."

"April, I knew you were shrinking into yourself, and I was just trying to prevent that from happening," he replied with glistening eyes. "I love you and I want us to figure things out. Worrying about losing you today, it made me realize even more how much I love you. I'm sorry for doing the wrong things and hurting you. Please, let's figure this out together. We'll do better going forward."

"I'm tired of doing," she sighed, closing her eyes and letting her hand fall limp inside of Theo's. "It's always *doing* with you, Theo, and never just *being*. I can't do it anymore. It's just not working."

Theo let his head drop while he squeezed her hand even tighter.

"April don't do this to me. Please, don't do this."

"I need to sleep," April said, suddenly drained beyond measure. She pulled her hand away and laid down, wincing as she turned to face the wall.

As sweet rest overtook her, the last thing she saw in her mind's eye was the face of Jesus as she imagined him. He was looking down with love as he untangled her from a thornbush, pulling spiky branches out of the wool that surrounded her body, bloody rivulets trickling down his hands.

- Chapter Twenty-Eight -

Her parents and Britney stayed the full weekend after the tornado, making meals and watching movies with her and even cleaning the house from top to bottom—for which her roommates expressed surprised gratitude. They were still mostly out of the house with their own busy lives, which suited April just fine.

The updates from Vanessa were encouraging. Seth was doing well, and although he was annoyed by all the activity in the house when their living room window got replaced and the entire first floor got professionally cleaned, he was physically fine and seemed emotionally secure. Other than now requiring the bathroom door to remain open when he needed to use it, he was going about his days with confidence. April thanked God for the answer to her most oft-repeated prayer in the days since the storm.

Theo had been gone when she'd woken up from her impromptu nap on Friday evening. Her mom said that he'd sat by her bed until they arrived.

"He said that you were really upset with him, so he wanted to give you space for a few days," she had explained, looking carefully at April's face for a reaction. April didn't know exactly what she was feeling, and she didn't know what her mom would have seen; all April knew was that one particular weight was off her shoulders but replaced with the new weight of unfinished business.

Patrick and Robyn stopped by on Saturday afternoon to deliver cinnamon buns and flowers. They stayed for a visit, which consisted of Patrick and Britney following Linus all over the house to clean up books and decorations and other items in his wake. April enjoyed the comic relief of the little toddler exploring this non-childproofed environment. Robyn sat with her on the couch while April's mom served coffee, and her dad mowed the overgrown lawn.

The freedom of speaking plainly was a new and overpowering rush, as if yesterday's honest conversation with Theo had unlocked something mighty from within. Yet her ribs wouldn't allow more than a few sentences to be spoken slowly at one time before she needed a break. Eager to share her thoughts with her closest friend and the mother with whom she shared a newfound, tenuous understanding, she brought her journal over to the couch and flipped it to that morning's entry.

"I'd like you both to read this," she said shyly. "And let me know what you think."

Robyn took the journal from April's hands, and April's mom sat down beside her. They leaned their heads together while the room fell quiet. April sank down into the opposite chair and slowly sipped her coffee, engaging her interest in the blue sky outside of the window while running those thoughts over and over in her mind.

I think I'm catching on to something. I think I've been running on a parallel road to where I was supposed to be. I thought I was running the race laid out in the Bible, and it probably looked the same on the outside, but I haven't been powered by God. I've been powered by the motivation of trying to be good enough. To not let anyone down. To feel like I can reach out and touch just a scrap of a sense of God's love for me, because I can't seem to hold on to any true sense of being loved, and I want it so bad, and it seemed like trying hard to be a good follower of Jesus would help me get there. But it hasn't, not really. I do believe God wants me to trust him, but I don't believe I've been able to because I'm not looking at him. I've been looking at myself this whole time, hoping me and my actions are good enough.

It was easy for me to accept the whole 'put others before yourself' idea because I hated myself. For not being good enough, and for not being an easy person to accept at face value. I didn't fully love others the way I thought I did. Instead I hated myself, and that made it easy to put others' needs first. It wasn't true submission. It was desperation. And it was breaking me down over time. I believed that this was part of God's design for maturing me as a Christian, so I accepted that he wanted me to keep on stuffing my needs and personality deep inside because that would help other people see how unselfishly he loves them.

Maybe I need to take a step back. Not from God or my faith, but from the way I've been operating in life. Maybe I need to learn to accept how much God loves me with no strings attached. Maybe I'll even learn to love myself enough, so that laying myself down for others truly is Biblical submission—truly is sacrificial love—and comes from the source of God's love. Not from my own insecurities.

"April," her mom said quietly, drawing her attention away from the window and toward the feet of the woman who had raised her.

"So anyway," April said, feeling self-conscious. "That's where I'm at."

"I'm amazed." Her mom shook her head and smiled. "One of my biggest prayers for my daughters is that you would both grow closer to God and realize how much he loves you. This is wonderful to read."

April's blush felt like a furnace.

"This is important stuff, April," Robyn concurred.

"I think…I think I'm going to break up with Theo," April said quickly, before she could change her mind about the declaration. She was done with letting feelings of inadequacy take the lead on her actions.

"No!" Britney exclaimed, making April jump. The teenager emerged from the kitchen, a half-eaten cinnamon bun in her hand and a look of despair in her face. "Don't do it, April! Theo is so awesome!"

April's mom stood up and put her arm around her younger daughter. "Britney, I know you've grown attached to him. But this is April's choice to make. You and I can discuss your feelings about it when we get home."

Britney looked at her mom with wide eyes, but the older woman's firm look under raised eyebrows prompted the upset girl to keep her thoughts to herself. She shrugged with a dramatic sigh and wandered back into the kitchen.

"That's a big decision," her mom offered carefully as she returned to her spot on the couch. "If you don't mind me saying so, I've suspected for a few weeks that this relationship isn't healthy for you. I'll support you either way, but if you end up deciding to stay together, I hope you'll *both* be willing to make some changes."

"Like what?" April asked, pushing down the defensiveness that was clamoring to colour her voice. Part of her wanted to explain what had occurred when she'd thought she might die—how the fleeting impression of leaving Theo behind had hammered home her need to be free of the relationship—but that moment was already half-buried in a pile of things she didn't want to relive. She left it there and focused on her mom.

"I think you have to be willing to stick to your guns every time you don't agree with him, even if it's uncomfortable," her mom said with thoughtful deliberation. "And I think he needs to learn how to turn himself down so he can really tune into you. Most of all, I think you need to keep a firm grip on your relationship with God. What you're saying today is the absolute truth. God's love for you is total and complete, and if you can keep your eyes on him, as you say, you will have the power to navigate the people-pleasing tendencies I'm afraid I've passed down to you." She smiled sympathetically. "And April, I know I said it already, but I'm sorry for not making enough space for you when you were growing up. I wish I could go back and help you see what I saw with you and Cosette."

April looked down. "It's okay," she said softly. "I'm just glad you and Dad are here. And I appreciate hearing your views on me and Theo now."

There was a frantic "No, no, no!" and a small crash from somewhere down the hall. The women laughed as Patrick walked back into the living room with a grubby-handed Linus in his arms.

"Let me guess. The plant?" April asked.

"Yep," Patrick sighed. "We've made quite a mess. I'm sorry. Robyn, can you…?"

"It's okay, I can help," her mom offered. Patrick handed the baby off to Robyn, and he went back down the hall while April's mom pulled the broom and dustpan out of the space beside the fridge.

"Your mom's wise," Robyn said once they had left. "And I have to agree with her, that I've been wondering if you and Theo were okay together. I'm sorry I didn't bring it up before, but I didn't want to mention it until I was surer. And then…" she trailed off, wiping dirt off her lips where Linus had just brushed his hand.

"Yeah, I know. Don't worry about it. I might not have been ready to hear it from the outside, but inside of me I had strong suspicions that something wasn't quite right between us." She swallowed past the lump in her throat. "And the thought of breaking his heart, and of missing him in my life, is awful. But I can't un-see what I've seen. I can't go back to the way it was before."

"Do you think he'd be open to a re-do in your relationship? Trying again, but with the things your mom just said?"

"I don't know. Maybe you can pass along some marriage wisdom?"

"Ha!" Robyn laughed humourlessly. "I wish. I thought I knew

so much, but these past few months have been rather humbling on that front."

"How are you guys doing?"

Robyn stopped to listen. Patrick and April's mom had started having their own conversation in the hallway. They seemed quite engrossed in whatever they were discussing.

"We're doing okay," Robyn replied quietly. "There's a lot to unpack, but we're saving those heavy topics for counselling. We both realize that talking about it without professional help might cause more problems at this point."

"And that starts on Wednesday, right?"

"Yes, the day before the windup," she said. "I've really enjoyed small group this summer, but I'm glad it's ending. Given our circumstances, I don't know if we'll have the energy to focus outside of our marriage for a while. And it would be harder and harder to keep things private, I think."

April nodded.

"Aren't we both glorious messes?" Robyn said with a wry smile.

"Yes," April replied, touching the hard little butterfly bandage on her chin. "Thanks for being messy with me."

"You're...welcome?" Robyn laughed loud enough to draw the attention of the others, who emerged from the hallway with the broom and an overflowing dustpan.

Linus clapped his dirty hands together and laughed along.

- Chapter Twenty-Nine -

On Monday morning, Patrick left for work. Robyn played with Linus and introduced him to the joys of finger-painting with chocolate pudding. She then spent the next half-hour trying to decide if the project had been worth the extra bath, the sticky mess that somehow found its way onto the white throw blanket in the living room, and the tantrum when she wouldn't let him eat the paper he'd painted on.

God, parenthood often makes me think about how we all struggle while you try to raise us, she prayed while cuddling Linus in the rocking chair, savoring the way he relaxed into her arms and dozed off. She lacked any motivation to put him in the crib for his nap today. If she could sit like this with him for an hour or two, it's not like the world would fall apart.

You give us good things, and we manage to mess them up. Yet I know how much your love wraps around us even then.

Robyn prayed for April, especially in her decision about whether or not to break up with Theo.

She prayed for her own marriage, and for Patrick's healing. It was still difficult to surrender control of this area to God, but he continued to make it clear that she was not to expect entrance where she wasn't yet permitted. Hopefully in time their intimacy would return. In the meantime, all she could do was pray, show her love, and wait.

When will I ever stop crying? she thought, annoyed with the too-familiar sensations of a wet face and tight throat. While grateful that she hadn't gone through with kissing Devon, she knew that even the temptation to go there had turned Patrick away from feeling safe to engage in this act of love with her. She knew it wasn't her right to ask one of him, and so she wouldn't. But she craved that contact to the core of her being. There was so much renewal and love to express to him whenever he was ready—and although she felt guilty admitting it to herself, she was desperate to know that he could love her wholeheartedly again.

* * *

Over the weekend, Vanessa had let April know that they would pay her for the full week of support but that she and Leonard were taking that time off work to stay with Seth.

"There are only two summer weeks left, so we know that you and Seth were going to part ways soon," she said, "but would you be willing to come over for a short visit with him sometime later in the week, when you're feeling up for it? We think it would do him a world of good to see you again."

"Absolutely!" April agreed, thankful that Vanessa had obviously trusted her when she had said she held no ill will or fear toward Seth. "When do you want me to come?"

They settled on Thursday, which meant April had a few days mostly alone. She filled her time by going for a few short walks, buying a new cell phone with money from Seth's parents, and trying not to notice the stares of the people who passed her by.

Although she kept in regular contact with her parents and Robyn, she hadn't yet replied to Theo's check-in text on Monday.

After much prayer and soul-searching, she knew what she had

to do.

Finally, she responded to him that she was doing okay physically. Then she ended the text with: We need to talk. Can you come over tonight?

Earlier in their relationship, when things were easier, she and Theo used to laugh at phrases like that. He called it "the most dreaded phrase a boyfriend can ever hear." April didn't want to use such a stereotypical cluster of words, but she hoped to ease Theo into their new reality as best she could.

A simple okay was his response.

Three hours later, just as she was pulling out some leftover chicken casserole from the fridge, Theo knocked on the door.

Her roommate, Dara, was in the kitchen, reading a magazine while she finished off the last of her salad. When Theo entered the house, a thick tension descended so suddenly that Dara took her salad into her room, shooting April a knowing look.

"Hey," he said sheepishly from the doorway.

"Hey," she replied. "Want some casserole?"

He stepped into the kitchen with heartbreaking vulnerability. "I'm not hungry right now." He looked at the floor, then back up at her. "I'm just here to listen to what you have to say."

He knew. The resignation was all over him. While that should have made it easier to bring up the topic, now she wanted to protect him somehow.

She closed the fridge door and stood up straight, looking Theo in the eye, then looking away.

"I think we should break up," she pushed out.

Fear and sympathy screamed *no, no, no!*

Everything else said *yes.*

The faucet dripped. There was a shuffling noise as Theo stuffed his hands in his pockets. He was dressed in his after-work clothes—a t-shirt and jeans. April had to ignore how strongly she wanted to place her hands over his upper arms and lean in to feel his heartbeat against her face.

Is this the right plan? she asked herself, already knowing the answer.

"It wasn't fair of me to jump all over you on Friday," she continued. "But I do think I needed to say what I did. I just wish I could have been calmer. But it's all true. And I want you to know it's not all your fault. I have a lot to learn about myself, and I need space for that."

Theo was staring at the floor. After a brief silence he asked, "So it's the old 'I need space' breakup, is it?"

April felt something crack inside of her, but she knew it wasn't her resolve.

"I'm so sorry," she said past the lump in her throat. "I don't know what else to say about it right now."

"I tried so hard," Theo said. "I really did, April. I'm sorry. I loved you. I still do."

"I tried so hard, too," April said. Her bruised ribs ached deeply as her muscles tightened. "But it's time to stop trying. I need to focus on myself and on my relationship with God. I need a fresh start. I think you do too. And…I don't know if you loved me, so much as you loved the idea of what you thought I could be. I can't fit into that."

Theo let out a long, shaky breath. "I'm sorry for being such a horrible guy," he muttered.

April closed her eyes. "I didn't say that." *But I also can't take responsibility for making you feel better.* "I'm sorry, Theo. I wish you nothing but the best, I really do, and…I mean, it wasn't all bad. We had…we had a lot of good times, too. So…thank you for the good times."

Their eyes met. His were reflecting a watery shine from the kitchen light. He opened his arms to her.

Unable to help herself, she walked into them and allowed him to wrap her in one final embrace. Crying against his shirt while feeling his emotion through the way he held her, she questioned the wisdom of allowing this hug. Yet their connection demanded this recognition before the send-off. They stayed like that for what could have been two minutes or half an hour. It was a unique kind of pain, full of too many layers to discern at once.

He kissed the top of her head and tightened his hold on her briefly while she stifled a wince, then he unwrapped his arms and stepped back.

"You take care," he said robotically as he walked backward toward the door.

"You too," she said, reaching over to lean against the nearest countertop.

Then he was outside.

The click of the door resonated with the finality of it all. Shock took over April for the second time in a week.

After the sound of Theo's car faded away, April was out the door like a rocket. She went for the longest walk of her life, ignoring her sore ribs as she focused on inhaling and exhaling and burning off the energy that wouldn't let her legs slow down until she found herself back at home, overwhelmed by her liberated yet broken heart.

- Chapter Thirty -

Even though the living room was the same as it used to be, the sun shining into the window was brighter than it was before the day that it broke, and even though it was nice to have Mom and Dad around all the time, it was not a vacation feeling—it was a heavy feeling. They were comfortable when he was lining and eating and going for walks and car rides with them, but they both had a presence with pressure that matched the pressure inside of him about wondering if the loud time and the window breaking would happen again, but he also knew that it was only going to happen once, like the time he went to Mom and Dad's wedding, which was new and strange and it happened just once so that was good, just like the loud time would only happen once. But why did April stay away so long this time?

But now Dad was telling him that April was coming over this afternoon, and that was the best news in a long time! Even though she was mean to him on the stairs and in the bathroom, that was just one time too, and he missed her.

When her car made noise outside and then shut off, and he could hear her walking up to the door, he was ready to see her—but then his wrist pain came back and he remembered when she grabbed him so hard.

When he heard her say "Hello" at the door he wanted to see her, but he didn't want to have wrist pain, and would she hurt him again? But Mom and Dad were here this time, and they would make sure she wasn't mean again. Lots of times they told him she was protecting him from the tornado. They said that she saved his life and that she was a hero, but even though he trusted what Mom and Dad said, it didn't feel like a hero would hurt or scare someone like April did to him on that day.

When April sat beside him on the couch he continued lining, just a little slower than before because his wrist was more sore than it was a moment ago, and the noise in his head got a little bit louder, but April wasn't talking and she wasn't putting her finger on his book, so he took deep breaths and was okay with her sitting there. He hoped she wouldn't get closer. She didn't, and he remembered that she almost never did things that he didn't want her to do. Except for that one loud day, but maybe she would never do that again. She was calm and peaceful right now, not like she was on that loud day when she tried to pull him down the stairs and locked him in the dark bathroom, and he remembered that she was almost always calm and peaceful with him—maybe she was still safe and good for him, like on the day she was proud of him for taking charge of their walk. Maybe she still liked him?

April leaned back into the couch cushions, content to be seated beside her friend. She couldn't gauge what was going on inside of his head, but she figured that, in terms of interaction, less was more this time around. Vanessa and Leonard had left them alone after the first few minutes of watching him carefully, satisfying themselves that both parties were at ease with each other.

The full force of breaking up with Theo sat like a ball of lead in her stomach, making it difficult to breathe at times. Doubts about the wisdom of her course had been plaguing her constantly, but in this precious moment, even that battle faded into the background.

Seth was letting her sit beside him. The victory of their closeness elevated her spirits immensely.

"I'm glad you're okay Seth," she whispered so as not to jar the silence. "I'm okay, too, and I'm so happy to be with you again today."

She let the silence billow back down around them. Seth's lining was still a bit slower than usual. The bruise on his wrist made her grimace, despite being prepared by his parents that she would see it.

"Can I come and see you again tomorrow? And bring a new book this time?"

Seth's unspoken assent reached her understanding. She didn't know how she knew, but she did.

Muffled conversation from the kitchen reached her ears. She wondered what his parents were talking about. She also wondered what they would think of the request she was going to make when she could get them out of Seth's earshot. It was an idea she had toyed with for a few weeks, then shelved as she wondered whether Theo would be okay with her taking time for it. Now it came back on a swell of energy, and she couldn't wait to put it to them.

* * *

That evening, April forced herself to get in the car and drive to Robyn and Patrick's house. As scared as she was about the possibility of running into Theo there, she didn't want to miss the small group's final gathering. If Theo turned up, she could stick like glue to Robyn's side or find a reason to excuse herself early.

It turned out to be an uncomfortable evening in almost every way possible, even though her ex didn't show. April found that she missed the way she used to lean into his social confidence. Listening to Samuel wax eloquent about his upcoming trip to Toronto to spend time with the love of his life scraped at a very raw nerve. Myla and Asher discussing their excitement about their baby struck her hard in the area of her heart where she had previously stored dreams about raising a family with Theo. Yvette was as quiet as ever, which meant that awkward silences between her and April stretched out several times when they found themselves alone in the lawn-chair circle. Faye was her usual brisk, no-nonsense self when she sat down next to April and asked where Theo was tonight. It took every ounce of energy not to burst out with a strangled animal sound around the handful of chips she shoved into her mouth just then.

The only redeeming factor of the get-together was watching Patrick and Robyn maneuver their way around the group. Patrick was stationed at the barbecue, while Robyn was dividing her time between chatting, restocking food supplies, and keeping tabs on Linus as he toddled around the small yard. There was an unspoken ease between them that April had never noticed before.

Their therapy must have gotten off to a good start—so good, in fact, that at one point when everyone else was occupied with one of Myla's funny stories, April glanced up at the barbecue just in time to see Robyn put a hand on Patrick's shoulder. He turned and smiled, planting a quick kiss on her lips. The way Robyn almost hadn't tilted her face up on time suggested that this was an unexpected move. The affection that blazed between their locked eyes shone so strongly that April looked away, feeling like an intruder on a sacred moment.

- Chapter Thirty-One -

The Ephesians study had been a very good one, full of encouragements and challenges. The people she'd gotten to know were great. Yet having discussions that kicked at the hard dirt of her performance-oriented faith, and developing a friendship with Robyn, were the two biggest and best takeaways from this summer's small group gatherings. How ironic that she had Theo to thank for forcing her into this, when it was his forceful ways that had eventually worn down their relationship.

Still, she couldn't fully lay the blame at his feet. She alone was responsible for knowing her worth and walking in the authenticity with which God had created her. It would take time and practice and a lot of intentionality, but the future was bright. Now that she understood that she was completely, unconditionally accepted and loved by the same God who had created the view before her, her burdens were becoming easier and her yoke lighter. For the first time in her life, April *knew* that nothing she did could ever make God love her any more or any less, and that nothing could separate her from his love.

From her seated position at the top of the hill, April gazed out at the horizon. The sun was low in the sky, casting long shadows behind the hay bales and trees that stretched toward her grandparents' farmyard. A slight breeze was keeping the season's final mosquitos at bay, caressing April's face in a tender way that made her close her eyes to meditate on the sensation. It was the final Saturday before classes were set to begin, and she had been enjoying a quiet visit in Baylor—a deep breath before the plunge of managing classes, homework, practicums, and everything else.

Robyn was planning to have April over for lunch every Tuesday until her maternity leave ended. At this point, April was still the only person, outside of Robyn's parents and in-laws, who knew about everything. April felt she had nothing to offer in the way of wisdom, but Robyn made it clear that April's nonjudgmental listening ear was one of her greatest gifts. In turn, Robyn's keen insights had been very helpful in connecting April's fledgling self-acceptance with truths from Scripture that bolstered her understanding of how God viewed her. Stepping over the threshold into trusting his love had been the sweetest homecoming she could ever imagine, but there was still a lot of work needed to keep her from running back out the door into old ways of thinking.

Seth's parents had been delighted with her request to see Seth regularly once the summer was over. Sunday afternoons from two to four became the agreed-upon schedule. It wouldn't be the same, she knew—but one day, when she was finished with her diploma, what were the chances she could find work at an agency that might provide Seth with a home or a day program? He only had four years left of high school before he would be looking for his next vocation, and possibly a new living arrangement if he and his parents decided to go that route. Saskatoon wasn't a big city; the chances of their lives remaining connected were optimistic.

Theo crossed her mind, as he frequently did, accompanied by an immense ache. Two days ago, he had texted her to ask how she was doing. She had sent a short and guarded response. He had reciprocated in kind, and they had left it at that. Somehow that exchange eased up a little bit of the hurt, but she wondered how long it would take for the entire wound to heal. People broke up all the time, she knew, but she'd never considered just how much the pain could affect a person's inner landscape.

God, thank you for being with me. I am hurting, and I'm okay. I feel broken up inside, and I am held by you. I am messy, and I am loved. I feel guilty, and I did the right thing. Thank you for not giving up on me, even when I thought I was one of the ninety-nine and didn't realize that I still needed rescuing myself.

April inhaled deeply and opened her eyes. The sun was still shining, even when her eyes were closed so she couldn't see it. Observing its brilliant effects on the scenery filled her with that painful longing she had once tried to describe to Theo; the same kind of painful longing that her Edmonton home aroused in her; and she decided that it was okay not to have words for it. Just feeling her feelings before God was enough, and she knew that he understood.

Finally, the sound of her mother's voice shifted her focus down to the yard.

It was time to go home.

Look for the second book of the
Seasons of April Trilogy

Coming in 2025!

About The Author

Kjersti Aicken spends a lot of time explaining how to pronounce her name (it sounds like "Chur-stee," or putting "church" and "thirsty" together). She has lived in both Saskatchewan and Alberta, and currently resides in Rosthern, SK, with her husband, Bryan, and three kids: Brielle, Corey, and Daniel. When she is not writing, she is probably percolating one of the many stories in the background of her head while she does other things.

Visit The Author's Website

kjerstiaicken.wixsite.com/author

Find her on social media

Facebook – Author Kjersti Aicken
Instagram – k.aicken

Or write

kjerstiaicken.author@gmail.com

Thank you to all my readers♥ - K.A.

Acknowledgements

I'm indulging an impulse to admit something: how surreal it feels to be typing these words. Who would have thought I'd be writing an "acknowledgments" page at the end of my own published story? Yet here we are—and "here" wouldn't exist without the help and/or influence of the following people:

YOU, the reader who saw fit to pick up my book! Your support and/or interest in this work means the world to me. Thank you for taking the time to go along on this journey!

My families, both the Friggstad side and the Aicken side—two of the most loving and loyal clans on earth. I'm forever grateful for the family I grew up in, and for the one I married into. Mom, Dad, Zac, Jenne, Gabriel, Lucas, Hannah, Jannaya, Graham, and Courtney; Gary, Sharon, Jaime, Lindsay, Jens, Kai, Mats, Nicola, and Sheena—you all rock!

My parents, Lorne and Janice—thank you for raising my highly emotional, sensitive, hyperactive and socially insecure little self with the type of full acceptance that I took for granted at the time (which is really as it should be). Your support of my writing hobby and your never-ending supply of paper was instrumental to where I ended up today. Thank you, and I love you both very much!

Sheila Erickson, my Grade Six teacher, who poured into my confidence as a young writer and facilitated the daunting journey of sharing my work with the public.

Each and every person in the community I became part of when I was a disability support worker. It's impossible to convey how enriching those eight years were, and how much they impacted the rest of my life.

Countless friends, peers, and mentors, who have taught me so much about life and conflict and relationship; about healthy love and how to recognize unhealthy patterns; about the interplay of self-esteem and our relationship with God, and all things faith-related. A writer's mind is like a big, bubbling cauldron that keeps everything that's put into it, and often the right ingredients rise up in response to the call of a story. I couldn't possibly separate my inspirations from so many sources, but I want to give respect to anyone who has ever walked with me in life, for any length of time, and allowed the richness of authentic connection to flow between us.

Author PD Janzen, who answered my questions about the process. I looked up from my first draft and blinked into the harsh reality that I'd have to figure out the business side of things. Our chat was informative and encouraging. I highly recommend her "Someone of Substance" trilogy! Check her out at pdjanzen.com.

My wonderful beta readers, who made this story far better than it would have been without their insights: Jannaya Jensen, Bryan Aicken, Wendy Kasdorf, Janice Friggstad, Sheélah Wall (check out her book review platform, the_library_upstairs, on Facebook, Instagram, and TikTok), and Terrie Hein. Thanks also to Terrie for printing off the beta hard copies—I'll try to make it more efficient next time!

Lisa Lee, whose attention to detail gave the wording, grammar, and consistency of my story a healthy boost. She can be found on Facebook at Lisa Lee Proofreading and Editing. I look forward to working with her again!

Nicole Hein, who took my author photo and somehow made me look like I wasn't even nervous.

Jannaya Jensen, who must have forgiven me for those early years of me squeezing her head in my armpit, because she put so much care into designing the most perfect cover for my story! I couldn't have come up with a more fitting image. Thank you for making me cry, sister.

Brielle, Corey, and Daniel—my sweetest gifts. There was a transition involved when this writing thing became a factor in our family life; I saw the adjustments you made. Thank you for adapting, and for asking questions about the book that probably seemed like it took forever to make. I love you three like crazy!

Bryan. My mind went blank with too many thoughts hitting it at once. Thanks for everything: for brushing the soil aside so I could see that this dream was still alive; for partnering with me on the business side of things with far more gusto than I could have conjured up myself; for being the rock-solid husband you are, and the most fun life partner I could ever have imagined. I'll save the ten-page love note for another time, or else this could easily turn into that!

And most of all, my gratitude rises up to God. Again with the mind blank. How do I put into words what you mean to me? Writing this story was a challenge at times, but you walked with me through it all. Our journey in this has been like a long and interesting worship session as I offer up to you the gifts and ideas you put into me. Thank you, thank you, thank you.

Manufactured by Amazon.ca
Bolton, ON

41079392R00173